Knights of Mendolon

A sequel to *The Beauty of a Beast*

by

Tony Myers

Knights of Mendolon

www.tonymyers.net

Acknowledgments

Whenever I write a book, gratitude is the emotion I feel more than anything else.

To my small group of dedicated fans, thank you so much for all your love and support. Your encouragement keeps me going. I can't say enough how grateful I am that you enjoy my books.

I love my family so much, and I am thankful for all their excitement and joy in writing these novels. I especially want to mention Hannah Beth, Anthony, Elliot, and Autumn Joy. I love you guys so much. You give me so much inspiration. To the love of my life, Charity, thank you for all your love and support. I appreciate all your help in reading it and editing it.

Also, while I'm on the topic of editing, thank you, Stephen, for once again coming out of retirement and editing the book. I appreciate all your hard work.

Thank you to the good folks at Waterloo Chick-fil-a for keeping me well-fed when I needed to get out of the office and write.

Lastly, I'm so thankful for my Lord and Savior, Jesus Christ. Writing this book was a joy, and He truly is the God of all joy and creativity. All glory goes to Him.

⋙⋘

To C.S. Lewis,

"You're never too old to set a new goal or to dream a
new dream."

Thank you.

⋙⋘

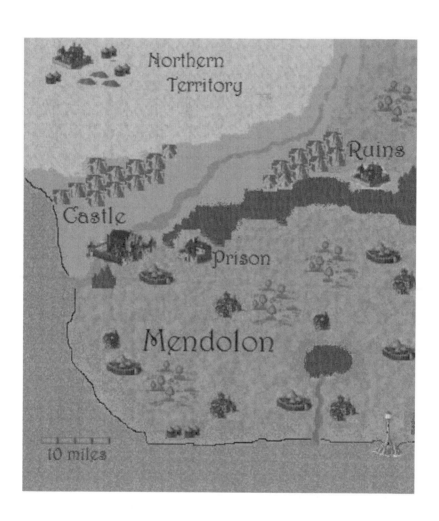

Corbeau de Lefevre

A short prequel

By

Tony Myers

1

The knight Corbeau de Lefevre sat in a tavern. His face was buried in his drink. He was in southeast Mendolon, trying to hide. He was far away from the castle, far away from any celebrations regarding the heroics of Michael de Bolbec. A month and a half had passed since the defeat of the Savage, and the people of Mendolon were still rejoicing that the threat was vanquished. Most of the victory had been attributed to Michael and the princess Belle, but with Belle now gone to Grimdolon, all the praise was now going to Michael de Bolbec, chief knight of Mendolon.

The jealousy stirred and continued to grow in Corbeau. Being in his early thirties, he was supposed to be the chief knight of Mendolon before Michael rose through the ranks. He had been completely passed over by Sebastian when the position was open three years ago. Michael was definitely the most skilled in combat, and his intelligence of battle strategy was beyond all others, but he was so young and inexperienced compared to Corbeau. In his mind, Corbeau felt cheated of the opportunity to be the chief knight. He respected Michael and followed his command, but this celebration was too much for him. He longed to be assigned to a post far from the castle and the western markets.

"More ale?" the owner of the tavern asked.

"Sure," Corbeau said, sliding his drink a foot away from himself. The owner then poured his cup full.

"Thank you," Corbeau said quietly. This tavern had been a retreat for him the last few weeks. Between walking the southern coast and casually reading at the small village library, this tavern was where he spent his time. Very few recognized him here, especially being this far from the castle. Being a knight, he was in great shape and had a naturally prestigious look about him, but without his armor on, he wasn't usually recognized by anyone. People would say he was handsome with his dark brown hair. Occasionally, a woman would approach him, but he was not interested. Finding love was the furthest thing from his mind at the moment.

Corbeau had been granted a long leave of absence after being attacked by the Savage at the Northern Ruins. He had been with his fellow knights when the mist fell on them, impairing their sight. The thought of the beasts attacking him haunted him. He was traumatized by the attack. Certain sights and sounds would set him off during the day, and at night he would dream of the attack.

He remembered it all too well.

⇜⇝

Corbeau took one last look around the courtyard. It appeared as if all the Savage's men had been captured and placed in the middle of the courtyard. All the knights were now regrouping with the men. "Have you seen anyone else?" Corbeau asked a fellow knight.

"No, we believe we've gotten all of them."

Corbeau nodded his head as he looked around the courtyard. He noticed Belle had taken Bernard in with her to the interior of the castle. He shook his head at the thought of it. In his mind Bernard was lowest of all the knights. For him to have received special assignments like this just for being the torch bearer was absurd. Corbeau didn't know what he would have to do to finally get the attention of his superiors.

"Where's Gideon?" he asked another knight, looking around the courtyard.

"Not sure. I saw him exit through the front gate. I think he must be checking the perimeter."

Corbeau walked toward the captured men in the middle of the courtyard. He wondered if he could get any information from them. He carried two swords on his back. He pulled them both and approached the men. A few of the prisoners noticed him but looked unafraid.

13

Right before he was about to speak to them, Corbeau heard the loud sound of the front gates slamming shut. He turned back to the men. The prisoners now had looks of terror on their faces. Their eyes flashed from side to side across the courtyard. Corbeau wondered what was transpiring. The other knights soon gathered around one another, trying to figure out what their next move would be. Gideon was the ranking supervisor, and most of the knights, not knowing that he was gone, waited on his command.

Corbeau began to notice the courtyard filling with a mist. "Steady men... steady!" one of the knights yelled. They all knew an attack from the Savage was coming soon.

The prisoners began to scream out, "No, you can't do this to us! After all we've done for you... you can't treat us like this!"

The mist got thicker around all the knights. Corbeau glanced from side to side with both swords in hand. It was just a few seconds later that he was completely blinded by the foggy mist. He held tight to his swords as he tried to stay focused. He felt fear begin to slip in. It was at that moment that he heard the first growl of a beast. It didn't sound like a normal beast from Grimdolon. It had an unusually vicious sound to it.

Without warning, Corbeau was knocked down from behind. He dropped one of his swords. He turned over as fast as he could and frantically tried to look for his sword. He wasn't thinking straight. Corbeau felt his mind beginning to play tricks on him. Sweat began to bead on his forehead as he breathed heavily. A kick then came to his side and he dropped his other sword. The fingers and claws of a beast wrapped around his head. The knight pulled his head forward. "Get away," he yelled out.

The beast then began to wrestle with him, pinning him to the ground. It laughed at him as it knew Corbeau's mind was playing tricks on him. The beast looked to be some type of werewolf creature. Once he caught sight of the beast, Corbeau covered his face in sheer terror. In his mind's eye it looked as if it was about to breathe fire on him at any moment. He pleaded in vain for the beast to stop.

The creature spoke in a vicious voice, "You can't stop us. We have weapons that are far superior to anything Mendolon possesses. You will all die." The creature then laughed again as it began to punch Corbeau in the head.

Images of Corbeau's life flashed through his mind as he thought surely this was the end. His eyes were blurry between the mist, tears, and a little bit of blood. The thought of death was somewhat relieving as it would be an escape from this present state of horror and terror.

Then very suddenly, the beast stopped beating him and just looked at him squarely for a moment. Corbeau turned his head and looked at the angry creature. Their eyes met briefly. Looking into the beast's eyes seemed to exaggerate any terror or evil he was feeling. Without warning, the beast stood up and ran away. Corbeau breathed deeply as he was now free from the eyes of the dreaded creature. A small part of him wondered if he was dead. His eyes began to clear as the mist started to thin out. The world around Corbeau still looked as if it was under water, but at least he could see more than just a foot or two in front of him.

He was shaking in fear as Gideon came and leaned over him. "Are you okay?" he yelled out to Corbeau, trying to get some information from his fellow knight.

Corbeau was wide-eyed and shook with fear. "Beast... beast... beast," was the only word that he could speak. The dreaded image of the beast consumed his thoughts... as it would every day in the coming weeks.

Corbeau took a walk down by the southern coast. He casually threw rocks into the sea as he walked at a slow pace over the sand. The sun was high in the sky. A few children were out playing in the sand. The temperature was too cold to swim today. Corbeau enjoyed walking along the coast at this time of year. The quiet atmosphere was very pleasant and just what he needed on days like today.

A passing thought came to his mind that maybe his days as a knight were coming to a close. Corbeau had taken the Savage's attack harder than the other knights. All of the others had completely recovered. He wondered if he ever would. Images of the beasts were still frequent in his dreams and often awoke him in the night. The inner fear of the Savage's beasts had only slightly diminished since that day.

Corbeau smiled as he passed a family playing in the sand. The family joyously played without a care in the world. The dad was playing a simple game of tag with his kids as they laughed and ran. The mother sat comfortably on the sand and laughed along with the kids as they ran from their father.

"Good day," the woman said as he passed. They didn't recognize him as a knight since he was in casual clothing.

"Yes, good day," Corbeau said in reply as he kept walking. He continued to hear their laughter as he kept moving. When he was about twenty feet away, he turned and took one last look at the woman sitting on the sand. She reminded him of his former wife, Renée. Corbeau still loved her. She had left him nearly two years ago after it was discovered that he had taken on a secret mistress. Now he was paying the price for that choice. Oh, how he wished Renée was still in his life. He could have used her love and comfort at a time like this.

The water splashed along the shore as he kept walking. Maybe it was time for a change for him. He could easily take a job as a blacksmith. Being the weapons maker was his duty as a knight. Corbeau came from a well-known family of blacksmiths in the southwest region of Mendolon. His father and his brothers still worked in a large shop in that area. Corbeau seemed destined to follow in his family's footsteps until things changed during his teenage years. It was discovered that he excelled in swordplay, and he even won a few competitions as a young man. When he turned twenty he joined the armies of Mendolon as a soldier, and it wasn't long after that that he was officially promoted to the rank of knight because of his superb skill with the sword. It was only a few months later that he was given the role of weapons maker. During his years of knighthood, he had forged numerous weapons. But he was now ready for a change.

Walking away from being a knight wouldn't be easy, but the more he thought about it, the more he knew it was the right thing to do. He could go back to work with his family while also working on winning back his wife Renée. He would do whatever it took to get her back. The quiet life with no more hectic missions sounded extremely pleasant at the moment. And above all, he liked the thought of ending his jealous feud with Michael de Bolbec. Sometimes the jealousy would keep him up at night and fill him with bitterness. He was ready to be done with that.

The more he kept daydreaming about this new life, the more sensible it sounded. A quiet life was what he needed. Corbeau continued to make his way down the calm beach. With this new resolve, the scenery seemed to be more enjoyable. The sun seemed brighter. The breeze against his face was soothing, and the continuous sound of the waves splashing against the sand was relaxing. It was the near perfect start he needed to a new life. Corbeau couldn't help but smile as he continued to walk.

It was settled. He would pack his belongings, head west toward the castle, and resign from the knights of Mendolon.

❧

After his walk along the beach, Corbeau quickly packed his belongings and left the quiet inn where he had been staying. A part of him was sad to leave. It had been the quiet getaway he had needed to help clear his thoughts. He had spent many hours reading in solitude. Corbeau would also miss the family that ran the inn as he had seen them most days. They would miss him as well. His steady payments provided much needed income for them.

Corbeau headed to the tavern that he had already visited earlier in the day. He hoped that he could catch a ride with someone heading west. He was now wearing his knight breastplate along with his two swords on his back. Even though he had planned to resign from knighthood, Corbeau hoped the people would see his armor and recognize him as a knight, and this would help in securing him a ride back west. He only carried a small bag over his back. It was filled with clothing and a few books. He was traveling light, so he wouldn't be a burden for anyone in his travels.

Reaching the tavern, Corbeau casually entered like he always did. He received a few passing glances from people as he walked toward the counter. Some of the folks in this small village knew he was a knight, but they had never seen him dressed like one. Corbeau simply nodded and casually smiled in return.

"You're lookin' a little more dressed up today," the scruffy bartender said as Corbeau came close.

"Yes, well... I'm heading out. Going home today."

"You finally goin' back home, are you?"

Corbeau spoke confidently, "I'm ready."

"I imagine they'd be happy to have you back."

"No..." Corbeau smiled slightly before continuing, "I mean I'm going back *home.* I'm done with knighthood."

The bartender nodded as he started to clean a cup. Corbeau usually ordered a pint of ale and drank it slowly at a corner table. The bartender spoke, "Knighthood gettin' a little hard on you?"

"I've done my duty, and now it's time to move on." Corbeau paused just a moment before continuing, "And besides the family business could use me as well."

Corbeau scanned the room and saw a couple dozen customers drinking casually. Everyone looked like a regular. None appeared to be travelers. Corbeau turned again to the bartender, "Say, do you know anyone passing through, heading west?"

The bartender bit the side of his lip as he poured the ale. "Nah... haven't heard of anyone, but I imagine if you wait long enough, someone will be passing through."

"Thank you," Corbeau replied quietly. He picked up his pint of ale and went to his corner table. He threw his bag beside the table and gently set his cup down. He wondered how long he would have to wait before someone came through. There was a window not far from where he sat. Corbeau could look out for someone who looked to be on a carriage. More than likely if he waited for a few hours he would find someone. If not, then he would just head back toward the inn for another night before trying again the next day.

Corbeau again scanned the small crowd of people in the tavern, looking for any sign of a traveler. The tavern was known for serving ale and a few wines, but it also offered a homemade stew that was popular among the customers. The place was well-kept and generally quiet. Families felt comfortable eating there. It was a far cry from other taverns located in other regions of the land where fights would break out on a weekly basis. This place was calm and Corbeau greatly appreciated it.

It was then that the door to the tavern opened suddenly and three men abruptly walked in. They looked angry and appeared as if they were seeking harm. Two of the men were average height with long hair. Their clothing was dirty and slightly torn. Corbeau noticed the bows and arrows in their hands, which were pointed toward the customers in a threatening manner. The people turned and gasped at the sight of the arrows. The other man who entered with them was about six and a half feet tall. He was muscular and bald and appeared to be in his mid-forties. On his face was a terribly angry look. It was obvious he was the leader of this company.

Corbeau knew right away who these men were. For the past month and a half, the soldiers and knights of Mendolon had been chasing the prisoners released by the Savage from Mendolon's main prison. It was obvious these were some of them. They were looking for hostages— anyone they could find to hold for ransom, someone they could use for negotiations.

The tall muscular man scanned the crowd before fixing his eyes on a young woman with blonde hair. "That one," the man spoke out with a deep billowing voice. One of the smaller men lowered his bow and approached the woman.

The young woman shook her head as she cried out, "No... No!"

A young man who was with her quickly stood to his feet. "You can't take her. You will have..." He couldn't say anything more as an arrow from the other outlaw flew through the air and pierced his side. He fell to the ground. The young woman put her hands over her mouth at the sight of the collapsed young man. Tears started to fill her eyes.

The bartender spoke out from behind the bar, "You get out of here. You aren't welcome here... You crooks." Another arrow was sent his way. He quickly dropped to the ground as the arrow stuck into the wall behind where he was standing.

"Don't call me that!" the leader yelled out.

The outlaw grabbed the woman and quickly brought her over to where the leader was standing. She was screaming frantically. The large man reached for the young woman and easily picked her up and threw her over his shoulder.

Corbeau knew it was now his time to strike. The woman's screaming and flailing was a distraction for everyone. Corbeau sprang to his feet and pulled his swords. He was right beside the men before they realized what was occurring. One of the outlaws tried to pull an arrow but Corbeau easily knocked it out his hands with a swipe of one of his swords. Corbeau then rotated his arm and cut the man across the chest. He fell to the ground, moaning in pain.

Corbeau turned to face the other smaller man who was trying to use an arrow as a sword. Corbeau easily blocked and knocked the arrow out of his hands. He was ready to strike again, but before he could, a kick landed against his side. Corbeau fell to the ground, dropping one of his swords. The kick took his breath away as it had come from the large muscular man.

"Let's move!" the large man yelled out to his companion. He then turned and left with the young woman still over his shoulder. Corbeau picked up his sword and ran toward them as the smaller man exited through the door and slammed it behind him. The man who had been slashed by Corbeau cried out as he held his chest.

Corbeau ran to the door and was about to open it before turning one last time to check on the young man who had been shot by the arrow. He was holding tight to the entry point of the arrow as he grimaced in pain. Others were starting to make their way over to him in order to help. The injured young man looked up at Corbeau as he saw the knight had stopped to check on him. The young man spoke through his agony, "Please, go... save my fiancé."

With a determined look on his face, Corbeau nodded confidently before opening the door and running out.

2

Corbeau ran through the door of the tavern. He could see the two outlaws galloping away on horseback. The young woman's hands were tied and she was sitting in front of the large criminal, who was the leader. Corbeau knew he would have to hurry as they already had a head start on him. He looked to his right and saw a horse tied up to a post. With no time to waste, he pulled one of his swords and sliced through the horse's rope. He quickly sheathed his sword and jumped on the horse. Giving the creature a hard kick, he galloped toward the outlaws.

The men were heading north through a lightly wooded area. They glanced over their shoulders to see the knight of Mendolon chasing them. After riding for two miles, the men could tell that Corbeau was gaining on them. This provoked the leader of the men to turn toward a more western path. There was a river that ran south for a few miles to the sea. Corbeau followed suit and chased them onto the trail close to the river. The captured young lady kept a desperate eye on Corbeau, as she recognized him as a knight. Any opportunity she could, she would try to sneak a glance behind her.

Corbeau was within fifty yards of the men when they turned sharply to their left and went over a narrow wooden bridge. It was barely big enough for a horse to pass over. They were headed to the western side of the river. Corbeau was taken off guard as the bridge came right after a curve in the trail. He couldn't see it until he was a few feet away, and this made him come close to missing it. His horse came to a near complete stop as he had to make the sudden turn left to cross the bridge.

The bridge was a little over thirty feet in length. It was wooden and sagged in the middle. At its lowest point it looked to be just over five feet above the river. It was made up of thick ropes and wooden planks that looked like they had been there for years. The horse was a little reluctant to cross, but Corbeau gave him a swift kick and the horse slowly trotted across. Its hooves were loud against the wooden planks and Corbeau wondered if any of them might snap before he got across.

Corbeau looked to the other side of the bridge to see the young henchman cutting through the ropes that held the bridge in place. The large, muscular bald man was a few feet away watching the progress. Corbeau knew he would have to hurry. He gave the horse a harder kick as it continued to the other side of the bridge. They were five feet away from the other side when one of the ropes was completely cut through. The horse started to fall to its side as the bridge under him was now gone. Corbeau was able to lunge forward and grab the rope to his right that was still in place.

For a brief second Corbeau held onto the rope suspended in the air. He could see that his horse's momentum had carried the animal forward and he had hit a downward sloping bank. The animal was greatly startled as his feet landed in shallow water, but thankfully he wasn't greatly harmed. Corbeau could see the young henchman coming toward him and he knew he would have to act fast. He swung his feet onto the hill and quickly pulled the rest of his body forward. Out of the corner of his eye, he saw the young man trying to quickly place an arrow into his bow. Corbeau pulled his sword just in time to deflect the arrow as it flew close to him.

The young henchman then pulled a small knife from his belt and ran toward Corbeau. He was holding it downward, attempting to fiercely stab the knight. As the young man got close, Corbeau pulled his other sword and caught the knife between his two swords just as the henchman tried to thrust it into him. Corbeau held it in place as his eyes met those of the young man. He could see the fear in the young man's eyes as he realized that he was no match for this knight of Mendolon.

26

Corbeau knew he had to act quickly as the leader could be on him at any minute. With great speed he moved to his right and pushed the knife to his left with his right sword. The young man stumbled onto his side. In one quick maneuver Corbeau took his left sword and ran it through the henchman. He fell to the ground in a brief moan of pain.

Turning around, Corbeau could see the leader trying to turn his horse to continue his journey north. There was no time to waste. Corbeau quickly ran toward the outlaw with the young woman. When he was just a few feet away he heard the young lady yell out to him, "No, stop!" It was too late. As he lifted his swords to engage the leader, the large muscular man threw a handful of dust into Corbeau's face. It briefly blinded him, and he fell to the ground.

"Let's move!" the man yelled to the horse. He gave it a hard kick as he continued riding north.

Corbeau wiped his eyes as they began to water. All of a sudden, he felt as if he was in a dream. Reality began to feel fuzzy. He climbed to his feet as he stumbled back toward the bridge. Through his blurred vision, he noticed the horse left from the henchman Corbeau had stabbed. He stumbled toward it.

As Corbeau approached the horse, he began to notice that the horse looked as if it was a vicious beast. He knew his mind was playing tricks on him, and it was at that moment that he realized that the powder thrown into his eyes was the same hallucinogenic powder he had encountered before with the Savage. His hands began to shake as he rubbed his forehead. "It's just an illusion... just an illusion," he said to himself as he slowly climbed onto the horse. He realized that this journey was now going to be a lot more difficult.

The outlaw was continuing to go north. There was a swampland located another mile from where they were. The criminal had been hiding out there before when he first escaped from prison. His hope was to again hide out there and possibly pass through it to the north in an effort to lose this dreaded knight that was following him. The swamp was dangerous. It was infested with different vicious snakes and creatures that dwelt on land and in the water.

This criminal's name was Brutus. He had been in prison for the last eight years before being released by the Savage a month and a half ago. He was originally sent to prison for the murder of three individuals, all criminals with whom he had disputes. Brutus had many followers through his years of crime. Even in Mendolon's prison, he had gained a following and was well-respected by most of the prisoners. Rarely did he have to engage in a fight as most of the time he had others that would do his bidding.

Brutus despised being called a crook. All his "crimes" he felt were justified. In his mind, they were necessities to help guarantee his survival. He never wanted to hurt anyone who was truly innocent. Even this young woman he had kidnapped, he hoped to release as soon as he was through with her as a hostage. In regard to his crimes, he would always try to ease his conscience and say to himself, "My hand was forced. I didn't have a choice. I am no crook." Truly he had come to a point where he could justify any action with these statements.

The edge of the swampland came into view. Confronting a knight in the tavern had completely thrown off his plans. Originally his plan was to simply head east with his henchmen to Grimdolon and then try to hitch a ride over the sea to a distant kingdom. But now that this dreadful knight was following him, his new plan was to make his way through the swamp and then exit to the east. From there he would go through Dragon Waste and head north to the Lost Mountains. If he ever found himself confronted by a company of knights or soldiers, then he would easily use the woman to negotiate safe passage. Having been out of prison for a month and a half, he promised himself to do whatever it took to never return.

The swampland was dark as thick foliage covered overhead. The ground was wet and sank in slightly when one stepped on its saturated soil. There were a number of ponds located throughout the area. Algae and other plant life covered most of the surface of the water on these ponds. Brutus preferred to stay away from the water because of the reptiles and other animals located in them. He knew his way around the area fairly well, and even though he had a small wooden boat, he favored walking the trails and taking the long way through the swamp.

The young woman was crying as he pulled her along by the arm. "Come on!" he yelled viciously. He knew the knight of Mendolon would be upon him soon, and he preferred not to take a chance with another confrontation.

"Please, no," the young woman pleaded as they entered the swampland. It was an extremely eerie area, and she had heard passing stories that the land may be haunted.

"Quit your cryin'." Brutus pulled hard on her arm as they wove through the trees in the direction of the center of the area. He pushed away hanging vines with his free hand as they walked. They'd only been walking through the area a few minutes, but the young woman could already feel a swarm of mosquitoes and various other insects attacking her legs and arms. She didn't know what was more painful, the bruise Brutus was inflicting on her arm or the continuous stream of insect bites on her flesh.

The path led them to a small pond covered in algae. Brutus stopped in his tracks. He looked to his left and then to his right. Knowing where both paths led him, he wondered which would be the best route to distance himself from the knight. His small boat lay not far in front of him. He only gave it a passing thought, as he knew it would be difficult to row forward and keep the young woman from jumping overboard.

After a few moments, Brutus once again squeezed the woman's bicep, pulling her to his left. "This way," he said, almost jerking the woman off her feet. The young woman was able to get one last look down the path from which they had come before being pulled aside. She saw nothing, but she could only hope that the knight of Mendolon was not far behind.

⁋⁋

Corbeau reached the edge of the swampland and slowly dismounted from his horse. He wiped his forehead as his sweat was beading. The hallucinogenic powder was still playing tricks on him. "It's just an illusion... it's just an illusion," he kept telling himself. He knew he would have to muster all the courage he could to enter this swamp while hallucinating. He gently patted the side of the horse in an effort to say "thank you." He didn't bother to tie up the horse. After being used by the escaped prisoners, he hoped the horse would enjoy a few days of freedom before being caught.

Approaching the swamp, Corbeau felt the darkness around the forest closing in on him. It was like the darkness had hands that were reaching out to grab him. In his mind the sounds of animals sounded loud and ominous. He shook his head, hoping to diminish the sounds in his mind. "It's not real," he whispered to himself.

Corbeau pulled one of his swords and cut down a vine as he stepped onto the faint trail, leading him into the area. Even though the hallucinogenic fears continued to exaggerate in his mind, he knew that the woman needed to be rescued and the escaped prisoner needed to be defeated. He took off running down the trail. He felt like the trees and the vines reached out for him as he ran through the wooded area. He knew he had to keep running because if he stopped to dwell on his fear, he would be consumed by it.

The trail twisted and turned for many yards as Corbeau ran through it. His boots splashed up bits of mud with every step. He didn't know where he was going or where the trail would lead, but he knew he couldn't give up. The knight of Mendolon was truly the only hope for the young woman to be found. He dreaded the thought of any harm or abuse happening to her.

Corbeau reached the edge of the pond. He saw both the trail to his left and one to his right. He quickly looked down both. They both seemed to eventually wrap around the pond to the other side. He wondered what other trails splintered off along the way. A passing thought of hopelessness entered his mind. There were many miles spread through this swampy area, and one wrong path could lead him in the opposite direction of the prisoner and the woman.

He was about to turn to his right, when something caught his eye. It was a small wooden boat on the edge of the pond, with an oar sitting in the middle of it. It looked like it had taken many trips across this pond. Corbeau stopped to think for a moment. Maybe a different approach was needed to catch his enemy. As a knight, he was taught to think a step ahead of those he was chasing. In this case maybe taking the boat through the pond would give him a good view of where both trails led. He thought it was worth a try. He pulled his sword and sliced through the old rope that tied it to a large root.

Corbeau began to push the boat off from the bank when he realized the water was rather shallow for a few feet. It would drag terribly if he tried to get in it at the moment. He braced his hands on the side as he pushed it forward. It moved easily. His feet went deeper and deeper into the mud with each step he took. As he walked he examined the boat to make sure there were no holes in it and that it would truly hold him.

The water began to get deeper until it was up to his knees. He kept going and after a few more steps it was up to the middle of his thighs. Corbeau knew this would suffice. The pond would only increase in depth after this point. He reached over to the far side of the boat and pulled himself in. He was just about to swing his feet into the boat when he felt pressure on his left boot. Twisting his torso, he brought his leg further into the boat and was startled by what he saw. He yelled out in fear. On Corbeau's leg was a vicious snake-like creature. It looked to be a cross between a snake and an eel. It made a strange growling sound as it tried to bite into his boot further. The growls were further exaggerated by the hallucinogenic powder. The creature was dark green with dark red eyes. Corbeau could see it was at least six feet long, but there was more of the animal underneath the water.

Corbeau's first instinct was to kick at it with his right foot. This only made the creature angrier as it continued to growl and tighten his grip with his teeth. The snake moved his mouth back and forth similar to a dog grinding his teeth on a bone. Corbeau began to feel the sharp teeth of the creature penetrate his leather boot and into his flesh. He closed his eyes tightly as he screamed.

Looking down at the creature, Corbeau looked directly into its eyes. He knew that it would not stop until his leg was gone. He turned his body on its side and stretched his arm back behind him. It was a very awkward position but he was able to grab one of his swords from his back. He twisted it around and stabbed the creature on its side. Its skin was thick and the sword didn't penetrate it much. He pulled it back and tried again. The sword went in a little further this time.

The snake growled as it loosened its grip. Corbeau was then able to kick it off his leg with his other foot. The knight quickly pulled his legs away from the creature and got onto his knees. The boat rocked from side to side from all the movement. The snake began to slowly pull himself back into the water. Corbeau was filled with anger at this point. With his sword in hand he lunged it forward, thrusting it into the side of the creature. It went in deep this time. A blackish-green blood-like substance oozed from its side onto the bottom of the boat. The creature gave a terrible shriek as it pulled itself completely off the boat and into the water.

Corbeau took a breath as he put his sword down. He hoped he had killed that dreaded creature. He examined his leg and saw that the creature had done considerable damage to his boot. Thankfully the damage to his leg felt only minor. Once this expedition was completed, the wound would need thorough cleaning, but he thought it would be fine for now.

His adrenaline was starting to wear down from the fight. Corbeau took a deep breath as he picked up the oar. He knew he would have to keep moving. A greater mission depended on him. Sticking the oar in the water, he slowly began to move forward. He looked down at the dark blood in the base of the boat. It looked to be a few pints. It smelled horrible.

After few minutes of rowing, Corbeau found himself in the middle of the pond. He moved the oar from side to side as he considered which direction to head. Putting the oar on his right, he felt it hit something in the water. He pulled it out and took a look over the side of the boat. He was quite surprised at what he saw. It was the snake creature following him. A stretch of dark blood flowed from its side as it swam beside the boat. Corbeau could see the creature's eyes glowing beneath the surface of the water. He looked angry. He looked hungry.

3

The pond was quiet. The water was still. Corbeau continued to row in the direction of a bank located on the far side of the pond. He kept looking around trying to see if he could spot anything that would give him a clue as to where the escaped prisoner and the woman might have gone. The effects of the hallucinogenic powder were just now starting to fade. Thankfully, only a small dose had been thrown into his eyes.

When Corbeau was within thirty feet of the bank, he noticed a small frog on a lily pad. He could hear a quiet croak from the creature as he got closer. In order not to disturb the frog, he stopped rowing for a moment as he passed by.

Corbeau stared at the creature sitting comfortably. All was peaceful. All was quiet. It was then at that moment that the snake sprang out of the water and attacked the frog, pulling him under in one quick motion. The snake went back underwater and everything was quiet again.

The bank was approaching quickly and Corbeau knew he couldn't get out of the boat with the snake anywhere close to him. He feared the creature would even climb a few feet onto the shore in order to strike. Another fight with that cursed animal was something he greatly wanted to avoid. He may not be so lucky with a second fight.

The boat stopped as Corbeau came to shallow water eight feet from shore. He checked around the boat and, sure enough, he saw the water clouded with the dark blood of the snake. He knew he would have to create a diversion. He slowly stood to his feet. The boat rocked slightly. Corbeau looked around and caught sight of the oar he had used to row. With the threat of snake in this pond, he knew he would not be using this boat to travel back over the pond. Holding the end of the handle, he twisted his body and with all his might, he threw the oar as far as he could toward the middle of the pond. The oar flew through the air and landed nearly thirty feet from where he stood. It splashed against the water.

Corbeau waited a few moments, watching intently to see what would happen. It was about six seconds later that the snake came up and twisted itself around the oar, thinking it was a fallen bird. Corbeau knew this was his time. Without a second to lose, he jumped out of the boat. The water was up to the middle of his shins. He ran as quickly as he could to the shore and kept going till he was on land and ten feet from the edge of the water. He stopped briefly to catch his breath. The knight was relieved to be out of the water.

Corbeau rested against a tree. This side of the pond was a thicker wooded area. The ground wasn't as moist, but there were more trees and denser foliage above. This area reminded him of a rainforest more than a swamp. The chirping of birds could be heard high above in the trees. He hoped that was all the animal life in this area and that there was nothing as vicious as the snake he had encountered.

About fifty yards away, Brutus hid among an area of thick shrubbery, watching the knight of Mendolon catch his breath. He held the young blonde woman in his arms. His thick hands tightly covered her mouth. A part of him thought about letting the her go. Maybe the knight would stop pursuing him. But then again, he may need this woman for negotiations later, particularly since he would be an especially wanted man at this point.

Brutus spoke in a harsh whisper to the young woman, "Shh… you be still now, ya hear? I ain't goin' to hurt you. I just need you as my puppet. You goin' to help me get away."

The young woman was frightened by her captor. She didn't trust anything he said. A part of her feared that he would kill her soon. She knew she would have to do anything possible to get away from this villain.

Brutus spoke again quietly as he continued to watch Corbeau, "We best be gettin' to go. Let's move along now." He slowly stood to his feet and began walking the opposite direction from the knight.

Brutus' grip loosened slightly over the woman's mouth. Few chances of escape would be possible. She decided to make the most of this moment. She moved her head away from her captor's arm and cried out as loud as she could, knowing the knight of Mendolon was within earshot. "We're here! Please help me! You are…" She wasn't able to say anything else as she was thrown to the ground. Her body hit with a thud against a fallen log.

"No, no, no! You weren't supposed to say that," Brutus said angrily, standing over her. "I told you, you're goin' to be fine." Feeling a little stunned, she looked up and saw her captor standing over her. His face was red with anger. She feared for her life.

Corbeau took off running as soon as he heard the woman yell. He had both swords in hand. Even though he had heard the voice of the woman crying out, he didn't know from exactly where it had come. He jumped over vines and fallen branches as he ran in the general direction of where he had heard the young woman's voice. Running through a bush, his face was scratched by a large thorn. He barely felt it as he kept moving as fast as he could.

After he had run about forty yards he came to a stop and looked around. All Corbeau could see were trees, vines, and low bushes in every direction. He listened carefully, trying to hear if the woman would call out again. He wiped the sweat off his forehead with his forearm. The knight heard nothing except the birds above. He knew he was close to finding them, and he didn't want this opportunity to slip away.

"Show yourself!" he yelled out. He listened carefully. He heard nothing in response.

Think...think... what can I do? Corbeau thought to himself. *How can I get a step ahead of this fiend?* Corbeau thought of seeing him in the tavern. He thought of him yelling out in anger at the bartender. He then remembered why this criminal got upset suddenly with the bartender. Corbeau decided to give it a try himself.

"Come out and fight me... you crook!" He stopped for a moment and looked all around him. "Where are you, you devilish crook?" He checked from side to side, but still he heard nothing except the sounds of birds and animals from the forest. He looked back toward the direction from which he came. Nothing had changed. Corbeau wondered if he had run in the wrong direction.

He took one step back toward the direction from where he came, when suddenly he felt a smash against the back of his head. He fell to the ground, dropping his swords. A thick log had hit him in the back of his head.

"No one calls me a crook," Brutus cried out with his deep voice.

Corbeau was stunned as he tried to climb back to his feet. He wasn't fast enough as Brutus was standing over him in a matter of seconds. He grabbed the knight of Mendolon, picking him up like a rag doll. He then threw him a few feet against a tree. Corbeau's arm and shoulder hit against the side of the tree.

Brutus picked up one of Corbeau's swords and quickly walked over to where the knight was lying. He raised the sword over his head. The knight moved quickly and grabbed a branch that was by his side. He raised it high just as the sword was brought down against him. The sword went halfway into the branch. Corbeau then twisted the branch to his side, pulling the sword from the hand of the escaped prisoner.

Corbeau shifted his body and with all his might threw a punch into the belly of the large man. Brutus groaned as he took a step backward. Corbeau then sprang to his feet and swung his right foot around and kicked his opponent in his side. Brutus stumbled slightly. Corbeau tried to throw another punch but his enemy was able to catch his arm before it made contact. He then bent the knight's arm backwards and grabbed him by the throat with his other hand. Brutus squeezed tightly. Corbeau couldn't breathe.

Brutus then lifted the knight into the air and pushed his body back against the tree behind him. He squeezed tighter against the knight's neck. Corbeau grabbed Brutus' hand, trying to pull it away from his neck. He knew he would have to act quickly as his brain was losing oxygen. Being that his feet were not on the ground, he sought to use that to his advantage. Pushing his legs off the trunk of the tree he was able to swing them forward and strike his enemy's stomach with his knee. Brutus let out a moan as he was hit, releasing Corbeau.

The knight of Mendolon fell to the ground and took a deep breath. Brutus was on the ground holding his stomach as the wind had been knocked out of him. Corbeau knew he had to keep moving. There was no time to spare. A thick vine was hanging off a tree not far from Brutus. The knight got to his feet and grabbed the vine. Brutus was moving slowly at this point, and before he could react, Corbeau had the vine twisted around Brutus' neck. Corbeau pulled it as tight as he could and then pulled his enemy to the ground.

Brutus rolled from side to side as his hands tried to loosen the vine. Corbeau kept pulling, trying to cut off any bit of air. "How do you like it now?" Corbeau said angrily.

Brutus then pushed hard against the ground and turned onto his back. Corbeau lost his grip on the vine and Brutus was able to easily pull it off. He then threw back his right elbow into the cheek of the knight. Corbeau fell to his side. Brutus, knowing that he now had the upper hand, sprang onto Corbeau and began delivering a series of punches onto his face.

Brutus was now moving like a madman as he continued to punch the knight of Mendolon. He didn't let up as he directed all his punches into Corbeau's cheekbone. "You didn't leave me alone," Brutus yelled out as he punched. "I'm just tryin' to get out of here." Corbeau felt his vision beginning to blur. He could only take a few more hits before he lost consciousness. With his right hand he felt along the ground, searching for something he could use. Mostly he just felt grass and mud. He frantically grabbed a handful of mud and flung it into Brutus' face. The outlaw hardly even flinched as the mud splattered onto the side of his head.

Corbeau went back to frantically searching for anything that could help him as punches kept being delivered to his face. His hand suddenly felt something hard. It had a sharp point on one of its end. Knowing it might be his only chance, he grabbed the small stick and quickly struck it into a soft spot on the back of Brutus' neck. It went in at least four inches sideways. "Aww!" Brutus screamed in pain. His plan worked as Brutus let up from his attacks so he could grab the stick out of his neck.

Corbeau, still dazed, crawled away from Brutus as best as he could. He then stumbled to his feet and began moving back toward the pond. He had a few moments as Brutus was still occupied with removing the stick from his neck. The stick had entered awkwardly under his skin, and blood was running from the back of his neck. Screaming in anguish, in one quick motion he removed the stick. The sharp end was covered in blood. The sight of it just made him angrier. He threw it aside and rose to his feet. His eyes were fixed on his opponent. He would not let him get away. Looking to his side, he saw one of Corbeau's swords. He quickly picked it up and ran after the knight.

Rain began to fall slightly as Corbeau ran through the wooded area. He was off the path and fought through many vines and branches. If he kept going this way he knew he would eventually arrive on the trail. His body hurt as the beating from Brutus had bruised him badly. As he continued to move, he looked back to see Brutus coming toward him, moving as fast as he could. Corbeau knew it wouldn't take long before he was caught by his enemy. He tried to pick up his speed but found it difficult with the throbbing pain he was enduring in his head.

Corbeau arrived at the trail. Fifty feet to his left he saw the small boat he had taken across the pond. Knowing it was his best option to lose his pursuer he ran toward it as fast he could. The boat sat in shallow water eight feet from the dry land, so he knew he would have to jump for it. He also hoped his momentum in landing would carry the boat into the middle of the pond.

Reaching the edge of the dry ground, Corbeau took a long jump toward the boat. He wanted to land on the farther end by the deeper water. He flew through the air and landed on his shoulder in the area he was hoping to land. Water splashed from side to side as the boat bobbed up and down. At first Corbeau thought the boat was going to tip, but it eventually steadied as it moved away from the shore. The plan worked. In just a couple seconds he was now at least thirty feet away from the dry land.

Brutus arrived at the edge of the pond and saw the knight floating away on the boat. He snarled angrily and gripped the sword tightly. He had been looking forward to putting an end to this menace. He stomped his right foot before yelling out, "You coward!"

Corbeau sat up in the boat to see his enemy walking away. He smelled something terrible. Looking at the bottom of the boat he remembered what it was. A plan quickly formed in his mind. He called out to his enemy, "Where are you going, you debased crook!"

Brutus turned around and walked back to the edge of the shore. He spoke quietly through a very angry expression, "What did you say?"

Corbeau rose to his feet, trying not to rock the boat. He hoped he looked like he wanted to fight. "I said you're nothing but a debased crook. You represent the worst of our kingdom." Brutus didn't say anything but just stood gritting his teeth. Blood continued to run down the back of his neck. He couldn't remember a time when he felt this angry. Corbeau continued, hoping his enemy would reach his tipping point. "Actually, I don't think you're worthy to be called a crook. You're just a large man who likes kidnapping poor, defenseless women. I hope you..."

"That's it!" Brutus shouted as he ran out into the lake. The sword was still in his hand as he easily made his way through the shallow water. Corbeau, all of a sudden, doubted this plan he had and began looking around for something he could fight with. Panic quickly came upon him. Brutus entered the deeper water and continued toward the boat. The water level was up to the middle of his chest. He reached the boat and grabbed the end of it with one hand. Corbeau backed away as far as he could, wondering if this would be his end.

Brutus raised the sword high in the air, when he suddenly stopped. He felt a strange sensation move up his body. With his empty hand, he reached into the water to feel the leathery skin of the swamp's snake wrapping around his torso. In his anger he had forgotten about the dangers of this water, and now he was paying the price for it. The snake began to squeeze his body tightly as he dropped the sword and screamed out in fear. Corbeau then watched as the head of the snake came out of the water and wrapped itself around his enemy's head, muffling his screams. Eventually, his head was completely covered by the snake's body. As the creature did its final lap, it stopped and looked straight at Corbeau sitting in the boat just a few feet away. The creature's red eyes glared at the knight of Mendolon. Corbeau looked back in fear, seeing the power of this creature. It was evil, and something in its expression looked as if it was enjoying itself. Corbeau would never forget this moment.

It was then without warning that the creature quickly pulled Brutus into the pond. They were both gone in an instant. Corbeau watched as he could see the ripples in the water as the creature with his victim moved out further to the middle of the water, long past the boat.

Corbeau breathed heavily. Between fighting with Brutus and seeing the snake again, he felt paralyzed, drained of energy. He collapsed in the bottom of the boat as he tried to catch his breath.

4

Corbeau lay in the bottom of the small boat drifting in and out of consciousness. He guessed it was around an hour before he felt awake enough to sit up. Now that his adrenaline from the fight was wearing off, he could feel every bruise and every cut. Touching his face, he could tell his eye was swollen. Nothing felt broken, but he knew he would have to see a doctor. Of first importance though was finding the young woman who had been captured.

As Corbeau sat up in the boat, he found that the vessel had drifted close to the shore beside a bush growing out toward the water. He was only about twenty feet from where he had jumped back into the boat. There was no oar in the boat so he would have to use whatever he could to get back to where he had jumped. He grabbed the bush and pulled it, propelling the boat toward the trail. Even the simple action of propelling the boat forward felt like a strain. He started to cough violently. His lungs hurt. A small part of him felt like giving up, but the thought of the young woman alone in the forest kept him moving forward. He knew she needed to be rescued.

Eventually the boat came to a stop in the shallow water, not far from where it was stuck earlier. He knew he would have to deal with the dreaded snake again. Corbeau brushed his hair to the side and took a deep breath. He thought he would try the same plan as before. The knight slowly removed his breastplate, hoping it wouldn't be needed anymore. He flung it sideways as far as he could into the middle of the pond.

Corbeau waited, and waited, and waited... and then eventually he saw the creature briefly come out of the water and take his breastplate under. Just the brief glimpse of the creature was enough to motivate Corbeau to quickly spring from the boat and onto the shore. He moved a few feet from the shore and once again stopped to catch his breath. He shook his head as he hoped that would be the last interaction he ever had with that terrible creature.

Corbeau began moving toward the area where Brutus had left the young woman. The plant life was quite a bit thicker than he remembered. His pain slowed him down. The bite against his lower leg was starting to bother him more. He found himself limping slightly. His feet sank an inch or two with each step as the ground was moist. Vines, small bushes, and tree branches all made the path difficult, but nothing was going to stop him from finding this young woman.

Corbeau de Lefevre arrived at the spot where he had fought with Brutus. He took a breath and looked around the area, trying to remember the exact spot from which his enemy had sprung. Looking down, he saw the log Brutus had thrown at his head. He tried to remember where he was standing and from what direction the log had come. The world was still a little blurry to him as he was still recovering, but he thought he knew the general direction of where to search.

A thick tree stood about fifteen feet from the area of the fight. It had to be where Brutus was hiding earlier. Corbeau headed toward it, fighting through branches. Reaching the tree, he checked around it and saw nothing. He was about to turn away and head back when he caught a glimpse of the young woman's arm. It was sticking out from behind a bush. He quickly ran to it and looked around to the other side of the bush. The woman was lying on her side unconscious. She was badly bruised, and one of her cheeks looked swollen. It appeared as if she was knocked out by Brutus before he came out to fight. Corbeau knew he had no time to waste. He gently picked up the woman, supporting her head as best as he could. She moaned slightly as he adjusted her in his arms. Corbeau walked slowly back through the thick woods. He knew this trip would be a longer one since he would have to find a different route around the pond and toward the area from where he entered.

The walk out of the swamp was a long one. Corbeau had to stop and take many breaks. His strength had been diminished during the fight with Brutus, and now more than ever he could tell how weak he felt. The young woman was his motivation. Through the whole walk out of the swamp she didn't wake up. She needed to be rescued. She needed a doctor soon. Corbeau feared she might have entered into a coma.

After an hour and a half, Corbeau found his way back to the same entrance from where he came. Coming out of the swampland, he could see it was starting to get dark. To his disappointment he saw that the horse did not wait for him to return. He had no other option but to walk back toward the village. It was close to nightfall and he knew they wouldn't make it far before darkness came upon them. Still he had no other choice; he knew he would have to continue on.

Corbeau carried the young woman down the road. He hoped he would find someone who could help. It was late, and the chances of meeting someone would be slim. He kept moving forward into the dark of night. Usually travelers would take a route a few miles to the south, but with the bridge out over the river, very few people would be traveling in this area.

It wasn't long before darkness had completely overtaken them, and Corbeau didn't know if it was delirium or reality but he thought he heard horses' hooves coming toward him. He would take the chance that this was in fact reality. He began calling out. "Help! ... Over here! ... Please!"

The sound became louder and after a while, he could see four men coming toward him on horseback. Corbeau instantly felt relief as the men came further into view. He didn't know exactly who they were, but he did recognize a couple of them from the small village from where the woman was captured. The same village where he had lived for the last month.

Corbeau sat on the ground and gently laid the young woman down beside him. He felt his body relax even further as he knew these men were coming to rescue them. The mission was complete.

کوچه

It was early in the afternoon on the next day before Corbeau awoke. He found himself back in the room at the inn where he had stayed for so long. His body was sore and his head was bandaged. It was obvious that a doctor had seen him. He thought about just rolling over and falling back asleep, but a part of him was curious as to the condition of the young woman. The knight pulled the covers off his body and swung his feet onto the floor. He could see that his leg had also been bandaged where he had been bitten by the snake. That was one wound he hoped was cleaned extremely thoroughly. Corbeau moaned as he stood to his feet. He felt as if his body had aged ten years as a result of his confrontation with Brutus.

Someone apparently had left a pair of sandals and a change of clothes for him. He gently slid them on and headed down the steps of the inn. All was quiet which wasn't unusual for this time of the day. Most people just came and stayed overnight. Few residents were around during the day.

Reaching the bottom of the steps, he noticed the innkeeper behind the desk. His glasses were on and he was fiddling with something small. Corbeau slowly took a step toward him. There was a creak in the steps and the innkeeper looked up and took notice. "You're awake," he said, excited to see the knight.

"Yeah," Corbeau said quietly. His voice was a little raspy.

"Do you need anything?"

Corbeau shrugged his shoulders, "I don't know.... I think I'm fine."

The innkeeper held out a cup toward the knight. "How about some water?"

"Sure, thanks." Corbeau gingerly grabbed the cup and drank it down. Finishing it, he set the glass down and wiped his mouth.

The innkeeper smiled through a white beard as he kept speaking. "You did an amazing thing for this town, saving that girl and all."

The mention of the woman caught his attention. "How is she?"

"Well... don't know for sure yet. Talk around town is that she's got a long road ahead of her, but they think she'll be all right."

"I see," Corbeau said, looking off to the side. He was relieved to hear this. His initial thought was that the young woman would never wake up from this whole ordeal.

The old man rubbed his chin as he continued to talk. "Our men found one of the outlaws badly wounded, just past the bridge. Do you know what happened to the big guy who was leading them?"

Corbeau just looked straight at the inn keeper and nodded. Thinking about that man's death, he didn't know quite what to say in response.

The innkeeper was curious for information. "Did he get away?"

"No... he definitely didn't get away. Let's just say he now rests in the bottom of a pond in the swamp."

The innkeeper was a little curious about Corbeau's answer, but the man could tell he was ready to talk about something else. "Well, whenever you're feeling up to it, the folks would like to see you in the tavern."

"Okay... thanks," Corbeau said quietly in response. A change of scenery might be what he needed He didn't like the thought of just sitting in his room alone, and besides, a pint of ale and a bite to eat sounded good. "Thank you."

Corbeau headed back to his room and changed into his extra set of clothes. He was feeling better by the minute. The night's rest had gone a long way in his recovery and getting food in his system would further help significantly. He knew it would take a few weeks before he was completely healed, but he was hopeful.

As Corbeau left the inn, the innkeeper yelled out to him, "Do you want me to take you to the tavern? I've got a wagon."

"No, thanks. I'll walk."

"You sure? You're limping. Here, let me take you," the innkeeper pleaded. Corbeau relented, knowing the old man wouldn't take 'no' for an answer. They quickly attached a horse and were on their way. The ride didn't take long as the tavern was only a quarter mile away. As they progressed further down the road, Corbeau was thankful for this ride. It would probably be a couple days before his legs would be up to walking this far.

Reaching the tavern, Corbeau slowly climbed down from the cart and began walking toward the tavern. After a few steps he realized the innkeeper was not coming. He turned and saw he was still on the cart. "Aren't you coming?"

The old man chuckled as he shook his head. "No. This is for you. I believe the folks will be glad to see you." Corbeau nodded without saying a word. He then turned and slowly made his way inside.

The knight found the place full of people, most of them engaged in robust conversations. The capture and rescue of the young woman was definitely the talk of the small village and would be for a long time. As he took a few steps toward the counter, folks began to take notice. Many stopped their conversations as they turned to see their hero walk amongst them. Corbeau smiled as he walked toward the counter. It was then that a middle-aged man in the crowd began to clap slowly. Others started to join in, and then others; more and more joined until the whole place was loud with applause for the knight.

Corbeau reached the counter as the clapping continued. The tavern owner poured him a pint of ale. "This one's on me," he said proudly. Corbeau took the cup and raised it high toward the crowd. He had a wide smile on his face.

To further honor their hero, one of the patrons in the crowd then began a chant, "Our – Knight!, Our – Knight!, Our - Knight!" The crowd quickly caught on and before long the whole crowd was then joining the chant. From now on, he would always be held in high regard in this small village, and he would always be their knight.

Corbeau scanned the crowd and saw the immense joy on their faces. It was a day of victory for them. He was thrilled to be a part of it. The chants continued, "Our – Knight!, Our – Knight!, Our – Knight!" He had to admit to himself too, that this recognition truly felt good. He smiled and laughed as he continued to receive their gratitude.

Two weeks had passed since the rescue of the young woman. Corbeau was now back working in the castle of Mendolon. Any thought of walking away from knighthood had ceased. He was a new man. All of his nightmares and anxieties from the Savage were now gone, and most of his injuries were healing. He was now planning to help the Mendolon soldiers with the capture of the other escaped prisoners around Mendolon.

Currently, Corbeau was walking the halls of the castle. This was his first day back. He had received a message from Hector to see him in the war room. Hector was now leading and organizing the effort to capture the rest of the escaped prisoners. There were many left that still needed to be found. The king wanted to be vigilant in capturing them before any other kidnappings or large crimes took place. Corbeau was eager to join the effort and get his assignment from Hector.

"Glad you're back, Corbeau," a couple of knights said as they passed him in the hall.

"Thank you," he said casually. The castle was a busy place today, and many people were excited to have him back and in good spirits.

A group of soldiers passed him as he descended the steps. "Welcome back. Congratulations on the rescue of the young woman," the men said.

Corbeau nodded, receiving this gratitude. He had received compliments like this all day. They were motivating, encouraging to hear.

Opening the doors to the war room, he found Hector sitting casually at the table. He was dressed in his usual dark green robe. His black hair was pushed back, and Corbeau could easily see the pale face of the king's advisor.

"Welcome, Corbeau de Lefevre. Conqueror of the dreaded Brutus," Hector said, with the hissing of his voice clearly on display.

"Greetings," Corbeau said, stepping further into the room. He noticed the room was dark. A candle sat in the middle of the round table where Hector was seated.

"Come, sit," Hector said, standing to his feet and offering a seat near him. Corbeau slowly made his way over to the king's advisor, wondering why this meeting seemed so secret. He figured he was just receiving his assignments.

Both men took a seat near one another as Hector continued. "How is your strength? Have you fully recovered from hunting that dreaded criminal?"

"Yes, I think I'm close. I'll be as good as anyone in chasing down these escaped prisoners."

Hector put his hands together on the table and leaned forward. "What became of Brutus?"

Corbeau looked off to the side. The dreaded memory of his death was not one he wanted to recount. "He's dead. A creature in the swamp killed him."

"Good," Hector responded, smiling devilishly.

The two men sat together in silence for a moment. Hector slowly tapped his fingers against the table as he seemed to be deep in thought. Corbeau was growing impatient as he was anxious to receive his assignment. He was ready to start a new mission and hunt down these prisoners. "Where would you have me go?"

Hector bit his lip as he thought carefully about what he was going to say. After a moment he spoke quietly, "I'm going to need your help. You're going to lead the soldiers in the capturing of the escaped prisoners."

"You want me to lead?" Corbeau asked in amazement.

"Yes, we have identified a few different locations where the criminals are hiding out. I want you on every attack. When can you be ready?"

Corbeau was stunned. He wasn't sure exactly what to say. "Why... why me?"

"I need a knight, and you are the one I trust the most. The others have been reassigned to different areas of Mendolon."

A flood of questions entered Corbeau's mind. He didn't know where to start. He had come a long way from just a few weeks ago, when he was thinking about giving up his knighthood. Now he was going to be a leader among the soldiers. Corbeau nodded as he looked straight at Hector. "Yes. I will lead the soldiers."

"Good, and there is one more thing."

"Yes, and what's that?"

Hector rubbed his chin and looked around one last time to make sure no one else was in the room. "Every time a mission is complete, I want you to report to me first about everything you see among the criminals. Miss no details. I need to know everything."

Corbeau was caught off guard by this statement. He was curious. "What... what am I looking for?"

Hector stood to his feet and pushed the chair back under the table. He hissed slightly under his breath as he spoke quietly, "Just do what I ask. Report to me first. Every detail."

Corbeau just sat looking at Hector, trying to think what to say next. Hector leaned forward, "Do you hear me?"

The knight slowly nodded his head. "Yes... report to you first. Every detail."

"Good. Now, be ready in the morning for your first assignment," Hector said as he abruptly turned and left the room. Corbeau watched every step as the king's advisor turned and left. He wondered what this new adventure would entail.

Knights of Mendolon

Book #2

By

Tony Myers

PROLOGUE

Once there was a kingdom called Mendolon. The kingdom was known for its company of knights. They were elite in their abilities and particularly their swordsmanship. Though the number could vary slightly, there were usually around twenty of them, and they were known as the fiercest protectors of the realm. Their history went back to the time of the kingdom's founding. These knights helped fight for the kingdom while also standing for truth and justice for the people. Through the years they had helped to keep Mendolon balanced and standing for righteousness.

The kingdom of Mendolon also had an army of soldiers, but the knights were a distinguished group from them. In order to become a knight, a soldier would have to be recognized by his peers for his abilities and character. He or she would have to go through various tests before being approved by the king. A vote could then proceed among the other knights to let him or her join the ranks.

The knights also had legislative abilities in the kingdom. If the king enacted a law that seemed immoral and unjust, the knights could call for a special council. After deliberating, if the knights still thought the law was unjust, they could call for a vote to repeal. This was rarely done. In an extreme case of a king acting wickedly, the knights could convene a council and call for a vote of no confidence against the king. It would take a hundred percent vote from the knights to overthrow the reigning king. This had never been done in the long history of Mendolon.

Throughout the years, the knights had faced many challenges, but the challenge of the Savage had proven to be their most difficult yet. The attack at the ruins had left many of them decrepit and weak, unable to fight their enemy as a collected whole. It took many of them a few weeks to completely recover. Thankfully, a handful of knights, along with the help of the beast, Jean-Luc, were able to get a step ahead of their enemy's plans and defeat the Savage. The kingdom was again starting to stabilize and work toward normalcy.

However, little did the knights know that their greatest challenge awaited them. A test was coming that would seek not just to destroy them as individuals, but would seek to destroy the very things the knights of Mendolon stood for—truth, hope, and justice.

♋︎⤸

Hector, the king's advisor, waited outside the castle gates. It was late in the evening and rain was pouring down heavily. He was dressed in black this time because he didn't want to be recognized by his green robe. A hood was also pulled over his head. He was waiting anxiously for news of the last raid. For the past six months, the soldiers and knights had searched far and wide throughout the kingdom of Mendolon to capture all the prisoners the Savage had released. There had been about a hundred prisoners who had escaped. So far, about two-thirds of them had been recaptured. Currently, Hector was waiting to hear word about a raid that had happened earlier in the day.

There were growing anxieties in the kingdom of Mendolon with the prisoners being on the loose. Many small thefts and acts of crime had been committed by these prisoners. Many of the villages throughout the kingdom took matters into their own hands, often capturing one or two stray criminals that were trying to blend in among the people. Thankfully among all the chaos created by the escapees, there had only been two instances of violent crimes against Mendolon's citizens.

The raid earlier in the day was for a group of a half dozen prisoners. They were hiding out in a mountainous area in the northeast region of Mendolon. Hector briefly heard that the raid went well and that the prisoners had surrendered when confronted by the soldiers. Once captured, the prisoners were interrogated before they were taken back to the prison. Oftentimes the interrogations led to more information concerning where other prisoners were hiding.

Hector's train of thought was broken by a knight coming up the road. He was in a hurry. He was dressed in battle armor except without his helmet. A red cape flowed behind him as he ran to meet Hector. His name was Corbeau de Lefevre. He was a knight in his early thirties. He had proven himself mightily in battle, and he was confident in his abilities. Maybe sometimes a little too confident. Four months ago, Hector had assigned him the duty of overseeing the soldiers in their attempt to capture the escaped prisoners. Hector was pleased with his work, and as the weeks passed by he had grown to trust Corbeau with more information.

Corbeau was out of breath as he approached Hector. "I came as soon as I could."

"Was the raid as easy as they said it was?" Hector said, hissing as he spoke.

"Yes, they surrendered without putting up a fight. It seems like these were just common criminals. Nothing out of the ordinary."

Hector was looking for more information. "Are you sure he wasn't among the prisoners today?"

"Yes, they were all fairly young prisoners and it was even more clear from the interrogation that they were just trying to escape to Grimdolon or to the Empire in the north."

"Curses!" Hector uttered as he shook his head in frustration. "We may never find this dastardly fiend."

"Well, take heart, my lord," Corbeau spoke through the heavy rain. "They did speak of an island off our coast where the rest of the prisoners are gathering."

"What? Tell me more."

"They said something of an old fort where they were hoping to gather supplies and eventually sail across the southern seas."

"The old Toulouse fort! When Sebastian became king he abandoned it, not seeing the need to station soldiers there."

"My lord, it sounds quite promising. I believe this is the best lead we've had yet."

Hector nodded, hoping Corbeau had received accurate information. There was one specific prisoner that urgently needed to be found. And Hector knew that no one was safe until he was found. "Let us hope that this is the end."

CHAPTER 1

Michael walked the rows of corn, picking the crop as harvest was upon Mendolon. He was sweating as he carried a large cloth bag over his shoulder almost full of corn. Occasionally he would help a farmer friend during this time of year. Working as the chief knight of Mendolon often came with stressful demands, and he found that working in the fields was just what he needed to help focus his mind. He looked forward to these times when he could completely relax.

He looked different as of late as he had his hair cut shorter and a light beard donned his face. He was dressed in old farm clothes with a bandana over his head. Many of the citizens of Mendolon wouldn't have even recognized him in this context.

The past six months in Mendolon had been a little hectic with the knights trying to capture the escaped prisoners. Michael had only been on one of the raids against the prisoners since Corbeau was now leading the soldiers and knights in the raids. Michael's time had mostly been spent reassuring the citizens of the kingdom of their safety. The people felt very reassured hearing directly from Michael that the Savage was defeated and the kingdom was working to capture the escaped prisoners. He took great joy in being the bearer of good news.

Many of the citizens of Mendolon had questions concerning Belle. They loved the princess and were quite alarmed by her absence. Whenever he was asked, Michael was honest. He told them who Belle really was, and that she had fallen in love with King Jean-Luc of Grimdolon. Most of the people responded with happiness for their princess but also with anger toward King Sebastian. The act of kidnapping a future queen of any kingdom was reprehensible, even if it wasn't an ally nation. Through it all the people appreciated Michael's honesty.

Michael picked his last ear of corn as he came to the end of the row. He walked to a nearby wooden cart and emptied his bag. Michael had worked nearly six hours as he had started a couple of hours before daylight and it was now mid-morning. He was done for now and was ready to head home. The old farmer who owned the farm approached Michael with a water skin.

"Thank you for your help today, Michael. I owe you a lot."

Michael took a drink from the water skin. He shook his head as he brought it down from his lips. "You don't owe me anything, Piers. Like I've said in the past, I look forward to these times in the field."

"Well, I don't know how I'd make it without you," the old farmer said smiling. He was getting close to eighty, and he kept finding his old farm harder and harder to maintain. The farmer, Piers, had been a family friend for a long time. Michael's father, Albert, even worked for him when he was a teenager. Michael greatly appreciated all the stories the old farmer told about his father.

Michael took a seat on the wooden cart and looked out into the distance as he drank the rest of the water. The old farmer turned to Michael, "Has ol' Sebastian sent you on any new excursions lately?"

"No, I've helped to settle a few land disputes in the east, but other than that, the last few weeks particularly have been quiet."

"Well, I hope you're not just sitting around getting old and lazy."

Michael laughed slightly, "Thankfully the princess built an extensive training ground. I've found it quite helpful in keeping my abilities fresh."

The farmer nodded his head. Michael could tell he was thinking about something specific. Piers took off his straw hat and took a deep breath. "Well... uh... Michael..."

"Yes?"

He spoke a little timidly, "Have you heard from her since she left?"

Michael looked down at his feet as he searched for the words to say. "No, I figured she made it safely to Grimdolon and found Jean-Luc."

Piers put a long grass blade in his mouth. He chewed it methodically. He and Michael were close, and he knew he could ask him anything. "Do you miss her?"

Michael bit his lip as he searched for the right words. He debated with himself about how honest he should be with his friend. He had plenty of time to think about her since he hadn't been on many missions lately. He figured honesty was the best route. "I do. Every day I think of her." Michael paused briefly before continuing, "But I'm comforted knowing that she's happy, and Grimdolon is where she's supposed to be." Piers simply nodded in return. He could tell this was a little difficult for his friend. He didn't want to pry much more.

The two friends sat in silence for a few minutes, enjoying the sunshine. It was a beautiful scene. There had been a lot of rain the past couple days and it was great to have some clearer weather today. The birds were out chirping. A few squirrels were running around the edge of the field. Michael was truly at peace.

Michael was then caught off guard when the farmer tapped him on the shoulder. "Yes," Michael said, turning to face him.

"My eyes aren't very good, but I think someone is coming up the road for you."

Michael turned to see where the farmer was pointing, and sure enough, coming up the road was a soldier in battle attire riding on a horse. "Hmm... yeah, I think you're right." Michael turned to face the farmer with a smile, "Maybe he's coming to see if we need any help with the corn."

The farmer laughed slightly, "Call me crazy, but I don't think my farm is a top priority for Mendolon soldiers."

As the soldier got closer, Michael could tell that it was Amis, the man he had rescued from the Savage at the prison. Michael jumped off the cart when the soldier was a few feet away. "Welcome, Amis, to whom do I owe the distinct pleasure of this visit?"

"Greetings, Michael. You've been summoned by King Sebastian."

Michael was taken aback by this sudden order. "Is everything all right? Do you know what this is about?"

The young soldier shook his head, "No, he just said to find you immediately. He said it was urgent."

Michael looked back at Piers sitting on the cart. The old man shrugged his shoulders as he continued to chew on the blade of grass. Michael smiled, knowing this peaceful day was about to take a different turn. A part of him wished he could go back and just sit on the cart with Piers.

The king was sitting on his throne when Michael walked into the throne room. A handful of soldiers were stationed around the room. Sebastian was wearing a long robe and his crown was sitting comfortably on his brown curls. Seeing Michael enter the room, he stood to greet him. "Greetings, Michael."

Michael simply nodded in return as he approached the king. The two had not been on friendly terms since the defeat of the Savage. Michael was angry at Sebastian for the kidnapping of Belle. The chief knight debated with himself many mornings about officially confronting the king about it with the other knights. A large part of him felt betrayed by his king. He wondered if Sebastian was hiding any more secrets.

The king looked toward the soldiers that were stationed close to the walls. "Guards, leave us." In full obedience, the soldiers turned from their posts and left the room. Michael was puzzled as the men left the room. He wondered why Sebastian needed the secrecy.

As the doors were closing, Sebastian continued, "Thank you for coming, Michael."

"You're welcome. King, what is the nature of this visit? Why the urgency?" Michael said, trying to get right to the point of this meeting.

The king calmly turned and walked to a small table stationed beside his throne. Michael could see a bottle on the table along with two cups. "May I offer you a drink?"

"No," Michael said quietly.

Sebastian slowly poured himself a cup of wine and took a small sip. He then turned to face Michael before continuing. "I need your help."

Michael looked at the king sternly. "Obviously it will depend on what you want me to do."

Sebastian shook his head. "Michael, please don't tell me you're still mad at me for kidnapping the princess of Grimdolon."

"What you did was reprehensible," Michael said firmly.

The king stepped closer to Michael and put his hand on his chief knight's shoulder. "It was what I had to do, my chief knight. Grimdolon is our enemy, and you know the power they possess in those mines. I had to do something drastic."

Michael looked off to the side as he didn't want to face the king. He had lost any respect he had for this man. Even though he had provided a stable realm for the people of Mendolon, Michael was tired of his manipulations and immoral tactics. If it wasn't for his love for the other knights and the people of Mendolon, Michael would have walked away from the kingdom long ago.

Sebastian continued, "Besides, think of this—for being an enemy princess, I treated her fairly. I made her my own daughter. I even let her pursue training as a knight. Surely you of all people can see that she was well taken care of."

Michael didn't know what to say. He had already grown tired of this conversation with Sebastian. Michael felt like even still he was being manipulated. He looked back at the king as he spoke, "What is it you want?"

Sebastian smiled as he patted Michael's shoulder. "Very well," he said, turning from Michael and heading back toward the small table. "As you are well aware Corbeau is leading the knights and soldiers in the raids against the escaped prisoners."

"Yes, I'm aware. I believe there are a few that are still unapprehended."

"That's correct," the king said with his back toward Michael. "I believe there is one last raid that will be conducted."

"And where's this?"

Sebastian turned again toward Michael, "Off the southwest coast of Mendolon. We have gotten word that a few dozen prisoners are taking refuge in the old Toulouse fort."

Michael rubbed his chin as he recollected the old fort. He had forgotten about it as Sebastian didn't see it as a priority to maintain. "Ok, what does this have to do with me?"

Sebastian took another sip from his cup. "I want you on this raid."

"With all due respect, Your Majesty, Corbeau seems to be leading these raids just fine. I could see my presence bringing some confusion among the soldiers as to who is in charge."

"Yes, I know Corbeau has been successful, but there is more to it than just simply capturing the last prisoners."

Michael was intrigued. "What do you mean?"

Sebastian stepped closer to Michael and spoke in a whisper. "I mean that something is happening behind my back."

"What are you talking about?"

"I've gotten word that during the raids Corbeau is secretly interrogating the prisoners once they are in custody."

Michael was a little confused. "How do you know this?"

The king laughed just a little. "Michael, you know the soldiers are loyal to me. Corbeau doesn't know he's being watched, but they see him."

Michael crossed his arms as he continued trying to decipher the meaning of all this. "Ok... why are you choosing to involve me?"

"I want you to find out what Corbeau is planning. Why is he operating in secret? I fear that there is something greater at work here."

"What do you mean?" Michael said, puzzled.

The king bit his lip and looked off to the side as he spoke quietly, "I'm not sure how this came about, but there is some sort of secret among the prisoners."

"Secret... what is this you speak of?"

"It's like the soldiers have some sort of hidden power among them."

Michael was stunned at this point. Confusion plagued him. "Tell me more, King. What of this power?"

"I don't know for sure, but it may have something to do but with a prisoner Hector had arrested years ago." The king paused a moment before continuing, "All I know is that these prisoners need to be captured before this power is let out."

Michael nodded his head, realizing the urgency of the king's request. He knew they would have to act quickly. "When do they leave for the fort?"

"In just a few hours... be ready to leave from the southwestern port."

CHAPTER 2

The ship was tossed by the rough waters of the ocean as it made its way toward the old fortress. A crew of soldiers manned the ship. Corbeau was at the helm looking out into the sea, his red cape flowing in the wind. He was waiting for the fortress to come into sight as the ship continued moving forward. Everyone was generally quiet, knowing some sort of fight would ensue once they arrived on sight.

Corbeau looked toward his men. He had brought sixteen with him. Some looked anxious while others tightened their armor, making sure everything was in the proper place. He wondered if this was their last fight with these prisoners. He'd been chasing them the last four months, and he hoped that this would be the end, and better yet, he hoped that he would find the one prisoner he was looking for. He unsheathed one of his swords and admired it as the light of the sun reflected off the blade. He gripped it tightly as he rotated his wrist. Corbeau usually carried two swords with him in battle, each just under two feet in length. They were his most trusted weapons.

"Sir, land is in sight!" a soldier yelled out, interrupting Corbeau's train of thought. Corbeau looked out to sea and saw the old fortress come in the distance. Every man stood to his feet and got their respective weapons ready. Some had swords, while others had bow and arrows. A few carried spears. Most had shields.

"Ready yourselves, men," Corbeau said. "We will enter together and move slowly as they will have nowhere to go." A few of the men nodded in agreement.

In the depths of the ship, a cloaked figure arose from among a collection of empty barrels. He had heard the men on the deck getting themselves ready. He figured the fortress was coming into sight. As a force of habit, he felt the daggers on his belt, making sure they were all in their proper place. Michael de Bolbec had sneaked on board before the soldiers came. He didn't have a definite plan in place for when he was on the island. He wondered when he should reveal himself to the others, or if he should try to stay in the shadows the whole time. Either way, he knew his main objective was to find out who Corbeau and Hector were looking for.

The ship ran ashore on the island, and the men quickly jumped overboard using ropes to guide them to the water. The water was just about at the men's knees. Only one would stay aboard the ship. Corbeau turned to the lone soldier before he jumped off, "Prepare the barracks in the lower decks. We hope to bring all the men back alive."

"Yes sir," the soldier responded. Corbeau nodded one last time as he jumped into the water. He was a little surprised to find that it was quite cold. Slowly he made his way through the water toward the shore. Many of his men were already on the small beach regrouping. Corbeau looked further on to the small fortress about fifty yards away. It was an old dilapidated, sand colored building. There were many holes in the walls, and one could easily see that a large portion of the roof had caved in.

Reaching the shore, Corbeau instructed the men one last time. "Remember to be careful. Through talking with other prisoners, I've learned the leader of this group is a man named Lin. He is from a kingdom in the far east and is trained in an ancient Eastern fighting style. He is very skilled, but he shouldn't be too much of a problem if we work together."

"Yes, Captain," the men responded in agreement.

"Ok, let's move in," Corbeau instructed as he moved toward the fortress. He was in the lead with the soldiers following in behind. Each man had his weapons ready just in case they were suddenly ambushed.

At this time Michael made his way to the upper deck. The lone soldier on board was watching his comrades as they made their way closer to the fortress. Michael calmly walked up behind the soldier as he was watching the others make their way further onto the land. "How many men did

Corbeau bring with him?" Michael spoke calmly, but it still startled the man.

The soldier turned and fell to the ground as he pulled his sword. He held out his sword toward Michael before realizing that he was standing before the chief knight of Mendolon. "Michael de Bolbec! What are you doing here?"

"Just checking on this raid... making sure everything is in proper order. How many men does Corbeau have with him?"

"There are seventeen of us total," the soldier said, still surprised from seeing the chief knight.

Michael simply nodded as he continued. He spoke quietly, "See to it that no one knows I'm here until the raid is over."

"Yes, sir," the soldier said obediently.

Michael looked toward the fortress to see the soldiers entering the building. He knew this was his time to leave. "I'll be back with the others," he said to the soldier as he jumped overboard into the water. His dark cloak still covered his armor as he made his way toward the fortress. He could see the last soldier entering the building. Michael decided to go around to the back to see if he could find a different entrance into the fort.

Inside the fortress, Corbeau and his men walked through the old building. It was completely silent. Corbeau felt a bead of sweat roll down his cheek as he made his way through a large open area. There was some old broken furniture by the side walls, and a few dusty tapestries lay on the ground. As they continued to walk, one of the soldiers spoke up to their leader, "Do you think they all left?"

Corbeau didn't immediately respond but instead continued to scan the room around him. He couldn't see them, but he knew he could feel their breathing. He abruptly came to a stop in the middle of the room. Gripping his swords tightly, he began to feel like he was in the midst of a trap. He called out to his men, "Shields up men!"

It was just a moment later that the men saw ropes coming down beside them, and down the ropes came the escaped prisoners with clubs and other makeshift weapons. Many of the soldiers were knocked down as the prisoners quickly slid down the ropes. A few others sprang from hiding behind the old furniture.

Corbeau was instantly engaged in a fight with two prisoners at once. Being a skilled knight, he was easily able to overpower them as they were amateur fighters. He moved at great speed and knocked the two prisoners' weapons out of their hands before delivering a fierce kick to the head of each man. He turned to face another prisoner, but found he quickly surrendered. Corbeau delivered a quick hit to the man's head with the handle of his sword. He knew he couldn't have him turning on him later.

He looked toward his other men and found all of them were engaged in the battle. Some were still on their backs from being knocked down from prisoners coming down from the ropes. Corbeau knew he would have to get ahead of this situation fast before the prisoners got the upper hand.

There looked to be about twenty-five escaped prisoners locked in this battle.

Quickly Corbeau ran and knocked down one of the prisoners who was on top of a soldier. He then turned and swiped his sword at the hand of another prisoner. He didn't even stop to see the damage he had done. Another prisoner took a swing at him with a club. It was swiftly blocked with one sword as Corbeau then used the other sword to pierce the prisoner in the shoulder. The man screamed out in agony as he dropped his weapon. Corbeau quickly spun and kicked the man with the heel of his foot.

Two other prisoners came against him with swords. He easily blocked both. The prisoners pulled back their swords and took another swipe. Corbeau quickly readjusted his stance and blocked their swords again. Lowering his body, he then spun and swept the legs of each man. They both fell, hitting their heads against the hard ground. As one of the men started to get up, Corbeau kicked him in the mid-section. The man fell flat on the ground.

Other prisoners started to take notice of Corbeau defeating many of their own. Many of the soldiers were also gaining the upper hand on their opponents, and the battle was quickly turning in favor of Mendolon's soldiers. Sadly, Corbeau could see that three or four of the soldiers looked injured, including one that looked severely wounded.

He scanned the room again to see the eastern man, Lin, run through a door. He knew he could not let him get away. The soldiers seemed to now have the prisoners under control. Corbeau quickly ran toward the man. He would have to be careful as this was the leader of the group and was known to be extremely dangerous

Corbeau ran through the doorway and saw no one. The room was very quiet. He looked around and saw a balcony up above. Much of the roof was missing in this room, which made it much brighter than the large room he was just in. Corbeau took a few steps into the room. He held both swords tightly. His attention was distracted by a raven that came and landed on the edge of the balcony. The bird turned and looked directly at the knight of Mendolon. Corbeau thought it was an odd scene.

It was at that moment that he felt a kick on his left side. He stumbled to the ground. He quickly put his swords up to block as Lin took a swipe with a staff. As their weapons met, Corbeau pushed back and rose to his feet. The prisoner swung his staff again, this time against Corbeau's side. Corbeau quickly jumped, missing the swing of the staff.

The eastern man, Lin, was short with dark hair and a mustache. His skin was very tan, and his clothes looked as if they hadn't been changed since he escaped from the prison six months ago. He moved with great speed that kept Corbeau on the defense. The way he used the staff was like a work of art. He tried to strike the knight with both ends of it. It took every ounce of Corbeau's attention to match the man's quick attacks.

Corbeau kept moving backwards until his body hit a wall. He was startled briefly, and Lin was able to land a strike from his staff against Corbeau's right arm. He dropped one of his swords before ducking from another swipe of the staff.

The knight quickly spun off the wall and held up his other sword as another strike from the staff was coming. As their weapons met, Corbeau grabbed ahold of the staff and tried to pull it out of his opponent's hands. Lin saw what was transpiring, and then delivered a fierce head butt to Corbeau's forehead. Slightly dazed, Corbeau stumbled backward. Lin then struck his wrist with the staff before landing a strong punch just above Corbeau's eye. The knight yelled out in pain as he dropped his sword and fell back a few feet.

On the ground, Corbeau tried to shake himself in order to gather his bearings. Before he could even look up, the prisoner came and pulled him up by his back armor. He then threw the knight into a dilapidated pile of loose stone and wood that had fallen from the roof years ago. Corbeau's body hit with a thud and flipped over the debris. He thought he possibly chipped a tooth as his mouth hit against a stone on the ground. He felt his mouth starting to fill with blood.

Lin walked over to where Corbeau was lying. He had his staff in his hand and he was ready to finish off this knight. Corbeau was now on his hands and knees, trying to get into some sort of a defensive position for what may be coming. Curiously, his left hand was on the stone that his mouth hit. Lin came and stood over Corbeau. He pulled his staff back to take one more violent strike on this knight. He was ready for this fight to be over.

Just before Lin was about to strike, Corbeau turned his body and with all his might threw the stone directly at the man's forehead. It hit perfectly, instantly causing a terrible wound just above his nose. Lin fell forward as he put his hand over the deep gash on his forehead.

Corbeau took a deep breath as he picked himself up. His body was sore from the fight, and he could feel that he indeed had chipped one of his top left teeth. He walked over and grabbed one of his swords. A passing thought came to his mind to run this escaped prisoner through and be done with him, but he knew this thought would have to be suppressed. This prisoner might have the vital information that he needed.

Lin tried to climb to his feet to engage Corbeau, but it was no use. He was terribly dazed from the rock. Corbeau was easily able to knock the staff out of his hands. He then reared back with all his might and struck the man directly in the forehead where he was bleeding. Lin moaned in pain as his body hit the ground.

Michael de Bolbec had entered from a back door of the fort and had made his way to the upper levels. Entering the balcony of the room of Corbeau's fight, he could see the knight with a sword in his hand. Blood was seeping from a wound over his eye. His opponent was on the ground moaning and on the verge of passing out. Michael watched casually from the shadows as his fellow knight reached down and pulled the defeated man up by his hair and held his sword to the man's throat.

Corbeau spoke angrily as the interrogation began, "Where is he?"

Lin's eyes were shut as he spoke through baited breath, "I don't know what you're... talking about."

"Yes, you do!" Corbeau shouted. He then slammed Lin's head on the floor. He screamed out in pain.

Corbeau walked over and put his knee in the man's back before continuing. "You know full well who I'm looking for. Is he here?"

Lin said nothing.

"Fine... have it your way." Corbeau then picked up his head and again slammed it hard against the hard surface of the floor. The prisoner continued to moan.

"You have one more chance before I use this sword on you," Corbeau said through gritted teeth. He held his sword to the back of Lin's neck. Again, Lin was silent.

"Speak!" Corbeau yelled as he pulled on the man's hair. When Lin refused to speak, the knight slammed his head against the floor again.

Michael could see that Corbeau was losing control of his emotions. He quickly stepped from the shadows and climbed over the balcony. Corbeau was too focused on the prisoner to take notice of Michael approaching. "Corbeau, I think you need to ease up."

Looking up, Corbeau was confused to see Mendolon's chief knight speaking to him. "Michael, what are you doing here?"

"I think he's had enough," Michael said casually.

Corbeau stood up from the prisoner. He was still breathing heavily from the fight. He threw his sword to the ground as he faced Michael. "How did you get here?"

"I hid in the lower deck of your ship."

Corbeau shook his head, somewhat frustrated that Michael was working behind his back. "Why are you here?"

"I'm trying to figure out what you're doing with these prisoners. Sebastian knows something is going on with Hector and..."

"Oh, so you are spying on me for the king."

"No," Michael said strongly. "The king did ask me to come along, but I'm here for myself. I wanted to know firsthand what's going on before I report back to him."

Corbeau turned to the side and spit a bit of blood from his mouth. He then looked directly at Michael, wondering how much he should say. He looked off to a side wall as he bit his lip. "Hector says that there's an escaped prisoner who is extremely dangerous."

"What? I haven't heard of this. Most of the prisoners were common criminals or followers of the Savage. The man you just defeated was probably the most powerful of the prisoners."

Corbeau took a step closer to Michael. He made sure no one else was around before speaking quietly. "Yes, the man we're looking for was arrested by Hector for something insignificant at first."

"What was it?"

"I'm not entirely sure," Corbeau said, shaking his head. "I think it was something to do with Hector's experiments. He was taking pages out of some of Hector's books, and he was stealing chemicals to go along with it."

Michael was a little confused. He took a few steps and paced as he processed this new bit of information. "That's odd that someone could get so close to Hector's laboratory and steal from him. He must've worked inside the castle."

Corbeau nodded his head. "Yes, he did."

"Well... who was he? Did he work with Hector? Was he an apprentice?"

Corbeau shook his head as he thought about the answer to Michael's question. "No... no he wasn't."

"Then who was he?" Michael pleaded, anxious for answers.

Corbeau stood in silence for just a moment before answering. He looked directly at Michael. "He did work in the castle, but he was the king's court jester."

"What?" Michael responded. He was shocked and quickly realized this dilemma was more complicated than he had first thought.

CHAPTER 3

Gideon walked among guests in a meeting hall of a southwestern village. He had just helped to settle a major land dispute among the villagers and government dignitaries. Tempers had been high, and at times this meeting had gotten out of hand with outbreaks of arguments among those in attendance. He was thankful that things ended in a calm and peaceful manner. He politely said "goodbye" to the residents as they left the main meeting hall.

Since the defeat of the Savage, he was assigned to represent the kingdom in different villages throughout Mendolon. He traveled extensively across the kingdom. Being in his late forties, he was the oldest of all the knights.

An older knight had retired after being attacked by the Savage at the Ruins. Now as the eldest knight, most of his duties now involved strategic planning and representation of the king. He found this new assignment particularly valuable with all the unrest in the kingdom regarding the escaped prisoners. His compassionate, fatherly personality was just what the kingdom needed at this moment in time.

A local governor approached him as the meeting hall was clearing out. The governor was in his late sixties. He had a smile on his face. "Gideon, my old friend, I don't know how you were able to settle that one. Those folks were quickly getting out of hand."

Gideon chuckled as he wiped a few sweat beads from his balding head. It was true that the meeting was on the verge of complete chaos. He hadn't shown it, but this particular meeting made him more nervous than any of the previous. "Well, I know my sword is always by my side if things were ever to get too far out of hand," Gideon said sarcastically.

The governor laughed again as he spoke, "Well I'd like to see that. You versus a bunch of farmers and townspeople, along with a few government dignitaries stuck in there."

"What do you mean 'you'? I was counting on you helping if the people started coming for me." This sent the governor into an even greater laugh. The thought of him in a battle was truly a hysterical thought.

Gideon and the governor continued to talk for another fifteen minutes. Their conversation was mostly about the meeting that just transpired but also about other matters of unrest in the community. They were deep in conversation when a servant gently grabbed Gideon's arm, interrupting them. "Sir."

"Yes," Gideon said turning to him.

"Soldiers are arriving at the southwest port."

Gideon was a little confused by the pertinence of this information. The arrival of the soldiers at port was unusual, but he was more struck by the servant's urgency. "Yes... I will see them as soon as I'm finished here."

The servant bowed his head as he spoke, "Much apologies, but I thought you would want to know that Michael de Bolbec is among those arriving at the port."

"Excuse me," Gideon said to the governor. He quickly turned aside to meet with the servant in private. They walked quickly down a nearby hallway.

Gideon continued as they walked, "How long have they been at port?"

"Not long, maybe thirty minutes. I came as soon as I saw them."

"And you're sure Michael was with them?"

"Yes sir. I have a carriage waiting for us outside."

"Good," Gideon said quietly. He pulled at the left side of his mustache in anxiety. Within the last couple days, he had received a valuable piece of information that he needed to deliver to Michael. With his new duties of settling disputes, he and Michael hadn't work together much lately. If he was this close, then Gideon wanted to be sure not to miss him.

Coming out of the meeting hall, he saw a carriage waiting for him with the door open. Without stopping he and the servant stepped in the carriage and shut the door. The driver immediately set out toward the port. It was less than a mile away, but Gideon knew he would be stopped frequently with questions from citizens if he tried to run or navigate the streets via horseback.

Gideon stared out the window as the carriage moved through the streets. It was a beautiful day in the southern region of Mendolon. He saw many people moving about on the streets. Many were men who were organizing and delivering various supplies of imports that were brought in from southern kingdoms. An odd mixture of smells struck Gideon as they passed a bakery that made an assortment of breads, and then at the next moment they were beside a couple of men pulling carts filled with fish. Commerce was great in this region as many merchants set up shops to serve the fishermen and crew men who brought in the imports.

The carriage stopped abruptly as a child ran out into the road. The mother quickly grabbed her son by the hand and pulled him to the side, scolding him along the way. As they traveled, the driver had to continue to stop periodically as people were constantly crossing back and forth in the street.

As they approached the ports, Gideon spoke to his servant, prying for more information. "Tell me. Who else is on this ship?"

"Corbeau was on board with maybe fifteen soldiers. I didn't get a clear look but from what I could tell, it looked like they were preparing to unload a number of prisoners."

"Hmm..." Gideon said staring out the window. "Are you sure there were that many soldiers?"

"Yes. Positive."

"Interesting... this must have been one of the last strongholds of the escaped prisoners. I wonder what they found."

They arrived at the ports. Gideon could see the soldiers' ship docking at the port. He could see Corbeau instructing the knights as the prisoners were taken off the ship. They were all tied securely with their hands behind their backs. Many of the soldiers and the prisoners looked injured. Even from afar Gideon could tell that Corbeau had been in a fierce fight as there was bruising around his eyes and a large cut on his forehead. His dark brown hair looked unkempt and disheveled.

The carriage came to a stop. Gideon immediately opened the door and stepped out. He made his way through the crowd of soldiers who were occupied with the prisoners. He continued to pull at the ends of his mustache as he looked through the crowd for Michael. It was apparent that the soldiers had been ambushed by the prisoners at the old fortress. There were varying levels of injury among the men. Five soldiers in particular came down the boat's ramp supported by others. They were injured significantly and would be taken immediately to the infirmary. It was at that time that Gideon saw the unfortunate sight of two soldiers carrying a stretcher covered with a sheet. He realized that one soldier paid the ultimate price during the fight. As much as he hated to admit it, it looked as if the Savage's actions were still responsible for taking lives in Mendolon.

Gideon watched the men closely before noticing the cloaked figure coming off the boat. His hood was off and he could easily see that it was his close friend, Michael de Bolbec. "Michael!" he shouted, moving toward him.

Michael turned to see his fellow knight as he came down the ramp. "Gideon," he replied, acknowledging his friend. It had been a couple months since they'd seen each other.

"What happened?" Gideon asked as he met Michael coming off the ramp. They began walking away from the ship toward a side street.

"There were about twenty-five prisoners at the old Toulouse fortress. They anticipated the battle and surprised our men. I was keeping a low profile."

They walked in silence for moment or two. Gideon could tell Michael was leading him to a secluded area. "Was the eastern man, Lin, among them?"

"He was. Corbeau engaged him in a fight and was able to defeat him."

Gideon looked over his shoulder at Corbeau. He could see the bruise around his eye. "It looks like Corbeau definitely met his match."

"Yes. He did, indeed," Michael muttered under his breath. He led Gideon to a quiet alley. He looked around one last time, making sure no one else was around. Michael continued speaking quietly, "Corbeau was looking for someone for Hector."

Gideon was a little confused. "What? Who was he looking for? A prisoner?"

"Yes. One that he arrested specifically over twenty years ago. Do you remember any of this?"

"No." Gideon rubbed the back of his neck. "But, in all honesty, we have arrested a number of people over the years."

Michael kept checking his surroundings, making sure no one was close by. "Not one like this. Corbeau said this prisoner worked inside the castle."

Gideon nodded his head. "Yes, there were a few castle servants who have stolen weapons and jewels over time, but I think many of those were released, and then those that..."

"No," Michael interrupted him. "Corbeau said they are looking for an old court jester."

Gideon stood silent, looking at Michael. He rubbed his chin as he thought about this prisoner. Michael quickly caught on that Gideon knew who he was referring to. He continued, "Gideon, you know who he is?"

Gideon pulled Michael further into the alley away from the main road. He wanted no chance of anyone overhearing what he was about to say. "He was our longest prisoner. Under Hector's orders he was always kept in solitary."

Michael was shocked. "He's been in solitary for over twenty years? What was the nature of his crime?"

"It was just before I became a knight. I don't know the fine details, but I believe he was stealing from Hector."

"What did he steal?"

"I'm not exactly sure. It was something to do with Hector's experiments." Gideon kept looking off to the side as he spoke. He twirled his mustache as if he was in deep contemplation.

Michael put his hand on his friend's shoulder as he spoke. "Gideon, tell me. Is there something more to this story?"

Gideon took a deep breath and shrugged his shoulders before speaking. "I don't know for sure, but there is something mysterious about this prisoner." He paused for a moment before continuing. "It's like there is some sort of unspoken legend regarding the court jester. Many wonder who he really is and where he comes from."

Michael started to pace slightly. It seemed funny that only yesterday he was out on the farm fields with Piers. His life now seemed full of mystery again. He walked back toward the end of the alley and saw Corbeau directing the soldiers as they continued to unload the prisoners from the boat and onto carriages. There was a very small prison in this southern part of Mendolon, but it was only big enough to hold half a dozen prisoners at the most. These men would have to be taken directly to Mendolon's main prison east of the castle.

Michael's train of thought was broken by Gideon. "Michael... as much as this is a mystery, I fear there is something else brewing among the soldiers."

Michael turned around and looked straight at Gideon. "What? What do you mean?"

Gideon took a step closer to the chief knight. "It seems like Sebastian is preparing them for a direct assault against Grimdolon."

"What? The citizens of Mendolon will never approve of any action like that. He will risk civil war if he tries striking the beasts. Besides, our knights will never go to war against Grimdolon at this stage."

Gideon shook his head. "I've got an inside source among the soldiers. He says Sebastian doesn't need the knights. Most of the soldiers will attack for him and..." Gideon paused for a moment. "He says he has the power of the Great Dragon."

Michael was struck by this comment. "This is crazy. The Great Dragon is a myth."

Gideon peered over his shoulder again before continuing, "Somehow he has the soldiers convinced. I don't know how he persuaded them, but they're swearing that he has this power."

Michael rubbed his forehead as he thought about what Gideon was saying. The Great Dragon was a supposed legendary creature that controlled the dragons. There was much debate as to whether it was ever a real being or not. Today it was seen as more of a power one could possess; a power to completely control the dragons of this world. A large part of him didn't believe what Gideon was telling him, but he did have to take under some consideration that it might be true, seeing that Sebastian at one time did convince a dragon to live east of Mendolon. More than anything, he wondered about the possibility of an invasion into Grimdolon. After pacing for a few seconds, he turned to Gideon and spoke quietly, "Okay, what's our next move?"

"You must go to the king, Michael. Persuade him not to go to war. He may listen to you above all else." Gideon spoke with great urgency. "Tell him the people will never stand for this behavior. Tell him that he will lose what little loyalty he has if he does this."

Michael nodded as he listened. He knew that Gideon was right. If there was anyone in the kingdom King Sebastian might listen to, it would be his chief knight. He would have to at least try. Any alternative was better than war with Grimdolon. "I'll wait a couple days and then I'll go to him in the castle. This might buy us some time. He's going to be expecting me to report back to him after this mission. I don't think he will advance with anything until he hears from me. I believe he first wants to know who Hector and Corbeau were looking for."

Gideon rubbed his chin as he thought about what Michael suggested. It sounded like a plausible plan. "I'll inform the knights of what we've planned."

Michael looked back toward the soldiers unloading the boat. They were beginning to finish the unloading process. He focused in on Corbeau as he was loading the last prisoner into a carriage. He was being harsh with the prisoner as he pushed him in. Michael spoke to Gideon who was standing behind him. "For now, let's keep this information from Corbeau."

"Why's this?"

Michael shook his head as he spoke, "As of late, he's been so preoccupied with hunting the escaped prisoners and searching for this court jester. I'd hate for him to accidentally mention our plan to the soldiers he's working with, or even Hector for that matter. We can inform him later, if all of us knights need to convene."

Gideon knew there was a lot of truth to what Michael was saying. "Yes, I agree. That sounds like a wise course of action."

The men stepped back into the street as they headed toward Gideon's carriage. They tried to be as casual as they could. Their plan of action could be treasonous if the king found out. They didn't want the soldiers to suspect anything unusual from the men. Looking straight ahead, Gideon spoke quietly to the chief knight. "What's your next move, Michael?"

Michael didn't break stride as he spoke, "I'm going to look as casual as I can... I'm going to see my family."

Many years ago...

The young boy was being pulled by a merchant through the streets. Even though he was only eight years old, this wasn't his first offense. He had often been caught stealing, and this time the merchant was through with giving this young boy mercy.

As they approached the young boy's mother, he started tearing up, knowing that he had disappointed her. His mother ran over to meet them. "My son, what did you do this time?"

"I'll tell you what he did," the merchant said angrily. "This little brat was caught stealing from me again."

"Oh, I'm so sorry. It won't happen again," the mother said sincerely. She was a poor lady who had lost her husband years ago. Since then the family had struggled providing for themselves.

"You're right. It won't happen again. Because if any of us merchants ever catch him stealing from us again, we will report him to the authorities, and he will be thrown directly into the dungeons."

The mother got down on one knee to comfort her son who was now crying heavily. She held him tight and ran her hand through his very light blond hair. "I'm so sorry, sir. I understand completely."

"You better be sorry," the merchant replied as he abruptly turned and left.

The mother was now left alone with her son. She looked at him squarely as she spoke with great tenderness. "Mamour, what were you doing? Don't you know he could have you reported?"

"I'm sorry, Mama. I know I shouldn't have, but he had some new things, and I just wanted them so badly." The young boy was referring to the new toys and trinkets that the merchant had at his shop. He was the only one in this northern territory that sold things like this.

"My son, you can't steal from the merchant. He needs to provide for his family too," she said quietly.

"I'm sorry, Mama... I'm so sorry." The boy continued to cry. The mother also felt tears begin to well in her eyes. She gently rubbed the young boy's blondish-white hair. She knew the struggle inside her son. It was as if he was always fighting within himself. Fighting to choose good over evil. She worried about him. She worried that evil would win.

CHAPTER 4

Michael knocked on the door to his mother's home. He waited just a moment before the door opened. She was surprised to see him. "Michael, my boy," she said as she embraced him tightly.

Michael returned the embrace. "It's great to see you, mother."

They hugged in the doorway for a moment or two before Michael's half-sister, Alecia, came running around a corner in their house to see her much older brother standing in the doorway. "Michael!" she yelled, running to see him.

"Hello there," Michael said as he bent down to give his young sister a hug. "How's my favorite girl doing?"

"Great! You want to come outside? Daddy built me a tree house. I put a rope up so I could climb down. It's not too scary. Want to see?"

Michael smiled as he rubbed his sister's hair. "Yes, I'd love to. I won't have to leave until tomorrow morning."

"Do you think you can stay for my birthday next week?" the young girl said with great anticipation.

"Unfortunately, I truly have to depart tomorrow morning. I'm needed up north."

"Oh, Michael, please!" Alecia said, clearly disappointed. Michael did visit often, but it was never enough for his sister. Even though there was a sixteen-year age gap between them, she always thought of him as her best friend in the whole world.

Seeing his sister's disappointment, he decided he would go ahead and give her the gift he brought. "I'm sorry, Sis," he held out the gift, "but maybe this will cheer you up." It was a square box about a foot in both length and width.

Alecia's eyes lit up as she took the gift from Michael's hands. "Oh Michael, thank you so much." She quickly got down on the floor to open it up. It was a Greek game board with colored stones for game pieces. It was hand crafted and sold at one of the shops by the southwest port.

"I figured we could play together," Michael said as his sister admired the gift.

It was at that time that his step-father came into view and approached him. "Michael, it's always a pleasure to see you," he said holding out his hand.

"You too, Bronson." The two men shook hands. They both greatly admired one another. Michael appreciated Bronson's care for his mother after his father was lost in battle. Michael was twelve when he died. He was now twenty-six. Throughout the last fourteen years, he would consider Bronson a great friend.

"What brings you out this way?" his mother asked, curious about this unexpected visit.

Michael looked toward the ground as he spoke quietly, "I imagine you heard about the prisoners that were brought in from the port."

"We did."

"The king had me on the boat. We seemed to have apprehended one of the last gatherings of prisoners at large."

"Was everyone okay?" his mother asked, concerned. "We heard there was a large number of them with the soldiers that came into the port."

Michael looked off to the side as he tried to think about what to say. Technically he wasn't supposed to say anything until the kingdom issued an official decree about the death of a soldier, but he knew that news would already be spreading concerning the soldiers' injuries. "There were many prisoners that attacked and one soldier was killed."

"Oh, I'm sorry to hear that. Was it just soldiers with you?"

"No, Corbeau de Lefevre was actually leading the raid. I just came on special assignment. I was exploring the old fort where the escaped prisoners were hiding. I wasn't even engaged in the fight."

Michael's mother, Helen, smiled as she rubbed her son's arm. She was thankful that her son was okay. Being the mother of the chief knight of Mendolon was no easy task at times. Any major battle or talk of war would directly involve her son. Through it all she determined in herself not to live in fear. She knew her son's service was greatly needed in the kingdom... just like her former husband.

Looking to quickly change the subject, she directed him further into the home. "Come now, Michael. We will have dinner ready soon."

Michael smiled in return. "I'd love that."

Helen led her son into the dining room where they enjoyed a small feast. The family conversed and laughed joyfully as they talked about various things. This was a common experience when the family was all together. Their meals traditionally seemed to last a long time as they took their time. Alecia particularly had a hard time finishing her meal because she had so much to say. She wanted to tell her older brother about everything that had occurred since he was last in town. Michael listened and took in every word. He loved his sister and truly missed her when he was gone.

After dinner the family retired to their backyard. Bronson sat comfortably in a chair by the house while the others walked along the edge of a wooded area. Alecia ran ahead of Michael and her mother. She was talking non-stop, telling Michael about various things that she found in the yard, and how her father had built her a tree house. She was anxious to show her big brother everything.

As she began to climb to the top, Helen spoke quietly to her son. "Are you sure you can't stay a few days, Michael?"

"No... I'm sorry to say I have to get back. The king will be expecting me to report back soon."

"I understand," Helen said, not wanting to pry further. "What has Sebastian been like as of late?"

"He's been stable... but... I don't know." Michael shrugged his shoulders and gently rubbed the sides of his blond beard as he searched for the right words to say. "He always seems like he is scheming, planning something behind my back."

"Yes, I know what you mean, my son. I've never trusted the man, and these recent revelations of the identity of the princess can't help his case with the people."

Alecia peeked out from a window in her treehouse. "Michael, Michael, look!" she yelled as she waved to her older brother.

"Hello... looks marvelous, Sis," Michael said, waving back. Alecia stuck her head back inside.

Michael turned back to his mother and spoke very quietly. "Mother, promise me this—if Sebastian ever gets out of control, you will seek refuge somewhere, either in Grimdolon or in a southern kingdom over the sea."

Helen was a little confused at this point. "Seek refuge. What do you speak of?"

Michael tried to smile. "Just a precaution. Sebastian is just so full of mystery and now learning that he captured

Belle when she was a child... I just don't want us to be caught off guard by anything."

Helen rubbed her son's arm as she smiled back at him. "Don't worry about us, my son. Gideon's been spending lots of time in these parts. We'll be well aware of anything occurring with the king."

"Michael, you coming?" Alecia shouted from up top in the treehouse.

"Be right up!" Michael responded.

Michael began to climb the ladder along the trunk when his mother spoke up, "Michael, speaking of the princess...have you heard from her since she left?"

"No," Michael said, shaking his head. "Not much information comes from Grimdolon. I just hope she's happy." Michael paused for a moment before continuing, looking directly at his mother, "No, in fact, something inside me knows she's happy."

"This is going to be so beautiful," Belle said with much excitement in her voice. She was admiring the ballroom of Grimdolon's castle. Currently it was under repair. There were odd tools and decorations scattered around, covered in sheets to protect them from dust. Jean-Luc and Belle were meeting with the royal decorators to discuss the final plans regarding their wedding in three weeks. Even though Belle was still a human, there was great promise that her form would change back very soon, and the wedding would go on.

"Belle, sometimes I think you would rather be one of the royal decorators as opposed to queen," Jean-Luc said casually.

She smiled back at her fiancé. "Well, now that you mention it. It doesn't sound like such a bad plan after all." The decorators all broke out with laughter hearing Belle's comments. For many years when Jean-Luc was a prince they had come to learn of his sense of humor. They were happy to see that the future queen shared the same trait.

"Oh, no you don't," Jean-Luc responded, "You agreed to be queen; therefore, you will be queen. You can't back out now." Belle laughed in response. She greatly admired her future husband's quick wit.

"Sir, if I may," one of the decorators spoke up. He was the oldest beast of the group. There was some graying in his fur, and a pair of glasses rested on the edge of his nose.

"Yes," Jean-Luc responded.

"We should probably venture outside to the gardens before evening approaches, especially with the plans of our queen." Belle smiled in return. The plan was for the whole kingdom to be invited to the wedding reception held in the gardens. There would need to be accommodations for a few thousand.

"Belle, my love, before this wedding is over, I fear you may drive our whole kingdom into poverty with your generosity," Jean-Luc said with a large smile on his face. Even though he often joked about her generosity, he greatly loved her good nature and spirit. He truly wanted to entertain any idea she may have.

The small group of decorators started to head outside when Belle grabbed her fiancée's arm. "Jean-Luc, before we go outside, let's just enjoy one dance."

Jean-Luc was caught off guard. "Belle, are you sure? This place is a mess."

"Come, Jean-Luc. It'll be fun." Belle pulled him toward the middle of the dance floor. She turned toward the decorators. "Could one of you play for us, please?" She pointed to a piano stationed along the wall. One of the female beasts stepped from the group of decorators and approached the piano.

Jean-Luc tried to object, "Belle, shouldn't we wait till everything is decorated and looking marvelous for the wedding?"

She ignored his comment as they reached the center of the dance floor. "Grab my hand, Jean-Luc, just like at the winter ball." He did as he was told. He couldn't hold back the smile on his face.

The beast at the piano started to play a beautiful Grimdolon melody. The beauty and the beast began to slowly dance around the room. Their eyes were locked as they spun and waltzed across the floor. The others stood around the edge and watched their king and future queen. Even amidst all the covered decorations and furniture, it was a beautiful scene. Looking around the room, Belle spoke quietly, "Picture it, Jean-Luc. The decorations, the people, the music... it's going to be a glorious event. Can you see it?"

Jean-Luc nodded just a little as they continued to dance. "I can, my love. I truly can." The couple were soon lost in their imagination, thinking about that day that would come. After everything they'd been through together, it all felt like a dream. For years, Jean-Luc had been waiting for the right time to rescue her from Sebastian. He couldn't believe he was now holding his true love in his arms. They had become great friends while he was in Mendolon, and now she was going to be his wife.

As the music ended, Belle threw her arms around Jean-Luc and laid her head on his shoulder. She closed her eyes as she ran her fingers through the hair of his mane. She felt as if she could have stayed in this moment for hours. "I love you, Jean-Luc," she said ever so quietly.

Jean-Luc gently rubbed her back. "I love you too, Belle," he whispered in her ear.

Belle released Jean-Luc as the decorators started to head outside toward the gardens. The king and future queen held hands as they approached the doors. Even though their marriage would signify strength and peace for the kingdom of Grimdolon, Jean-Luc looked forward to the simple moments more than anything. None of the diplomatic business regarding their marriage mattered at this moment. He was just thankful he was going to be walking hand-in-hand each day with his beautiful bride.

Jean-Luc and Belle were following the decorators when a servant approached Jean-Luc. "Sire."

"Yes," Jean-Luc responded, a little caught off guard.

"One of our doctors would like to meet with you."

Jean-Luc turned back toward Belle who was now waiting for him by the outside door. "I'll catch up. You go on ahead."

"Ok," Belle said, smiling. She then turned toward the decorators and followed.

The servant led Jean-Luc to a nearby hallway where a beast, who was a doctor, was waiting for him. He was dressed with a brown coat over his shoulders. He appeared worried. This made Jean-Luc concerned, especially considering this was an unexpected visit.

"Doctor, what is it?"

"Sir, we've been doing tests on Belle's blood…"

"Yes, I know that," Jean-Luc interrupted. He was trying to stay patient, but his anxiety for information was taking over.

"It doesn't look good. It looks like everything that we've tried isn't working."

"What? What do you mean?"

The doctor adjusted the glasses on his face. "Her blood shows no change in composition or in its characteristics."

A worried look came over Jean-Luc's face as he processed what was being said. He took a deep breath. His voice was raising. "Doctor, tell me openly. What does all this mean? What are your next steps?"

The doctor looked directly into Jean-Luc's eyes. There was a sad look on his face as he contemplated what exactly to say. A few moments passed before he spoke up quietly,

"Your majesty. I'm very sorry .... but it means that the princess cannot be changed back into a beast."

Jean-Luc was stunned. He couldn't believe what he'd just heard. He turned and looked back through the windows on the other side of the ballroom. Tears started to fill his eyes as he caught sight of his bride in the garden.

CHAPTER 5

Jean-Luc sat on the windowsill in a forgotten tower of the castle. He was looking out to the west in the direction of Mendolon. Even though he was forty feet high, he was unafraid. It was a beautiful night. The stars were out, shining bright. He had spent many nights here when he was a teenager, thinking about the lost princess of Grimdolon. Growing up, it was always such a mystery in his life. He would wonder what she would be like, or if she would ever have any desire to return to the land of beasts.

His violin was in hand and he played a soft, slow piece. This was his normal routine when he needed to be alone and think. Since very early in his childhood Jean-Luc had played the violin. Most beasts were gifted in the arts and particularly music, but the violin was one of the more rare instruments played by beasts. Jean-Luc had picked it up naturally, and he found that it was something he greatly enjoyed.

At this moment Jean-Luc found that he needed his violin more than ever. He felt completely dejected knowing that the one he was destined to be with would be a human forever. Thoughts kept passing through his mind, wondering if she would still love him. Would she even be accepted by the citizens of Grimdolon? Maybe she would just want to go back to Mendolon? Jean-Luc tightly shut his eyes as he tried to suppress the thoughts.

He looked out onto the land of Grimdolon that lay in front of the area known as Dragon Waste. Even though it was late, a few of the houses still had lights shining from them. He wondered if any of them could ever hear him when he played from this tower late at night. Occasionally he would hear a comment from a castle servant that they heard him playing. He hoped it hadn't kept them awake.

As his piece came to a close, Jean-Luc gently put his violin down beside him and reached for a bottle sitting on the windowsill. He took a quick drink. It was a sweet wine made from the juice of Grimodolon apples. It was a rare delicacy even for the king.

He set the bottle down and looked over toward his violin sitting beside him. He didn't know if he could play another piece. The words from the doctor entered his mind again. He closed his eyes once more and tried to think of something else. A gentle breeze blew against his face. It took him back to his childhood when he particularly loved to come to the tower and watch the snow fall on winter nights. What joy it would be to be a boy again.

Jean-Luc's thoughts were broken when he heard a voice behind him. "I heard your song on the way up. It sounded beautiful."

"Hello Belle," Jean-Luc said with a bit of sadness in his voice.

Belle walked over to where Jean-Luc was sitting. She gently sat down facing him. "This is a lovely, quiet spot you have, Jean-Luc."

He looked down at his feet and took a deep breath. "Belle, why are you here?" These last few months she had lived with her family near the castle. It was odd to see her here so late as it was now past midnight.

She spoke quietly, "What happened today after our dance? You never came outside to the gardens."

Jean-Luc rubbed his forehead as he searched for the right words to say. "I... I..."

Belle, seeing that he was nervous, reached for his hand. "You can tell me... anything."

Jean-Luc looked out onto the world. He tried to think of the right words to say to his future wife. He wondered how she would receive the grim news from the doctors. He decided just to tell her directly. "The doctors said the medicine isn't working. They say there's been no change whatsoever in your blood."

Belle nodded in return before speaking. "Okay, so what's our next step?" she said optimistically. She seemed unmoved.

"I'm sorry, Belle, but there is no next step. The doctors have tried everything they could, and nothing's working. There's nothing medically or scientifically that we can do to turn you back into a beast."

"Jean-Luc, don't talk like this. There are other things the doctors can explore. We'll try new options."

Jean-Luc shook his head. "There are no other options. I'm sorry, we did all we could."

The two sat in silence for a few minutes taking in the discussion they just had. Belle had detected that something had gone very wrong in Jean-Luc's conversation with the doctor. If it had been good news, he would have told her right away. The doctors were optimistic most of the time as they were constantly trying new medicines and minerals found in the mines. A few times they had even guaranteed their king that their formula would work. Jean-Luc had always been hopeful that Belle would be a beast before their wedding. He now sat on the windowsill of this tower feeling hopeless.

After a few minutes Belle spoke up, "Jean-Luc, may I show you something?"

He nodded slightly as he turned to face her. From a small bag by her side, she took out a small dried flower. "What's this?" Jean-Luc said curiously.

"It's the rose you gave me before the winter ball."

Jean-Luc adjusted his glasses as he looked at the brownish color of this once beautiful flower. "You saved it all this time."

"I did... and it's something I'll never part with."

"I'm... I'm just surprised you've kept it all this time."

"Yes, and do you want to know why I will forever keep it?"

Jean-Luc turned to look her in the eyes. He spoke quietly, "Tell me why, my love."

Belle paused for a moment, twirling the old rose in her fingers. It brought back many good memories. "It was amazing that you as a prisoner of Mendolon were able to get me a rose for the ball, and also that you were able to have some of the finest attire a guest could have."

Jean-Luc laughed a little at the memory of it all. "It was such a wonderful evening... all until the explosion went off and... such."

"Yes," Belle paused for a moment. "But the reason I keep this flower is to remind myself that love finds a way. There was no way you should have been ready for that ball, but somehow you were able to do everything needed to be a wonderful companion. Just in the same way that you should've never been able to save me the way you did. Love found a way, Jean-Luc. Love will always find a way."

Belle reached for his hand as their eyes met. Jean-Luc softly wiped away a tear that was rolling down her cheek. It was at times like this that he was reminded of her inner beauty. She was truly greater than all the legends that were told of the Princess Mendolon. At that moment Jean-Luc knew that they would be all right. He didn't know what would happen, or how this current situation would be resolved, but in the end, he knew that their love would overcome. Love conquers all.

"Thank you, Belle," Jean-Luc said smiling. "Thank you for everything."

She didn't respond. She simply rested her head on his shoulder as they looked out onto the land of Grimdolon.

Michael abruptly opened the throne room doors and walked in confidently. Two days had passed since the raid on the Toulouse fort. He was dressed in his full battle attire. It was the same specialized grey suit Hector had made him for attacking the northern ruins. He wanted to look as official as he could be standing before the king. Sebastian was on his throne, drinking from a goblet. His crown rested atop his brown curls, and his long robe stretched to the floor.

"Welcome back, Michael," Sebastian said, trying to sound affectionate.

"King," Michael responded emotionless. He knew he would have to remain focused as he had a lot of ground to cover with the king.

The king arose from his seat. "I heard the last raid on the prisoners went well. Corbeau was able to defeat the eastern man."

"Yes, I approached Corbeau after the fight. You're right. Corbeau and Hector were looking for a prisoner Hector arrested years ago. He wasn't among those at the fort."

The king nodded slightly as he took a sip of wine. Bringing down the cup, he spoke confidently. "I knew it. They were hiding something from me all this time. This is pure treason to command an operation like this behind my back. Corbeau will surely face my wrath for this."

Michael held up his hand in an effort to calm Sebastian. "King, I think you need to relax. They were executing exactly what you asked them to do. They were simply trying to capture all the escaped prisoners."

"Michael, don't be so naïve."

"No, listen to me," Michael quickly interjected. "There is a prisoner, a court jester in fact, that Hector arrested years ago for stealing formulas from him. They were simply trying to locate him. He is dangerous and capable of a variety of experimentations."

The king threw his goblet against the floor. "Oh, come on, Michael! Do you think of me as a fool? Can't you see that this court jester has figured out some sort of special formula to use as a weapon?"

Michael was a bit confused now. "Yes, but I don't see your point."

Sebastian shook his head in frustration. "Hector and Corbeau want this power for themselves!" he shouted.

"Your Majesty, please. You're not thinking rationally. You commissioned them to capture all the prisoners, and that is simply what..."

Sebastian stepped toward Michael and stuck his index finger in his face. He spoke slowly, "I will not... will not be caught off by anyone seeking to overthrow my reign."

Michael chose to say nothing in response. He simply waited for Sebastian to calm down and back away. After a few moments, Sebastian retreated to his throne where he sat down comfortably. He seemed more relaxed, and Michael thought this was his opportunity to speak up. "King, I will implore you to ask Hector directly if you think he is hiding something from you."

"Well, Michael, that is not an option at this point."

Michael was a little confused. "What are you talking about?" he said quietly.

"Because I had him arrested," Sebastian said firmly.

"What? What for?"

"For not talking to me," Sebastian said, leaning forward. "I approached him about this secret mission of his, and I could tell he was hiding something from me."

Sebastian stood again and walked to the small table beside his throne. He calmly poured himself another cup of wine. Michael watched in silence. He didn't know what to say in response. For Sebastian to arrest his most trusted advisor was truly an extreme measure. Michael realized that Sebastian most likely knew more about this prisoner than he was letting on. Many scenarios passed through his mind as to what might happen next. Instinctively he felt his hand slowly reach for the handle of one of his daggers. If the king was truly out of control, then he definitely didn't want to be caught off guard.

The tension in the room continued to rise when Sebastian turned to face Michael. He seemed calm again. Michael removed his hand from the hilt of his dagger as the king stepped close to the chief knight. He simply reached up and put his hand on Michael's shoulder in an effort to ease the tension. "Listen, Michael... as king I have many affairs I'm currently dealing with. I don't want to worry in the slightest about this court jester's abilities falling into the wrong hands. After things calm down around the kingdom and I complete some of these tasks, then Hector will be released and restored to his position. Simple as that."

The king smiled as he tried to reassure his chief knight. Michael wasn't believing any of it. He knew that Sebastian was holding back information. Realizing that the king was a little calmer now, he decided to get to one of the main points at hand. "King, you talk about many tasks that are at hand. Does one of these include invading Grimdolon?"

The smile quickly vanished from the king's face. He removed his hand from Michael's shoulder. "Who told you that?"

"Word gets around, your majesty. Do you really think the citizens of Mendolon will approve this act of war?"

Sebastian took a few steps back and simply shrugged his shoulders. He took a sip of wine from his new chalice before speaking. "Michael, as I said before, I have many threats coming that I must deal with. With the power the beasts possess in their mines, it's only a matter of time before they come for us. This new king, Jean-Luc, will be no different. As soon as he has enough power, Grimdolon will march on us."

Michael quickly objected, "But the people will never approve of such action!"

"I'm sorry to say, but I don't need their approval. The soldiers are loyal to me. They will go to war for me no matter what the people say."

Michael bit his lip as he shook his head. The king was going too far this time. Michael always knew that Sebastian hated the beasts of Grimdolon. He just never thought this day would ever come when they would be on the cusp of war. He feared where this would all end. "I'm sorry, King..."

"What?"

Michael spoke as firmly as he could, "I'm sorry. You know I don't approve of this action. I will not be following you into this battle, nor will I authorize any knights to follow you. In fact, by order of the knights, I will strictly forbid any of them to assist you in these efforts."

Sebastian took another sip of his wine and licked his lips. To Michael's surprise the king still seemed unusually calm. "Well, Michael... if that's the way it has to be... then fine. I've never forced you to do anything you didn't approve of." The king hesitated just a moment before continuing, "That will be all from you. You can go."

Michael stood for a moment trying to think if there was anything else that could be said. Nothing came to mind. "Be gone!" Sebastian spoke, breaking the silence. Michael simply turned and walked through the throne room doors back into the hallway. The doors echoed as he closed them tightly.

Michael proceeded to walk down the castle's hallway. He kept thinking about his conversation with Sebastian. He wondered if there was anything he could have said differently. It all seemed to happen so fast. A lot of ground was covered, and the thought of Hector being arrested had caught him off guard. The king seemed to be a step ahead of Michael at this point.

His mind quickly changed directions as he now thought of what his next move should be. Michael wondered if he should gather a brigade of knights to approach the king and try to change his mind. Under Mendolon's law, if a majority of knights objected to the king's plans, then by law the king's orders could be changed. This was one route to take, though it would be risky because the knights who objected would be seen as disloyal to the king. Another plan would be to try to inform the townspeople of Sebastian's plans and try to raise a revolt on the king's order. This was extremely dangerous as Michael may be accused of trying to take over the kingdom. A half-dozen other scenarios passed through Michael's mind as he walked through the hallways of the castle. He smiled and nodded at the people he passed. Many of them he hadn't seen for a while as he hadn't been at the castle much recently.

Michael's train of thought was interrupted when a soldier called out to him. "Michael!"

"Yes," Michael said, turning to face the man.

The young soldier stepped closer to Michael as he spoke in a whisper. "I think we found him."

"What? Who are you talking about?" Michael said, confused.

The soldier looked off to the side, making sure no one was around. "The mysterious prisoner Hector was looking for."

"You found him?"

"Yes," said the young soldier. He couldn't have been older than nineteen. "We have him locked in the dungeon. We were just about to interrogate him when we heard you were here."

Michael also looked around to make sure no one was watching. "Take me to him?"

"Certainly."

The two men proceeded through the castle in the direction of the dungeon. Michael tried to act as casually as he could. He didn't want anyone reporting to Sebastian that they saw Michael walking through the castle in a hurry.

Reaching the top of the steps to the dungeon, a troop of five more soldiers waited for them. One of them spoke up as Michael approached, "We just brought him in, Sir."

"How did you find him?"

"He was hanging around the markets. He tried to blend in, but he clearly stood out. He gave himself up when we approached him."

"Hmmm...." Michael was puzzled by this situation. "This is curious. Let's see what he has to say."

Michael walked down the dark stairwell to the dungeon below. All six soldiers followed in behind him. A few torches along the wall lit the way. As they continued to descend, Michael wondered what he would say to this new prisoner. He also thought about this mysterious special 'power' of the court jester. Did he already possess it? Or was it something he was trying to gain? What would he do if he refused to talk?

"Which cell is he in?" Michael asked when he was a few steps away from the bottom.

"First one on the left," one of the soldiers answered.

Reaching the bottom, Michael quickly turned to his left and found the door to the prison cell open. A torch in the hallway of the dungeon clearly showed it was empty. Michael was confused, "Where is he?"

It was at that moment that Michael felt a kick against his back. It came from one of the soldiers. He fell forward into the cell. He quickly turned himself onto his back. One of the soldiers reached for the cell door to close it. *I must act quickly,* Michael thought to himself.

CHAPTER 6

Michael quickly slid himself a few feet forward and kicked the cell door with all his might as it was about to close. It hit one soldier with great force and he fell backwards. The others looked on and before they were able to react, Michael was able to jump to his feet and spring toward one of the soldiers. He swiftly delivered a punch to the soldier's nose. The man collapsed as blood immediately started to pour from his nostrils.

It had all been a setup. Sebastian had long had this trap in place if Michael had not agreed to join him in his pursuits. The rank of soldier was different than knights in that knights were given some authority and governing power over the realm, whereas soldiers were simply troops who followed the king's commands no matter what. These men didn't even know the real reason why they were attacking Michael. They were simply doing the king's bidding.

The other four soldiers rushed at Michael and pushed him against the bars of the cell. "Chain him up!" the one in command shouted. The soldier that had been hit by the door slowly started to get up. Michael had not noticed it before, but he had brought with him a chain that had cuffs on each end. He knew that if he was shackled in them, there would be no escape. He would have to think of something quickly.

With all his might, Michael threw his head forward in order to headbutt the soldier holding his left arm. The soldier was only mildly hit, but it was just enough for him to release some of the tension on Michael's arm. The chief knight then drastically pulled his left arm downward out of the soldier's grip. He quickly reached for a dagger, and in one quick motion pointed it upward and stuck it into the right arm of another soldier who then immediately let go of Michael.

Before the other soldiers could react, Michael pivoted his body and struck another soldier with his left elbow. He was moving at great speed. With his right hand he grabbed that same soldier by the hair and rammed his head into his left knee. Michael then grabbed the bars with his left arm and swung his body to the left, and in the process delivered a fierce kick to the head of one of the soldiers.

Michael's back was turned as the soldier with the dagger in his bicep grabbed him around the neck from behind with his uninjured arm. He squeezed tightly. Another soldier was getting to his feet and was starting to draw his sword. Michael knew he would have to act with extreme precision to get out of this situation. He quickly reached over and slightly twisted the dagger in the soldier's arm. The soldier screamed in pain as his grip was loosened. Michael was then able to reach over his back and threw him into the soldier that was coming at him with the sword.

From behind, another soldier was approaching with a drawn sword. Michael quickly moved to the side as the sword hit against the bars of the cell. He then reached up and grabbed the soldier's head and slammed him against the bars of the cell. The soldier fell unconscious to the ground.

Another soldier was then rising to his feet and pulling his sword. Michael grabbed his own sword off his back as he approached the man. He truly didn't want to hurt any of these soldiers. They were simply pawns in a larger game that was occurring. The soldier charged forward with his sword. Michael easily stepped out of the way and knocked the sword out of the soldier's hand with his own. The soldier then tried to throw a punch at Michael. It was easily blocked. Michael then took the young soldier and threw him into the bars of the prison cell close to the doorway. Michael delivered a quick kick to the man's head. He fell to the ground unconscious.

Michael took a deep breath and wiped his forehead with his sleeve. None of the men were moving at this point so he thought he would take a quick moment to gather himself. He truly felt sorry for the men that lay at his feet. He hoped he hadn't injured any of them seriously.

"Michael... Michael!" he heard someone call from the other end of the dungeon. Michael quickly ran toward the end of the hall toward Jean-Luc's old cell.

The dungeon was dark, but there was one torch that lit the way. As he came close to the cell he could see the dark black hair and green robe of a man grabbing the bars of his cell. "Hector!" Michael called out.

"Listen to me, Michael. You've got to get out of here. Things are more drastic than you imagine."

Michael nodded his head. "I've heard Sebastian is looking to strike Grimdolon."

"Yes, but that's not the problem!" Hector shouted back. "There's a prisoner on the loose, who..."

Michael interrupted him, "Yes, I know, the old court jester you had arrested years ago."

"You must find him. Years ago he was caught stealing from my book of potions and mixtures. He's trying to create a specific concoction that will give him immense power."

"It sounds like another Savage is on the loose."

"No, you fool. This is nothing like the Savage." Hector stuck his face as far as he could through the bars of the cell as he continued. "The Savage had a clear objective. He sought to take over this kingdom. This jester is different. He was hired to wreck havoc on everyone. All he seeks is madness and anarchy."

Michael nodded in return. He knew he didn't have much time and would need to gather as much information as possible. "Who hired him?"

"I don't know. Possibly the northern emperor."

"The emperor? What would he want with our kingdom?"

"You imbecile, listen to me," Hector was getting frustrated at this point. He naturally didn't like Michael and was quickly losing patience with him. "You are missing the point. If this jester gets the last ingredient to his potion, there will be no limit to the destruction he can cause."

A noise was heard from the other end of the dungeon. Michael turned to see one of the soldiers rising to his feet and stumbling up the steps. He knew it would only be a matter of time before there was a manhunt all over the castle for him. "Hector, I have to go. They'll be after me soon. Where should I look for the jester?"

"You must try the great forest, north of Grimdolon."

"The Forest of Saison?" Michael said, astonished. Never before had he been to that great and mysterious forest.

"Yes," Hector continued to speak with urgency. "It's the last place he could be hiding, and besides, there are rumors of something irregular occurring there."

"Okay... I'll see what I can do," Michael responded as he turned toward the steps.

Hector reached out and grabbed Michael's arm before he could leave. He looked directly into Michael's eyes as he spoke. The hissing in his voice was strong. "Michael, you must be careful in confronting the court jester. This power he possesses will destroy you. Be extremely cautious... do not let him attack you."

Michael pulled away from Hector's grip. He knew that for Hector to warn him like this, it must be tremendously vital to stop this menace. He spoke quietly, "Hector, I'll do everything in my power to stop him. I promise."

The king's advisor looked sincerely at Michael as he gave one last encouragement, "Be careful."

"Thanks!" Michael called out over his shoulder as he ran toward the stairwell.

Jean-Luc was in an upper room of the castle looking through various scientific and historical books. He was trying to see if anything had ever been written regarding the transforming of humans to beasts. Surely if he went back far enough he thought he could find something. The origin of the race of beasts dated back a few hundred years. It was a time when men were carelessly working with various chemicals and formulas, not taking any precaution to what the results of their experiments might be. They also sometimes mixed sorcery into their experiments, adding a whole new level of danger.

Jean-Luc realized that the current book he was reading added nothing to his search. He abruptly closed it and took it back to the bookshelf. He reached up higher for another book. A mound of dust fell from the shelf onto Jean-Luc's sleeve. It was obvious that these books had not been referenced in a while. He was thankful that beasts were generally controlled and less intrigued in finding new formulas. The only exception was in regard to finding new compositions in regard to medicines.

As Jean-Luc was walking back from the bookshelf, he heard the gallop of horses coming toward the castle. He adjusted his glasses as he saw the small troop coming up the road. There were three beast warriors coming toward the castle on horseback. They were dressed in battle attire. The curious thing was that on the back of one of the horses was a covered figure of some sort. It looked as if the warriors had killed something and were bringing it back to the castle. He couldn't explain why, but something inside of him had a bad feeling about this visit. He abruptly left and went downstairs to welcome the warriors.

Jean-Luc quickly made his way outside the front gates to meet the warriors. Usually the king would always have at least two guards by his side when leaving the castle, but this time he was in such a hurry that he didn't even summon anyone to accompany him. The warriors were dismounting from their horses when Jean-Luc walked up. He recognized all three of the beasts, but only knew the oldest by name. His name was Etalon, and he was a leader among Grimdolon warriors. "Welcome," Jean-Luc said as he approached the beasts.

"Your majesty," Etalon said in a deep voice. He was surprised to see the king alone.

"I saw you coming up the road. May I ask what is the nature of the visit?"

"We were stationed on the northern border, just west of the orchards."

"Do the other warriors know you left your post?" Jean-Luc asked.

"Yes, your majesty. We've had extra guards stationed there for the past few days."

Jean-Luc was a little puzzled. "Extra guards?"

Etalon nodded as he listened to the king's questions. "Yes, we've heard of strange rumors coming out of the Forest of Saison. We wondered if these were true or not, but we thought to add a few extra guards just in case any of it was true."

Jean-Luc put his hand on Etalon's shoulder. "Listen, you know Saison is a strange place. Rumors are always abounding. The Noe creatures keep to themselves, and there's no interaction with the humans that live there." It was true. The Forest of Saison was truly a place of much mystery and uncertainty. All four seasons occurred in the Forest year-round in different quadrants of the forest. The southeast contained the spring. The southwest was the summer. The northwest was the fall, and the northeast was the winter. One could feel the effects of the seasons by standing on the border of the forest by the different quadrants.

The small creatures called the Noe inhabited every area of the forest. They looked like thin, two-foot-tall guinea pigs that walked on their hind legs. They communicated to one another through various squeaks and whistles. It was unconfirmed but it was said that their touch could bring on a feeling of peace and rest. Twenty-five years before, an official group of researchers from Mendolon went to explore the Noe creatures. They never returned. Others from various kingdoms also ventured into the area over time, never to return.

The oldest warrior beast continued, "No, your Highness. It is nothing like that. We have gotten word that strange creatures are exiting the forest and attacking animals and scaring travelers before returning back to the forest."

"What kind of attacks? Are any of these verified?"

He shook his head. "We actually haven't been able to yet."

"Okay." Jean-Luc rubbed the edge of his chin. "I'm a little confused. Is there anything to confirm if any of this is true?"

All three warriors looked at one another at that moment. Making eye contact, they all nodded in agreement. Etalon slowly turned to face his king. "This is what we want to show you, King." Etalon slowly walked to the horse that was in back with the dark blanket covering a figure. Jean-Luc followed him.

"Did you catch one of the creatures?"

"Well, um..." The old warrior beast stumbled over his words as he thought about what he was about to say.

Jean-Luc scratched the side of his head as he was a little puzzled. "Etalon, your hesitation is quite puzzling." He shrugged his shoulders. "Usually that is a fairly easy question."

Etalon looked straight at Jean-Luc. "Normally that is... but this is a different situation. One of those creatures attacked one of our guards. We were able to take off the creature's head."

"What happened to his body?" Jean-Luc said, a little afraid to ask.

Etalon pulled back the blanket for Jean-Luc to see. "The body actually ran for a couple miles before collapsing."

Jean-Luc stared in wonder at the creature's head that lay before him. Many questions filled his mind.

Michael ran through the castle like a fugitive on the loose. He was heading toward the southside door of the castle trying to escape as fast as he could. As he moved down the hallway, a young soldier approached him. He had a sword in his hand and aggressively took a downward swipe toward Michael. The knight easily moved to the side as the sword hit the ground.

His hand went instinctively to his daggers before realizing that was not the best option. He'd hate to leave any lasting damage on this young soldier. Instead Michael quickly grabbed the collar of his shirt with his left hand and pulled him close. With his right fist he delivered a swift punch to the side of the soldier's head. He fell to the ground in pain.

"Sorry," Michael whispered as he ran off. He hoped that going toward the south exit was his best plan of action. It was apparent that Sebastian had informed all the soldiers to attack and to try to capture Michael de Bolbec if he was seen. From Michael's perspective, he wished to meet up with as few of them as possible. He didn't want to hurt any of them.

Michael had run further down the hallway when another soldier approached him. Michael was about to attack. When the young man held up his hands. "Whoa! Stop," he said to Michael. Michael quickly realized this was Amis, the soldier he had saved from the Savage six months ago.

"Amis!" Michael said, happy to see his friend.

"Michael, Sebastian informed all of us soldiers this morning to be on the lookout for you. He said you were going to meet with him and offer terms of surrender. He says you're trying to overthrow the kingdom."

Michael put his hand on Amis' shoulder. "You know all of this is false, my friend."

"I know. There are some of us that can see Sebastian is growing power hungry. He says he's gaining the power of the Great Dragon."

"I've heard. Listen to me, Amis. You have to help me get out of here."

He nodded as he spoke, "Michael, he's assembled most of us guards along the north and south exits."

Michael thought for a moment about what he was to do. He needed a new and drastic plan of action. "Well, I guess I will have to go through the east gate. Thank you," Michael replied as he began to run away.

Amis was a little stunned. "But Michael... that's the main castle gate. That's insane."

137

Michael yelled back toward his friend, "I guess they won't be expecting me then!"

Michael found the castle mostly empty as he made his way to the main castle exit. He knew there would be a few soldiers stationed out front, along with a wooden carriage that patrolled the front gate. He hoped all would be taken by surprise. Getting close to the gate, he passed a couple servants. They looked quite confused to see the chief knight of Mendolon running through the castle. He simply ran past them, not stopping to tell them not to let anyone know about him.

With great speed Michael ran out one of the front doors into the courtyard area. Two guards were waiting, both with a sword and shield in hand. Neither was facing the door from which Michael came. He ran onto them quickly. He jumped in the air and kicked one on the side of the knee, buckling it at an awkward angle. The soldier screamed out in pain as he grabbed his knee.

Turning to face the other soldier, Michael pivoted as the soldier was taking a swipe with his sword. Michael then grabbed the soldier's shield and rammed it upward into the soldier's forehead. It cut deeply into his flesh. Michael quickly crouched down and swept the soldier's legs out from under him. His head hit hard against the ground. The other soldier was still holding his knee. Michael easily turned and delivered a hard kick to the head. The soldier fell unconscious. Michael grabbed the fallen soldier's shield, thinking he might need it.

Michael exited the outer wall of the castle to find the patrol carriage about twenty yards in front of him. *Just my luck,* he thought to himself. Two arrows then pointed from two small windows of the carriage.

"Fire!" shouted one of the soldiers inside the carriage.

Michael held up the shield for the impending arrows. He waited just a moment before realizing no arrows were coming. He peeked over the top of his shield to realize that "fire" didn't mean "shoot" in this instance, but rather literal fire. A soldier appeared from behind the carriage carrying a torch. He stepped close to the arrows and lit the ends on fire. They quickly lit up in a blaze.

"Surrender, Michael!" the soldier with the torch shouted.

Michael took a deep breath. He was a little frustrated but he knew what he had to do. He took off running toward the carriage in a sprint. The soldier shouted again, "I said surrender!" Michael did not stop. "Surrender now!" he continued to yell.

The soldiers with the arrows didn't wait any longer. They let their arrows fly. Michael wasn't easily intimidated. He simply held up the shield as the arrows were deflected. Someone yelled, "Stop!" one last time as Michael approached the carriage. Coming within a few feet of the carriage, he jumped in the air with the shield held high and with the full weight of his body behind the shield he hit the top of the carriage. Thankfully, he hit it just right and the carriage fell on its side. Michael now found himself lying on the side of the carriage. He heard the soldiers groan inside.

He quickly stood to his feet as the soldier with the lit torch climbed on the carriage and approached him. Michael jumped back as the soldier took a swing with the torch. He barely had time to react before the soldier swung at him a second time. "Focus, Michael," he whispered to himself as the soldier was preparing to strike again. This time Michael was able to react in time and grabbed the soldier's wrist as he took another swing. Michael immediately pulled the torch down against the wooden carriage. It easily started to catch fire. The soldier then looked up at Michael, wide eyed and a little scared. Michael wasted no time in punching the soldier square in the nose. He fell back awkwardly off the carriage, leaving the burning torch behind.

Michael quickly jumped off the carriage and sprinted toward the edge of a wooded area. He looked over his shoulder as he stepped among the trees. He could see the two soldiers escaping the inside of the carriage that was now in full blaze. Both of the soldiers' clothing were on fire. They proceeded to help pull their comrade who had carried the torch away from the carriage. They then jumped on the ground and began rolling around in the grass, trying frantically to put out the fire.

Michael knew he would have to escape to Grimdolon. Jean-Luc needed to be informed that Sebastian was coming for him. He knew that escaping over the border would require help. Many allies crossed his mind. The king would probably have many of the knights' residences searched. Maybe all, save one, that was now living on the border of Mendolon and Dragon Waste... his old friend, Bernard.

CHAPTER 7

Bernard sat in his quiet cabin painting a picture. He was dressed in his old painter's shirt with a beret on his head. He held a small brush in one hand and a palette in the other. His picture was a beautiful waterfall scene flowing over a mountain. He enjoyed painting scenery like this. It tended to relax him, not that his current job was particularly stressful. After the defeat of the Savage, he was relocated to work in the far eastern part of Mendolon. His duty was to patrol the area known as Dragon Waste. The land technically belonged to Mendolon, but it was still undeveloped. Sebastian wanted to make sure no one took advantage of it and tried to claim it for themselves. Every other day Bernard would hike through the territory, searching for anything unusual. So far, most of his searches had turned up nothing. On one occasion he saw a poor beggar woman who was making her way to the southern shore. He simply let her go.

Painting now filled his days. He was becoming quite skilled at it. There was a small village a half mile from his cabin where he would sell his pictures to a merchant who would then sell them at the markets around the kingdom. He also made sure to send one back to the castle every month. There was a servant girl whom Bernard had been pursuing for a while. He hoped these paintings would further help win her heart. Bernard finished the last stroke on his painting and sat back to admire it. *Peaceful. Just peaceful,* he thought to himself.

His train of thought was broken when he heard a knock on his door. This caught him off guard since he'd never had a visitor before. Bernard was curious. He gently put down his paintbrush and palette and walked to the door. *I wonder if this visitor is from the kingdom or a commoner?* Opening his front door, he was surprised to see... no one. He was perplexed. He looked further out his front door and still saw no one. A woodpecker sat on a nearby tree. Bernard wondered if that was what he heard. He simply shrugged his shoulders as he shut the door. A part of him was happy no one was there as he was enjoying his peace and quiet at the moment.

As the door closed he felt an arm go around his neck. "Shh... don't make a sound. We could be watched," the mysterious voice said.

"Who... who are you?" Bernard said in a trembling voice.

"Bernard, it's me, Michael," said the voice.

Bernard pulled away from his friend's arm and turned to face him. "Michael, how are you doing, my friend?"

"Shh... you must be quiet," Michael said in a hushed tone. "Soldiers are after me." It had been two days since Michael escaped the castle. He looked quite disheveled due to the fact that he hadn't slept or eaten much. Soldiers were patrolling the whole kingdom in search of Michael de Bolbec. Reward posters were starting to be posted in various villages around the kingdom, seeking to find the chief knight. Michael knew that Bernard now lived an isolated life. His residence probably wouldn't be searched since very few even knew where he resided.

Bernard continued, seemingly ignoring his friend's pleas. "My friend, it's so great to see you. Come, let me show you what I've been painting."

"Bernard, we don't have time. I need your help. Sebastian's growing power hungry and seeks more power by the day. He currently has the soldiers hunting me."

Bernard smiled in return. "Michael, Michael... you are too worried. I'm sure it's not quite as bad as you make it sound. You need to relax. Come, let me show you my paintings."

Michael wasn't sure what to say at the moment. He realized that his friend had spent a little too much time alone in the woods. "Listen, we don't have time for anything like this. You have to help me escape to Grimdolon. Sebastian is going to plan a surprise attack on the beasts. We must warn them before they start to advance. Time is limited."

"Michael, don't you realize that a lot of these struggles work themselves out. Just approach Sebastian and tell him you're sorry and offer him a good diplomatic solution. I'm sure he'll understand. Maybe..." Bernard looked off to the side for a moment. "Maybe paint him a picture."

Michael rubbed his forehead. He couldn't believe what he was hearing. Bernard often took to new ideas quickly. Michael wondered what kind of books he'd been reading as of late. "Umm... how about this, Bernard? You escort me through Dragon Waste in the back of your horse cart. If any soldiers approach, just tell them you are gathering firewood for your house. Hopefully they won't think anything about it."

Bernard looked at his friend with a slight bit of pity. He put his hand on Michael's shoulder as he continued to smile. "Okay, I will do this for you, my friend, if this is truly what you want, but..." Bernard paused as he shook his head. "You must really find a way to get this stress out of your life."

"Good. Let's mount up and leave at once."

"Calm down, Michael." Bernard was not in a hurry in the least. "Let's first get these wounds clean and then maybe have a bite to eat. The worries of this world can surely wait for just a few minutes."

Michael tried to think of something to say to object, but the words did not come. He took a deep breath, "Alright, but let's be quick."

The two knights made their way through Dragon Waste. Bernard was on the front of a cart, pulled by a horse. He knew these trails through the thick woods by heart. Michael was lying down in the cart, covered by a blanket made from animal skin. He had a few sticks and branches on top of him just to give the top of the blanket an authentic look of someone gathering sticks. It was a very uncomfortable ride because with each bounce of the carriage he felt another stick jam into his back. Michael knew he would have to stay situated like this for quite a while since the trek through Dragon Waste would take a few hours.

Michael was very thankful for his friend. Before leaving, Bernard had fed him and even helped him clean his wounds that he had acquired through his fight with the soldiers in the castle. Though he was still tired, the little bit of nourishment he received would hopefully be enough to get him to Grimdolon's castle.

They were about five miles from Grimdolon's border when Michael felt the cart come to a stop. Michael wondered what was causing the hold up. It was just a few moments later that Michael decided to peek out from under the blanket. He could see Bernard crouched down with his hands cupped, looking at a small animal. Michael was perplexed, "Bernard, what's going on?"

"Oh, there is a little rabbit here whose foot is tangled in these vine roots. He probably didn't realize the area was muddy and then hopped into the..."

"Bernard! We don't have time for this. The rabbit is going to be fine. He's survived many years in this area. He's probably more scared of you right now."

Bernard paid no attention to Michael. He just keep ministering to the rabbit. Michael's focus was then changed as he heard horses galloping toward him from the eastern border. He looked closely to see that it was three Mendolon soldiers coming toward him. He quickly ducked back under the blanket. The soldiers were the border guards who lived on the far east side of Dragon Waste. There was a small outpost located on the border where four guards could live while the border was watched.

The men rode close to Bernard before stopping. The three soldiers were dressed in traditional soldier armor. "Greetings, sir," they said to Bernard. Seeing that Bernard was a knight, he automatically was their superior.

Bernard stood up from the rabbit who was still caught in the roots. "Hello, men. What brings you back this way today?"

The men dismounted and approached Bernard's cart. The one that seemed to be the leader spoke up, "We received a message that King Sebastian has ordered the immediate capture of Michael de Bolbec. There is talk that he seeks to raise a rebellion against the kingdom. King Sebastian wants to bring him in for questioning."

Bernard nodded his head and shrugged his shoulders. "Well, the king hasn't been fond of him for some time now."

"We understand, sir. There is talk that he might try to contact you."

"Yes, we are long-time friends, but I do live in peace and seclusion now. Our paths don't tend to cross much."

The men stood in silence for a while looking at each other, not knowing exactly what to say. Bernard thought they all looked as if they wanted to say something, but no one had the courage to speak up. After a few seconds, Bernard decided to break the silence. He started walking back to the cart as he spoke, "Well, men, I do hope you find him. I know he does some farming by the..."

One of the men stepped in front of Bernard, interrupting him. "I'm sorry, sir, but we're going to have to check your cart."

"But..." Bernard tried to speak. The soldier put his hand on Bernard's chest stopping him from going further.

"I'm sorry," the soldier said. The other two soldiers approached the cart. It was obvious that Sebastian had warned them that Michael might try to contact Bernard and use him to help himself escape. Everything seemed to be in slow motion as they approached the cart. Bernard was nervous as the two soldiers slowly got into position on each side of the cart. They pulled their swords and looked directly at one another. They each grabbed a side of the blanket as they began to count silently, *1... 2... 3*. The blanket was quickly pulled aside and the men saw... nothing, save for a few sticks and branches.

Bernard let out a sigh of relief as he smiled back at the supervising soldier. "Well, I guess there was nothing to worry about after..." He stopped mid-sentence as he saw one of the soldiers on the side of the cart fall to the ground. Michael then emerged from under the cart on the opposite side where the soldier was still standing. It was apparent that Michael had escaped when Bernard was conversing with them. Michael then delivered a fierce punch to the soldier's stomach before rising and hitting him directly in the face.

The soldier in charge then approached Michael. The chief knight grabbed the blanket off the cart and flung it in the soldier's face, hiding his line of sight. Michael then sprang forward and tackled the soldier against the ground. The blanket covered his head and body. Michael landed a hard punch against where he thought the head of the soldier lay. Looking up, Michael could see the other two soldiers quickly approach him with swords drawn. Michael pulled two daggers from his belt. He wasn't going to throw them, but he thought he could at least use them to guard against their swords.

Michael steadied himself and got into a defense position when suddenly the soldiers stopped about seven feet away. Michael was puzzled as to why they stopped. The men held their swords steady, not approaching, but not attacking either. Michael was deeply focused on the men when he heard Bernard yell out, "Michael, watch out." All of a sudden, Michael felt a kick against his back. He fell forward from this sudden strike from a new soldier. The soldier jumped on his back and held him down as the other two approached to help. This new soldier had been hiding in the woods, observing from the side, waiting in case they needed a surprise attack.

"Hold him down, men. Don't let up!" one of the men shouted. There was even a sword pointed toward his back. Michael eased up and assessed his situation. He quickly thought through his options. Originally, when he had swept the legs out from under the first soldier, he hoped he could've spread the men out during his attack and thus fight them simply one or two at a time. Michael hadn't anticipated an ambush from this soldier hiding in the woods, and now he was paying the price. He would have to think quickly.

"Grab the chains!" a soldier shouted as they continued to hold him down. One of the men went to his horse and grabbed a set of chains to restrain him. The soldiers kept talking, "The king is going to give a grand reward for this."

"Yes, much gold was promised if he was found. I just didn't think..." The soldier wasn't able to finish his sentence because in that moment an angry Bernard ran forward and pushed the soldier holding the sword against Michael's back. He fell to the side. Bernard pulled his sword as another approached him and took a swipe. It was easily blocked. With the situation changing, Michael was able to roll another soldier off his back. He quickly grabbed a handful of dirt and threw it in the man's face, stunning him. He was then able to pull a dagger and thrush it into the shoulder of the man. The soldier screamed in agony. Michael glanced back to see Bernard fighting with another of the men.

Bernard yelled as he fought, "Michael, this is all your fault! I wanted to paint a picture!" Bernard was easily able to overpower the soldier and knock his sword out of his hand. The soldier then surrendered, dropping to his knees. Bernard shook his head as he knew this soldier couldn't be allowed to follow him. He took a step forward and with the handle of his sword he hit the soldier on his head. He fell to the ground unconscious. Bernard turned to see that Michael had taken care of the other men. They all lay on the ground beside him. One was grabbing his head, moaning.

"Thank you, Bernard," Michael quietly said before putting a dagger back in his belt.

Feeling quite angry, Bernard shook his head as he went and sat on the front seats of his cart. Michael continued with a bit of sadness in this voice, "Bernard, I'm sorry I got you involved in this ordeal. I didn't know what else to do."

"I was attaining peace, Michael! I was just... I just... I wanted a quiet life. I was painting a picture!"

Michael took a deep breath as he looked out into the woods. He wasn't sure what to say at this point. He hoped the words would come as he spoke as sincerely as he could. "Bernard, I'm sorry, but hopefully things will quiet down... after we warn Jean-Luc about the upcoming battle, ... then catch this devious villain, the court jester, ... then thwart any grander plan King Sebastian might be orchestrating, ... then help Grimdolon defeat an attack from Mendolon's soldiers..." Michael paused for a moment before looking up at Bernard. "And maybe somehow save the world in the process."

150

Bernard couldn't help but laugh just a little at the irony of Michael's words. Though he still felt a little angry at Michael, he knew that his friend needed him more than ever at this point. He now smiled as he looked right at Michael and spoke, "I guess not much has changed after all."

"Yeah, I guess not, my friend," Michael replied with a smile.

"All right, well, there's no time to waste." Bernard held out a hand to the chief knight.

Michael climbed aboard as the horses began to trot. They moved just a few feet forward when Michael spoke up abruptly, "Wait, Bernard. Stop the cart."

"Why, what's wrong?"

Michael quickly jumped off and ran to the edge of the woods. Bernard wondered what he was doing. He saw the chief knight kneel to the ground. He was methodically working on something. Bernard leaned forward trying to catch a glimpse at what Michael was doing. This was puzzling because he knew that Michael was in a hurry. Whatever he was doing must've been extremely important.

It was just a moment later that Bernard saw the little rabbit hop away into the forest. He had completely forgotten about it during the fight with the soldiers. Michael quickly climbed back onto the cart and shrugged his shoulders. "Sorry ... on second thought, I just couldn't leave the little guy stuck like that."

Bernard nodded his head. "Well... I guess we had time for the little rabbit after all," he said as the horses trotted down the path.

Many years ago...

The boy was becoming a young man. At age sixteen he found himself torn between decisions of right and wrong. He was a leader among his friends which made him a power for both good and evil at times. Currently he found himself in between two shops in one of his kingdom's markets. Five of his friends were doing his work. A boy in their school was constantly bragging about his wealth and using it as a means to demean others. Mamour thought this young man needed to be corrected. With the help of his friends, Mamour was giving him a beating while also checking his pockets for money.

"Please, stop," the rich boy pleaded as the beating continued. He was currently on the ground trying to hold his hands up in order to stop the process.

One of the boys stepped closer and raised his fist. *"Where's all your money now? It doesn't seem to be much help."*

A younger boy in the bunch brought Mamour a few coins that they found in the rich kid's pockets. *"We found these. I don't think he has much more."*

"Check his other side!" Mamour shouted out to those near their victim.

The boys picked up the rich boy like a rag doll and ran their hands through all his pockets. They then threw him down hard on the ground. The boy groaned in pain. One of the friends spoke out, *"He's got nothing more on him."*

Another boy walked up and kicked the rich boy in the side. *"You should've brought more,"* he said with a sarcastic tone.

One of the older boys followed suit with another kick in the ribs. *"I thought you were richer than this. You disappoint us."*

The group of boys then went forward to each deliver a kick to his side. They were all laughing and making crude comments as the jeering continued. Mamour looked on. He marveled at the power he had over these boys. This was all his doing. He planned this attack. He planned the place. He planned the person. He was the one in charge. He reveled in the power as many passing thoughts came to mind.

Mamour was then caught off guard when a simple question came to his mind, What would my mother say to me if she saw what I was doing? *It pierced his heart. He couldn't bear the thought of it. She would be severely disappointed.*

"Enough!" *Mamour yelled out to the group. The boys kept going, not hearing him amidst all the ruckus. He took a step closer to the group.* "I said enough!" *Mamour pulled the boys away from the victim who was curled up in a ball on the ground crying. Mamour couldn't take his eyes off the boy. He knew he was responsible for all of this. The other boys just stood looking at their leader, curious about the sudden stop of the beating.*

Mamour pointed to two of the younger boys in the group. "You and you, I want you to pick him up and take him home."

The two boys looked at one another briefly. They were confused. One of them spoke up, "But his family will come after us if they see us come close."

Mamour took a deep breath of frustration. He was ready for this to be over. He hated what he had done. "Well, then... just take him close to his home and leave him. He's had enough."

The oldest boy objected, "But we got him here. We're not finished..."

"I said he's had enough," *Mamour said emphatically.* "We're done here." *He then turned and walked away from the others. Never to join them again.*

CHAPTER 8

Belle and Jean-Luc met in a large meeting room of the castle with a few Grimdolon warriors. There was also a beast present that specialized in animal sciences. Currently, they were discussing what to make of the animal's severed head that was recovered after it attacked the warriors in between Grimdolon and Saison. There was much talk as to what type of creature it was. It looked to be some type of wolf with reptilian scales starting to form around the neck. Its teeth were larger than a normal wolf, and his blood appeared to be a strange dark brown color, but it started to look green as it thinned out. Even though this creature was dead, the look on his face was still one of anger and vengeance.

The scientist worked in silence while all the others looked on. He was a beast in his late seventies. He had a large beard that was almost completely grey. At this moment he worked closely with a magnifying glass and a small knife, exploring every part of this creature's head. Every once and a while he would say something quietly under his breath, "Interesting... Fascinating."

After a few minutes of silence, Jean-Luc and Belle's eyes met. Jean-Luc rubbed his chin as he shrugged his shoulders. "Well... I guess at least we have one more option for the main dish at the wedding." Belle gave a half-hearted smile. She knew her fiancée well enough to know that at this point he was trying to lighten the tense mood in the room.

The animal scientist spoke out as he continued to work, "Even though I've never seen anything like this in regard to his scales and teeth structure, the most fascinating thing about this creature is his blood. It doesn't bear characteristics of anything I've seen."

Belle asked a question, "Do you think this creature could be of some type of wolf?"

The scientist readjusted his glasses and then rubbed his greying beard as he began to speak, "It's extremely hard to say because of this blood. It's cold, and it has started to turn the skin yellow under the fur on his head. It will be very interesting when we start to examine the bone structure and its scales."

"Well, that should make for an interesting evening." Jean-Luc's comment was slightly sarcastic, but truthful. "You'll have to inform me of your findings."

"I will, Sire." The scientist then turned toward the warriors, looking for more answers. "What kind of fight did he give you?"

The warrior Etalon stepped forward from among the others. "The animal came on us in a fury, with great speed. We were able to put three arrows in him before he reached us."

"Did that slow him down?" Jean-Luc asked.

"Not at all. He kept running forward, undeterred by his injuries. When he reached us, he latched on to the arm of one of our warriors."

"Is that when you severed the head?" Jean-Luc asked.

Etalon shook his head. "Not at first; we weren't able to. He pulled our fellow warrior to the ground and dragged him around by the arm."

The scientist's eyes grew wide. "He was able to pull one of our warriors to the ground?"

"Yes, he was able to drag him a few feet toward the woods. We quickly pulled our swords and began stabbing the body of the creature as fiercely as we could."

"Did it faze him?"

"No ... in a final effort I swiped at his neck. I knew something was odd when the head didn't immediately sever." The beast paused for a moment and took a breath before continuing, "It took four or five more swipes before the head fell to the ground."

Jean-Luc turned and paced toward a nearby window. He couldn't believe what he was hearing. It truly was puzzling. Grimdolon's warriors were large beasts with great strength. For one to be thrown around by this strange wolf-like creature was astounding, especially given the fact that the creature was being attacked during the process. He wondered what would be his next plan of action. Being a relatively new king, external threats like this one were a new test for him.

Belle broke the silence, "Etalon, what became of our warrior that was attacked? Is he going to recover?"

The warrior beast shut his eyes tight as he spoke, "I hope so... he is in great discomfort at the moment, and it's like a sickness lies over him."

"And what about his arm?"

Etalon took a deep breath and nodded in return. "I'm sorry to say, but I think the doctors will have to remove it."

"Are you sure?" Belle asked with deep concern in her voice.

"Yes," Etalon said quietly. "The creature destroyed every bone in the arm, even eating a few of them in the process."

Jean-Luc turned from the window and faced all the others. There was obvious fear on everyone's face. "What are we dealing with here?" Jean-Luc said under his breath. Little was known about the territory of Saison, but surely, he thought, in all the rumors of the territory he would have heard of a creature like this. He wondered if this was some type of rare species that lived in its northern parts far from the borders of Grimdolon. His mind was growing in curiosity.

Everyone was then startled when a castle official abruptly entered the room, "Sire."

"Yes," Jean-Luc responded, puzzled about the meaning of the official's entrance.

"We've captured two men from Mendolon approaching the castle."

Belle spoke up, "From Mendolon? Who are they?"

"We immediately took them into custody and therefore didn't get their names. They gave up their weapons without a fight. I believe they are knights of Mendolon."

Without speaking another word, Belle left the room with Jean-Luc following close behind. She walked quickly to the throne room by the castle's entrance. Turning a corner, she entered the throne room and was pleased to see her two friends, Michael and Bernard. They were on their knees with their hands tied behind their backs. Grimdolon warriors were guarding them.

"Michael! Bernard!" Belle said, running over to them. She lifted up the hem of her dress she ran. Reaching the two knights, she bent down and gave both men a hug. Even though she greatly loved living in Grimdolon, she missed her fellow knights very much, particularly these two.

Rising to her feet, Belle addressed the warriors that stood over them. "Release them immediately." The beasts wasted no time in untying the men and helping them stand.

Jean-Luc spoke as he entered the room. A company of castle servants followed behind. "My good friends, Michael de Bolbec, and Bernard Descoteaux. How I truly missed you, fellows." He walked over and embraced both men. He couldn't hide the smile on his face. "I'm sorry about the ropes and all the precautions. I just have to be a little careful with folks coming from Mendolon... as you know, your king did kidnap my future wife."

"No offense taken ... thanks for having us," Michael responded, rubbing his wrists.

Jean-Luc continued, "Shall I prepare a feast? We have excellent cooks in Grimdolon. Bernard, I know how much you like ground beef with bread. For old times' sake, I could have our chefs make it for us. Michael, I like the beard. It's a good look for you."

Michael stepped forward, interrupting Jean-Luc's talk. "Thank you, Jean-Luc, but I must inform you that this is not just a friendly visit. Sebastian is ordering Mendolon's soldiers to march against Grimdolon."

Belle was the first to object, "What? He can't! Even the soldiers that are most loyal to him wouldn't march against us without great cause."

"I would guess there are some that will refuse, but he has many of them convinced that he possesses the power of the Great Dragon."

Everyone in the room was taken aback by Michael's comment. Many of them didn't believe in the Great Dragon, much less think that the power rested with King Sebastian of Mendolon. "You can't be serious," Belle objected.

"I'm afraid so. He's threatened them with it. Many of them know that he made the small dragon live between our kingdoms for many years, and now they think he is using that knowledge to his advantage. The soldiers are convinced he has power over all the other dragons of the world."

Belle continued to object, "But historically, dignitaries have been known to make deals with dragons. That's all Sebastian did with the small dragon in Dragon Waste."

"Yes, I think you're correct, Belle, but you know as well as I that Sebastian can be persuasive. I would imagine that many of the soldiers feel threatened by this new claimed power, and since most of the ideas concerning the Great Dragon lie in legend and myth, Sebastian is able to exaggerate the extent of any power that he has."

Belle put her hand over her forehead as she shook her head. She was perplexed as she took in what Michael was saying. Many of the Grimdolon warriors were murmuring at the mention of the Great Dragon. It was all overwhelming. Etalon's mind quickly went to battle strategies and what the best plan of action was for defending the kingdom since Mendolon soldiers would greatly outnumber theirs.

Jean-Luc took a deep breath. He remained calm and thought it was best to go somewhere to further talk in private. He spoke up, "Very well, why don't we continue talking over a bite to eat? Even if Sebastian is trying to wreak havoc, I'm not going to let him spoil my dinner." He held out his hand toward the dining room. "Shall we?"

Jean-Luc, Belle, Michael, Bernard, and Etalon ate together in one of the castle's banquet rooms while the castle servants served. Michael didn't eat as he was getting

161

everyone caught up on how Sebastian's soldiers would attempt to attack Grimdolon. He also explained everything he had heard about this mysterious court jester. Everyone listened intently while they ate. A part of Belle was disappointed with the dinner. She was very happy to be with her friends and she wished they could've just sat and talked about how they were doing personally. She missed them.

At the present moment, Michael was detailing how Sebastian's armies would advance. "The majority will come just north of Dragon Waste while others will advance through ships, most likely arriving on your southeast shore."

"How many soldiers will he bring against us?" Jean-Luc asked.

Michael leaned back in his chair and rubbed his light beard as he thought. He wanted to give Jean-Luc the best estimate he could. "I would think that he will only have half his army. A few hundred will refuse to strike, and many of the soldiers he will keep behind to guard the castle. I'm going to guess about a thousand."

Etalon stood to his feet and turned to Jean-Luc. His deep voice spoke out, "The biggest army I could possibly muster would be six hundred. We would be greatly overmatched."

Belle quickly interrupted, "Etalon, I've seen both armies. I've been around Grimdolon. Yes, Mendolon comes against us with bigger numbers, but Grimdolon's warriors are stronger and better equipped than the soldiers of Mendolon."

"Belle's right," Jean-Luc added adjusting his glasses. "What we lack in size, we make up for in ability. Our warriors are most astute in the areas of combat and battle strategy."

Etalon nodded in approval. Though in his heart he still feared their numbers were greatly too low, he was a respectful warrior that rarely ever questioned a command from his superiors. "How should we station our warriors?"

Michael spoke up, "I'd recommend we place a brigade of your fifty best archers on the southeastern shore to intercept any soldiers arriving by boats. This will slow them down as they try to come to shore. Have a hundred other warriors join them."

Etalon was now standing as he listened to Michael lay out his plan. "Yes, go on."

"I would then place most of your soldiers on the northwest border since that seems to be the best route for Mendolon's soldiers. Bringing an army through Dragon Waste would be very difficult, especially on the eastern side with the dense woods and rocky soil."

Jean-Luc was the next to speak, "I will be informing most of our residents to take refuge in either our castle or the old fortress to the south."

"Hmm..." Michael leaned back in his chair and assessed this new bit of information. He quickly readjusted his plan. "Well, I guess a hundred will need to be kept guarding the old fortress. How secure is it?"

Etalon replied, "Very secure. The doors are made of iron, and they are double layered in every entrance."

"Excellent. Also, keep a handful of warriors patrolling the mines and the orchards, just in case Sebastian tries anything irregular." Michael then turned to face his fellow knight. "Bernard, I'm going to have you head back to Mendolon. Hopefully the knights are already reconvening. We are going to need their help in this fight."

Bernard dropped the turkey leg that was in his hand. "Are you sure that's a good idea? I mean, we did just beat up a number of soldiers in the woods. Now they'll be looking for me also."

"Yes, Bernard. It'll take a little while before word reaches all the other soldiers that you're working with me. I want you to find Gideon and have him bring the knights to our aid."

Belle spoke up, "About how long do we have before the soldiers are at our borders?"

"Not long. I would guess they will be at our borders in two days. Gideon made it sound like Sebastian has been planning this attack for some time now."

Belle looked over at her fiancée. He was running his fingers through the bottom of his mane. He seemed calm and under control. As Michael continued, Jean-Luc quietly reached for a cluster of grapes that were sitting on the table. This battle would be his first main act as king. Even though Belle was fearful for the citizens of her new kingdom, she took comfort in Jean-Luc's wisdom and poise. It was much different than anything Sebastian ever exhibited when planning for a battle. If it wasn't for the strategic planning of

Michael and Hector, Mendolon would've been overpowered a long time ago.

Etalon spoke out, "Chief knight Michael, where will you be stationed during the battle?"

Michael took a deep breath as he looked off to the side. Belle knew him well enough to know that he was struggling with what he was about to say. He was known for his complete honesty and honor. Michael was trying to think of the right words. He sat back in his chair. Jean-Luc, always a master of observation, saw what was occurring and spoke up amidst the brief period of silence, "Let me help him out here... Michael will not be with us during the battle."

Bernard quickly objected, "What! Michael, we can't do this without you. None of us are as brave or as smart as you."

"Bernard!" Jean-Luc interrupted, holding out his palm to further his point. "Let me stop you there; apparently encouragement might not be your gift today."

The young knight blushed a little, realizing his words were a little too strong. "Sorry," he mumbled under his breath.

Jean-Luc continued addressing the others, "I anticipate Michael is going to head north to look for this court jester."

Etalon stood up. "Michael, like the others, I must object. We will need you in this battle. We will be greatly overnumbered and your skill in battle..."

Belle spoke up, interrupting Etalon, "It's okay." Her voice sounded particularly soft against the deep voice of

Etalon. "Michael wouldn't do this unless there was a great need."

Michael nodded before speaking, "Yes, this court jester needs to be found and done away with. I fear what I will find in Saison." It wouldn't, by any means, be an easy battle, and a part of him wished he could stay with his friends and fight. He knew he would be a great help, but the threat of the court jester sounded too serious to simply let go. Hector's brief words in the dungeon stuck in his mind. Defeating the court jester was the first priority.

The group was caught off guard by a sudden knock on the door. They all turned to see the castle servant, Jonas, peek his head through the door. "Sire, guests have arrived at the castle."

Jean-Luc took off his glasses as he turned toward Jonas. "More guests? Can't we just eat in peace? Hopefully this isn't another attempt by Sebastian to ruin our dinner."

"Well, Sire, this one you will want to know about. It's the knights of Mendolon."

All in the room were shocked at this news. "What? Here in Grimdolon?" Belle was astounded.

Jonas continued, "Yes, they arrived at our border and submitted themselves to our guards. They asked to be brought to the castle. They said they're here to help."

Instantly, much excitement filled the room. They were all relieved to hear this news. Jean-Luc calmly stood to his feet and wiped his mouth with a napkin. He was smiling. "Well, then, this is definitely good news... on second thought, let's pour the wine and welcome our new guests."

CHAPTER 9

The knights arrived at the castle under Gideon's leadership. All twenty were now present. There were two knights that had been watching the northwest border, but even they came with the group. Gideon had anticipated the possibility of Sebastian not accepting Michael's proposal of delaying action against Grimdolon. When word broke out that Michael was now a fugitive, they all met at the old northern ruins before proceeding through the northern route to Grimdolon.

Jean-Luc and Belle welcomed them by serving a luxurious Grimdolon meal. Everyone ate heartily while Jean-Luc, Etalon, and Michael continued to talk through battle plans and assignments. The beasts greatly welcomed the help from the knights of Mendolon. The beasts knew they were men of honor and that their abilities in battle were known all over the world. Few could rival them.

The current battle strategy was for the knights to spread themselves out among the different troops of warrior beasts throughout the kingdom. Most would be among a large group along the road just north of Dragon Waste. Others would be in the southeast among the Grimdolon archers, looking for soldiers who would arrive via the ports. This is where Gideon would be stationed. A few other knights would be stationed at the castle while others would be at the southeastern fortress helping to secure those who had taken refuge there. The plan was that if the soldiers ever broke through to the borders, the knights and beasts would retreat to the castle or the fortress, depending on their location.

It was now getting late in the day, so Michael decided to wait until the morning to start his journey to Saison. He had hardly slept the last two nights, and though the mission was urgent, he knew that he would need to be at full strength for the journey ahead. Currently, he was shaving his face in his castle room. He found it relaxing doing this simple task in the mist of the chaotic situation he now found himself in. The blade slid down his face, trimming his beard.

As he reached for a nearby cloth, he heard a knock on his door. "Come in."

Michael watched closely as the door slowly opened. He wondered who it would be. He instantly recognized

Corbeau, dressed in full battle attire, passing through the door. Michael thought he looked a little timid even though he was trying to project strength. "Hello, Michael."

"Greetings," Michael responded.

Corbeau calmly stepped into Michael's room and sat on the edge of the bed. "Trimming your beard, I see."

Michael nodded slightly as he wiped his face with a towel. "What do you need, Corbeau?"

Corbeau stood back up and took a deep breath before speaking. "I want to go with you to the forest and..."

"Bernard will go with me to Saison," Michael interrupted. "Now that all of us knights have arrived, he will be free to travel with me."

"Michael, please," Corbeau pleaded, taking a step toward the chief knight. "You know my abilities are more skilled than Bernard. He hasn't even been in any sort of combat over the last few months."

Michael thought about objecting to this last statement, knowing they had just fought a group of soldiers in the woods, but decided otherwise. "They need you here. Your skill will be a great help if the soldiers penetrate the borders."

"No! Listen to me." Corbeau spoke urgently. "I've been chasing this court jester for the last four months. I want to find him. I have to find him."

Michael turned to face his fellow knight. He didn't know quite what to say. "What are you doing? What are you trying to prove, Corbeau? We all know of your abilities."

Corbeau gritted his teeth as he hit the wall with the bottom of his fist. "Hector gave me this assignment. I was the one leading the effort. I should be the one to catch him."

Michael shook his head as he bit his lip. Corbeau often struggled with jealousy and pride. Michael knew it was beginning to get the best of him. "Since you can't see it, I'll tell you honestly." Michael spoke softly, trying to calm him, "This is becoming an obsession. It's getting the best of you. You need to stay here."

Corbeau took another step closer to Michael. He knew his fellow knight was right, but didn't want to give in. He decided to speak honestly. "If you know what an obsession really is, then you know you can't stop me. I'm coming with you."

As much as he hated to admit it, Michael knew there was much truth behind what his fellow knight was saying. He knew Corbeau well enough to know that if he ordered him to stay, he would end up running off and following him to Saison. Corbeau was always extremely devoted to the tasks he was given. Most of the time this was a great asset in his work as a knight, but sometimes his devotion was so strong that it clouded his judgement in other areas. He oftentimes refused to be reassigned to different missions, even if it was for the betterment of the team. This was one of those instances.

Michael took a deep breath as he wiped his face one last time. He decided to give in to his fellow knight's request. "Corbeau, we will leave at first light. We'll head for the southwest region of Saison, the summer section of the forest."

"Thank you," Corbeau said quietly.

"But make no mistake that I will still be taking the lead. You will follow me."

"Of course," Corbeau replied, holding out his hand. He wished he could object to this statement, but mainly he was just thankful to still be on the hunt for this villain of Mendolon.

Michael stood staring at his fellow knight. He wondered if he had done the right thing. A part of him wanted to take back everything he had just said, but in the end, he knew that Corbeau would be a huge help amidst any unpredictable foe they might face in the forest. He broke the silence with one last command for his companion, "Be sure to have enough supplies for a two-day journey. I hope to find those who have settled among the Noe creatures. From there we can regroup and see if we can find anything."

Corbeau was perplexed. "But... no one has ever seen the settlers since they entered Saison."

Michael smiled briefly. "Well, I don't think anyone's really looked for them for fear of going missing themselves."

Corbeau couldn't think of anything else to say. In the end he would have to follow Michael on this expedition. "Okay, I will do as you say."

"Thank you... sleep well," Michael said to Corbeau. His fellow knight nodded his head in return as he turned to walk away. A daring task lay before them in the morning.

As Corbeau opened the door to leave, he wasn't able to shut the door. Etalon pushed his hand on the door, not allowing it to be closed. He and Corbeau stared at each other as one passed out of the room and the other entered. Michael saw it all transpire from the mirror in front of him.

Etalon carried himself as officially as he could. When he had fully entered the room, he addressed Michael like a true servant of the king. "Sir, the king awaits your presence in his upper study."

"Is everything okay?"

"Yes, the king thinks there is something you need to see before you travel north."

"I'll be right there."

❧

"Jean-Luc, you called for me," Michael said as he entered into the upper study. Jean-Luc was sitting comfortably in a chair.

"Yes, there is something I want you to see before you journey north." Jean-Luc stood and walked to the far side of the room, away from the door where Michael entered. Michael could see a large sheet covering something on a table at the side of the room.

"Is this the creature's head you were telling us about?"

"It is. I thought you ought to see it before you travel north."

"Okay," Michael said quietly as Jean-Luc stepped into position to remove the sheet.

172

Jean-Luc continued, "Brace yourself. It is quite hideous."

As Jean-Luc removed the sheet, Michael was struck by the vile appearance of the creature before him. Something that directly caught his eye was the sheer look of hatred that appeared in the creature's expression. He took a step closer to examine it. He spoke softly, "What... what is this brood of evil that is before us?"

Jean-Luc adjusted his glasses as he stepped around the table to where Michael was standing. "I've been wondering the same thing since the day he came close to our border. Particularly, the scales under the fur around his neck are like nothing I've ever seen. None of my scientists can identify him either or even classify his species for that matter."

Michael reached out and touched the creature's fur. "Unbelievable," he said in wonder.

"Isn't it though? At first, I wondered if someone had given me a bit of the Savage's hallucination powder," Jean-Luc said in jest.

Michael lowered his head toward the creature in order to examine everything closely. He looked carefully at the neck structure along with the blood coming from the creature's muscles. "Very interesting," he said under his breath. He then spoke directly to Jean-Luc, "What did you say happened to the beast who was attacked by this creature?"

"Unfortunately, an infection spread throughout his body. It looks like he might lose his arm."

Michael shook his head in despair. It wasn't the answer he wanted to hear. He rubbed his forehead as he contemplated the nature of this creature. There were many unknowns about the Forest of Saison. He had heard many rumors about things that lived in the region. He wondered how many more of these creatures he would be facing in the forest.

As Michael continued to think, Jean-Luc broke the silence. "Michael, before you enter into the territory, I want to fit you with better armor."

Michael quickly countered, "The armor Hector made will suffice. The mobility of it is a great advantage in battle."

"Maybe, but..." Jean-Luc walked to the other side of the room. "I have armor plates for your forearms along with a helmet." Jean-Luc picked up the plates from a nearby table. Michael walked over to join him. He took them from Jean-Luc and placed them on his arms. They made his arms heavier, but he knew it would be a help in case he fought one of these vicious creatures.

"And now the helmet," Jean-Luc said holding it out. Michael grabbed it from his friend's hands and looked at it closely. It was black in color, a slight contrast from his dark grey armor. It covered his head and a portion of his face. It left an opening for his eyes and his mouth. He slid it on his head easily. "I'd say it fits well," Jean-Luc said with satisfaction.

"Great, thanks, Jean-Luc. Well, I think it might be time for me..."

"One more thing, Michael." Jean-Luc said, holding up his index finger.

"Yes, go on."

"What you've told me so far about this court jester is very intriguing. He doesn't sound like someone to be trifled with. I would suggest you do not try to fight him conventionally, but rather try to outsmart him."

"Like what you did to us in Mendolon?" Michael said with a slight laugh.

Jean-Luc thought for a moment before answering. "Hmm, yes, very similarly, but do be careful. You will want to stay a step ahead of this fiend."

Suddenly a knock was heard at the door. Jean-Luc turned. "Come in."

The door opened and the servant Jonas opened the door fully as he entered the room. "Sire."

"Yes, Jonas."

The small beast spoke timidly, seeing that the king was with Michael de Bolbec. He felt badly for interrupting. "As you requested, I've prepared your leisure room with our best cakes and pastries."

"Ah, wonderful," Jean-Luc said in return. He turned to Michael and spoke politely, "Shall we? Grimdolon desserts aren't something to be missed."

Michael shook his head. He smiled slightly as he spoke, "Jean-Luc... a battle is coming to you in a few days. Isn't there something else you should be doing with your time?"

Jean-Luc simply shrugged his shoulders as he walked to the door. "Michael, it's late in the day. We'll start tomorrow. Come now... there's nothing like the delicacies of Grimdolon to help relax one's demeanor before a few days of hard work. Won't you come?"

Michael stood quietly for a moment before taking a deep breath. He then calmly took off his helmet and motioned toward the door. "You lead the way."

Michael sat in Jean-Luc's reading room. Bookcases lined the walls. Comfortable seats were spread over beautiful rugs. A fire burned steadily in the fireplace. The knights had already been through the room earlier and had helped themselves to the Grimdolon desserts. Jean-Luc encouraged them to eat their fill and enjoy themselves. He was thankful for their help in coming to his kingdom's aid. He wanted the knights of Mendolon to see their finest hospitality.

Currently Michael was relaxing comfortably in a chair, listening to Jean-Luc tell stories to Gideon, Belle, and Jonas about some of the strange meals Bernard had brought him while he was in prison in Mendolon's castle. Gideon, Jonas, and Belle were laughing hysterically while Bernard sat blushing. Jean-Luc spoke with great jest in his voice, "So then I had to explain to Bernard... bless you, my boy," he said briefly to Bernard before continuing, "that we are not like beasts of the field. We like to cook our food." Belle and Gideon continued to laugh. Even though Bernard was embarrassed, he couldn't help but smile at some of the things he once did.

Michael leaned his head back and rubbed his eyes. He smiled as he listened to Grimdolon's king. He was tired but yet found this banter relaxing. He admired Jean-Luc and specifically how calm he could be, even in the midst of threats that were coming against his kingdom. His demeanor and poise were qualities to be admired. Jean-Luc continued with the story, "Then Bernard asks if I could come to the kitchen and help him in the food preparation. I then had to remind him that I was a prisoner and letting me into the kitchen was not a good idea."

Belle brushed a strand of hair out of her eyes as she continued to laugh. Even though she had heard this story before, the way Jean-Luc told it seemed to bring it to life every time. Michael couldn't take his eyes off of her as she smiled and laughed. He thought she looked incredible in that moment. She was dressed as the queen in an extravagant purple dress, but that was not what made her truly beautiful. Her inward beauty seemed to shine out as she laughed and smiled. She could light up any room with her pleasant demeanor. Michael turned to face the fire. He was glad his good friend, Belle, was happy. He missed her in his life, but at the end of the day her happiness was what he wanted for her most of all.

The laughter continued in the background as Michael began to slowly fall asleep. Tomorrow he had a big mission ahead of him, but for now he would sleep in peace.

Many years ago...

Mamour's bags were packed—he was moving south. He was now an adult and wanted to pursue becoming a prestigious knight of Mendolon. It was his dream. His kingdom was an ally of Mendolon. He would first try to find work inside the castle and eventually try to join the ranks of the knights. His swordsmanship was subpar, but he figured his intellect was enough to be a valuable asset to the knights.

He had already said goodbye to his mother and was out the door walking away. His blond hair was blowing in the wind. There was a bag over his shoulder as he walked from his home. His plan was to travel south and then see if a traveler would carry him further south into Mendolon. He hoped to be there by tomorrow evening.

"Mamour!" he heard someone call out from behind. He turned to see it was his mother coming toward him. Mamour didn't respond but simply waited for his mother to catch up with him. "There was one more thing I wanted to give you before you left."

He was curious. "What is it, Mother?"

She opened her hand and showed him a silver necklace. Mamour recognized it instantly. It was the one she wore every day. It was given to her by her father when she was a young girl. The shape was a six-pointed star that was hand crafted by a blacksmith. It was expensive and a gift that she greatly valued. Mamour objected, "Mother, I can't... that's yours... I... I..."

"I want you to have it, son," she said, putting it in his hand and then closing his fingers around it.

Mamour was stunned; he didn't know what else to say. He simply stood there looking at his hand and then back to his mother's face. A part of him wanted to give it right back, but he knew that for his mother to do this, she had a very special reason. She continued, "Please take it. You will always have it to remember me by when we're apart." She stopped briefly as a few tears started to roll down her face. "Remember to always do good. It's a harsh world, and we need more people standing for what is honorable and true, even when it gets hard. Choose good, Mamour, choose good."

Mamour felt tears beginning to well up in his eyes. He gripped the necklace tightly as he looked up at his mother. He *held up his arms and embraced her. He whispered quietly in her ear, "I will, Mother. I will."*

CHAPTER 10

Michael and Corbeau left early the next morning for the Forest of Saison. It was close to twelve miles from Grimdolon's castle to the edge of the forest. Jean-Luc had given them two horses to ride. With the horses running at a decent pace, they hoped to arrive before the middle of the day. The land directly north of the castle was reasonably flat after one left the rocky terrain of Grimdolon. For the most part this area was free of travelers as well.

Even though they packed light, both men were well equipped for their journey to the forest. Michael was wearing his dark grey armor that Hector had made him for taking on the Savage. He also wore Jean-Luc's arm plates, and he had the black helmet stored away. Corbeau, on the other hand, wore his traditional knight armor bearing a thick chest plate but also no helmet. His red cape flowed behind him as he rode toward the forest. They packed just enough food to last them a day and a half.

Both men felt a bit of apprehension as neither had been in Saison and had often heard legends about the area. The added mystery of the court jester compounded things even more. Michael wished he had gotten more information from Hector about the jester's background. He wondered about the power he might possess.

After riding for nine miles, Michael slowed his horse. They were on the edge of an open plain and a small forest. The Forest of Saison was only a few miles away, and Michael thought it would be best if they stopped for food. As Michael's horse stopped, he turned to address Corbeau. "Let's stop briefly before we arrive at Saison." Corbeau simply nodded in return and dismounted. Even though he thought this was a good idea, it always upset him a little to take orders from Michael. He was five years older than his fellow knight and thought he was more qualified to be the chief knight of Mendolon.

"How's your horse riding?" Michael said as he removed a small loaf of bread and apples from a side pouch.

"It's fine," Corbeau said, brushing the dark hair out of his eyes. The temperature outside was warm, and both men were sweating a little in their respective armor.

The two men sat in silence, eating the food they had brought with them. Michael knew of the jealousy in

Corbeau's mind. At times he didn't know how to deal with it. Thankfully their working relationship was good, and though Corbeau challenged Michael's leadership from time-to-time, he completed all his assignments flawlessly and was very reliable in battle. After five minutes, Michael broke the silence, "Have you heard from Renée lately?"

Corbeau looked squarely at Michael. He had an irritated look on his face. His relationship with his ex-wife was still very strained, and he didn't like Michael bringing this up with him. "No, I haven't," he said in a matter-of-fact manner.

"Hmm. Sorry to hear," Michael responded, trying to speak as compassionately as he could. "I did see her fairly recently. The farmer I work with sells his wheat to..."

"Michael, drop it," Corbeau interrupted, clearly upset.

"Ok... I was just asking, hoping progress had been made with you reconciling with her."

Corbeau looked off to the side and shook his head. He debated with himself whether to further respond or not. He took a deep breath before looking directly at Michael and spoke quietly. "She responded to one of my letters a few months ago, not long after I rescued the young woman in the swamp. She knows I've been leading the hunt for the escaped prisoners. I hate to think how everything might change with her after Sebastian tries to invade Grimdolon."

"Yeah," Michael nodded as he spoke. Life would surely be different now that the knights left Mendolon and were no longer operating under the king's control. In theory, the knights had the power to call a vote of no confidence against the king, but they knew this would be difficult to organize with Sebastian's dangerous and reckless attitude. Michael continued, "After the soldiers try to invade Grimdolon, and we defeat this jester, Gideon and I have a plan to go back to Mendolon and lead a judicial overthrow of Sebastian's reign. It's been a long time coming, and the people should agree with us."

"How do you know the people will go along with you?"

"There's no way the citizens of Mendolon will agree with this invasion of Grimdolon. They're angry at the king. Many of them know that Belle was kidnapped as a child. If we put up a full vote of no confidence, the people will follow us."

Corbeau spoke quietly, "I fear Sebastian won't allow us to get anywhere close to the castle and will have everyone turned against us."

"My hope is that after the invasion, Gideon and Jean-Luc can somehow turn the defeated soldiers in our favor."

"I think you're optimistic, Michael. These soldiers are..."

Corbeau stopped as Michael stood to his feet. He was looking into the nearby woods. "Show yourself!" Michael yelled out.

"What's going on?" Corbeau asked as he also stood and drew a sword. He looked in the same direction as Michael, trying to see what his fellow knight saw. He saw no one.

Michael drew a dagger. "This is your last chance. Come out and no harm will come to you."

Just a moment passed before a figure started moving in the woods not far from them. Corbeau looked closely and saw a figure dressed in all black, and he was moving toward them. Michael's eyes were keenly fixed on him as he stepped from the woods and stood calmly. The knights weren't able to see his face due to the fact that he was wearing a black helmet.

Corbeau was the first to speak. "Who are you?" The man said nothing in return.

Michael turned to his fellow knight. "I don't know who he really is, but this is Sebastian's personal assassin. The king calls on him whenever he has a special assignment in the north."

Corbeau was shocked. He had heard stories about the assassin but had never actually seen him. No one knew where he was from or what abilities he had. Many of the knights didn't speak favorably of him as they had a hunch that Sebastian's assignments for him were full of dishonesty and corruption. "What does he want?" Corbeau asked.

"I don't know," Michael spoke, still holding his dagger in his hand. "Take off the mask!"

The assassin shrugged his shoulders before unstrapping his helmet and removing it slowly. The two knights could see that the face exposed was a man with white hair and a white beard. He looked to be around sixty years of age. There was a relaxed look on his face. Seeing the man's face, Michael lowered his dagger, feeling no threat from the assassin.

"Greetings," he said calmly.

"Why are you following us?" Michael asked sternly.

The assassin just looked at Michael, not saying a thing. Michael spoke again. This time a little louder. "Why are you following us?"

"I don't answer to you, Michael de Bolbec. You know I serve the king of Mendolon."

Michael instantly pulled another dagger. He was in no mood for this. If this assassin was serving Sebastian, then he would need to be seen as an instant threat. "I'm warning you, assassin. This is your last chance. Why are you following us?"

The aged assassin pulled a sword from his side and braced himself. Corbeau pulled his other sword too. The knights approached the assassin as tension rose. The assassin looked squarely at Michael and saw he was not bluffing. He let down his sword, knowing that he wouldn't be able to take on either of these two knights, let alone both at once.

He quickly spoke to stop the approaching knights, "I'm not exactly following you, but I do want the same thing you do."

"And what's that?" Michael asked.

"I'm trying to catch this villain, the court jester. Sebastian wants him found."

Michael continued questioning the assassin, "What does Sebastian want with him? He's no longer in Mendolon."

The assassin sheathed his sword as he spoke. "Just like you, Sebastian sees him as a threat. He wants him vanquished."

Michael didn't trust what he was saying. Sebastian was selfish and didn't worry about things that didn't affect him directly. Michael wondered if this was some sort of plot against him. "You can leave and reassure Sebastian that we'll take care of the jester." Michael spoke in an authoritative voice. "Oh, and while you're at it, tell him the armies of Grimdolon and the knights of Mendolon are ready to fight against any force he brings against them."

The assassin stood emotionless. His gaze was fixed directly on Michael. "The king will want to see that I disposed of the court jester personally."

Michael took a step closer to his opponent. The daggers were still in his hands. "Let me make this clear to you. If I see you following us again, then we will not hesitate to engage you in a fight and be assured that you will lose."

No one said a word for a few moments. Corbeau sheathed his swords as he could tell that the assassin was not going to bring a fight at this point. The assassin slowly picked up his helmet and put it back on his head. Michael didn't take his eyes off him as he spoke, "We're going to be leaving now. I will warn you again. Don't come anywhere close to us."

The assassin nodded as he turned back toward the woods and walked away. Corbeau didn't know what to say as Michael stood staring at the assassin until he was completely out of sight. He was wondering what was going through Michael's mind at this point. He could tell the chief knight was deep in thought.

Michael took a deep breath before speaking quietly to his fellow knight, "We're done here... let's keep moving."

❧❧

Hector lay on the floor of his prison cell rubbing his head. A voice was calling out to him. He woke with a massive headache. He had been knocked out in the early morning hours of the day. It took him a moment to remember where he was and what he had been doing the day before. He saw blood on the collar of his jacket which brought back the memory of what had happened.

"Get up," the voice continued to call out to him.

Hector raised his head and was surprised to see king Sebastian standing in front of him. "Sire," he said with a weak voice.

"Did you warn the knights about my invasion of Grimdolon?"

Hector stumbled to his feet. "You give me far too much credit, O King." Hector stopped briefly to cough. "You misread your loyalty. Not everyone is in agreement that Grimdolon needs to be conquered."

The king paced in front of the prison cell. He was wearing a long burgundy robe and his crown sat on his head. He slowly stroked his beard as he took in what Hector was saying. He decided to change direction in the conversation. "What did you tell Michael de Bolbec before he escaped?"

Hector hissed as he threw his hand down in a dismissing manner. He didn't want to answer any more of the king's questions. The prison cell was empty except for a small bed in a corner. He took a seat on the edge of his bed and put his head in his hands.

The king continued, "Did you send him after our court jester?"

Hector looked up at the king with an angry look. He said nothing.

"Hector, do you think I haven't heard about him? A few of our soldiers who were with Corbeau hunting down the escaped prisoners informed me that a secret side mission was occurring. With a little research and spying by some of my most loyal soldiers, it was easy to discover who you were looking for." The king stepped closer to the prison bars. He continued to speak condescendingly to his chief advisor, "You see, Hector, you really shouldn't underestimate people's loyalty to me."

"What are you planning?"

The king snickered before speaking. "I will rule Mendolon unequivocally. Once Grimdolon is defeated and I own their mines, there will be no stopping me. I will even put to death any talk of an organized rebellion against me by the knights."

Hector shot back quickly. "The people of this kingdom will never follow you. The knights won't even have to judicially overthrow you. The citizens of the kingdom will rebel on their own."

The king smiled and shook his head. "Hector... no one will challenge me once I own this power of the jester. I won't even have to use it. The threat of me possessing it is enough to keep the people under my control."

Hector ran his fingers through his oily black hair. He was utterly frustrated. "You don't know what you're talking about!" he shouted. "You don't even truly know what the jester possesses."

The king stayed calm. He pulled on the top edges of his robe. A part of him pitied Hector for underestimating his plans. He was about to walk away when he paused to speak one more time with his advisor. "Hector, what happened to you, my old boy? For a long time you were helping me plot against Grimdolon. You could've been right beside me as I took complete control of the whole kingdom. It would've been a glorious moment in your pathetic life."

Hector didn't say a word. He turned to face the wall, not wanting to see the king any longer. Sebastian shrugged his shoulders. "Goodbye... enjoy your cell, Snake," he said as he walked away.

Sebastian was only able to take a few steps before Hector spoke up. There was great hissing in his voice. "The moment you, O King, started dealing with dragons, I saw the evil you truly have planned for this kingdom and this world. You're going to destroy yourself and all who follow you. You know where dragons come from, and still, that doesn't stop you. You are truly evil, O King."

The king didn't even turn around as he heard Hector speak. He stood for a moment before speaking calmly. "I find it very ironic, Hector de Serpent, that you of all people are calling me evil."

Hector did not respond as the king left the dungeon. He put his hands over his eyes as he thought about everything the king had just said. The biggest fear came to his mind. He feared that the king had already won.

CHAPTER 11

Michael and Corbeau arrived at the edge of Saison before midday. Besides meeting the assassin, the rest of their journey had been uneventful. It was an overcast day which led to a cooler temperature for which they were both thankful. They had arrived at the southwestern side of the forest which was the summer quadrant. Michael didn't know where he would find the court jester as the area was roughly twenty miles wide and fifteen miles long. His hope was that he could find some of the people that had settled there years ago. Maybe they would have some insight into the jester's location.

Upon arriving, the two knights were quite surprised by what they saw. Around the edge of the forest was a twelve-foot-high log wall. Thick ropes were used to tie the logs tightly together. The dense foliage of the trees rose above the wall.

The two men were both perplexed as they dismounted their horses. Corbeau was the first to speak, "Have you ever heard of this wall?"

Michael shook his head. "No... it must be relatively new. I've been here to the edge of Saison a few times and I don't ever remember this."

"Do you think some of the people got word about the released prisoners and decided to build this wall to keep them out?"

Michael stood silent for a moment as he approached the wall. He put his hand on one of the logs. He wondered what was the meaning and purpose behind this new structure. "I... I don't know."

Corbeau walked over close to where Michael was standing. He could tell he was deep in thought. "Do you think we should just climb over or break through?"

Michael looked off to the east and observed the terrain. "No. Let's head east and see how far this goes."

The men rode slowly toward the east. The wall was quite a structure. Though it wasn't impenetrable, the sheer length of it must have required a few months of steady work. Michael had heard legends about the Noe creatures that lived in the forest. He wondered if this wall was to keep out people who were curious about seeing the creatures. But yet another thought crossed his mind that this was some sort of plan created by the court jester. Maybe he was the mastermind behind this structure.

After riding for three hours, the men arrived at the spring quadrant of Saison. It was just a few yards later that the wall stopped. The men could see more clearly into the woods. It was obvious now that the season was spring. The foliage looked green and fresh. It also looked as if rain had fallen recently in this territory. There was no trail, but there was plenty of room between the trees to ride the horses through the area. "Let's move in," Michael said calmly. Corbeau nodded his head as they entered the forest. Michael put on the black helmet Jean-Luc had given him the day before. He didn't know what he would face inside this forest.

The forest seemed pleasant enough at first. Michael and Corbeau decided to head west back toward the summer section. Both men could feel the heat rise instantly as they passed into the region. Birds chirped overhead, squirrels and chipmunks ran about along the ground. Everything seemed normal in this area, except that both men had a general feeling of uneasiness. They couldn't explain it, but both felt as if they were being watched. At times they would quickly look to the side and briefly see a pair of eyes watching them. The eyes would then quickly disappear after a brief glimpse from the men. This kept them slightly anxious.

Both men couldn't help but examine the area as they moved about. They had both heard legends about the Forest of Saison, but neither had ever entered. Even though he currently felt anxious, overall Michael enjoyed exploring new areas. A part of it was his boyhood sense of adventure, while another part was his duty as the chief knight. He felt responsible for knowing the world and the areas around the kingdom. He wanted to be a true leader among the knights in regard to the knowledge of this world. This exploration of Saison was one he didn't think any knight had experienced since his father.

Corbeau spoke suddenly, "Michael, do you see that?"

"I'm seeing a lot of things. What are you talking about specifically?"

Corbeau lowered his volume. "Up ahead about thirty feet, there is something on the ground."

Michael looked closely, and he saw an animal lying on the ground. It wasn't moving. Anywhere else this would have been just a common sight, but here in Saison they hadn't seen anything like this so far. "Let's check it out."

Both men dismounted and approached the animal. As the men got closer the creature did not move. Moving even closer, they could see that it was a deer. It had been killed and left here mostly intact. It was as if something had killed it and just left it alone. It truly was out of place from anything else they had seen in this forest. Michael was the first to speak, "This is odd."

"I agree," Corbeau said while looking closely at the animal.

Michael bent down and turned his head to the side to look more closely at the dead animal. "Look at these marks along its back. These are clearly teeth."

Corbeau knelt down beside him. "Yeah... but what could've done this? It looks like some type of... shark bite or something like that."

Michael thought back to the creature's head he had seen in Grimdolon's castle. He wondered if this could be the work of that creature, but then again it seemed like that creature could have eaten this deer whole. As he continued to examine the animal, he kept asking himself the question, *Why was this animal killed?* A number of possibilities came to mind. It was a mystery. He looked closely at the animal one more time before the answer suddenly came to mind.

Michael quickly rose to his feet. "Corbeau! We must get away. This is a..." He wasn't able to answer because from the woods arose a fierce bear-like creature. It became obvious that it was all a trap. Michael was able to jump backward while Corbeau fell. The bear quickly raised his paw to strike him. Michael, moving as quickly as he could, removed a dagger from his belt and struck the bear in his palm. The dagger didn't go in far, but it was just enough to distract him. Corbeau got to his feet and ran to where Michael was standing.

Both men were then able to get a better look at the creature before them. It was a bear, but it was by no means a normal bear. He was enormous, roughly around ten feet in high and very bulky. His fur was dark and it was incredibly coarse, almost like grass. The creature's eyes were red and his teeth looked sharp, and from them dripped some sort of green substance. His claws also looked longer than any other bear. All of these characteristics were strange, but none compared to the overall look on the bear's face. As a whole the creature looked vicious, angry. It was as if his desire was to kill, not just for food or for sport, but purely for hatred.

"Get ready, Corbeau," Michael said holding a dagger in each hand. Corbeau quickly pulled both of his swords.

The bear looked at the men closely and kept snarling. He was ready to kill. The bear squinted his eyes slightly. Michael could tell he was about to spring on them. "Watch out!" he yelled.

As if on cue, the bear leaped for them. The knights jumped away from one another; Michael to the left and Corbeau to the right. Both men felt the ground shake briefly as the creature landed. The bear then turned to Corbeau. He took a swipe with his paw. Corbeau leaned backwards as the claws barely missed him. He then rotated his arm forward and thrust one of his swords into the arm of the creature. The blade went in about three inches. A thick dark green substance flowed from his wrist. The bear roared loudly.

Michael then sprang forward with his daggers in his hands pointed downward. He drove them into the back of the bear. The creature reared back and turned to see what was behind him. Michael moved with the creature and stayed behind his back, so he wouldn't be seen by it. He saw that neither of the daggers had gone in deep. Michael then quickly pulled one of them out and jabbed it again into the bear in the same spot. This time it went in all the way to the hilt.

Corbeau then moved forward to run the creature through with one of his swords. The bear was now moving more frantically. With a hard backhand swipe, he made contact this time and knocked Corbeau backwards. The force of the bear's strength sent the knight through the air ten yards. Corbeau hit hard against the ground which took his breath away.

Michael knew he had to keep the bear distracted. Thankfully, he was still behind the creature, out of sight at the moment. He pulled another dagger, quickly moved to the bear's side, and with all his strength pushed it downward into the foot of the creature. The bear turned and looked down to see the dagger in his foot. He continued to roar viciously. Michael was now in full sight of the bear. He would have to think quickly in order to keep this bear from pouncing. He pulled another dagger and looked for a place to throw it. So far, the skin of this bear had proven to be remarkably thick. Looking at the bear in the face, he noticed a spot on the creature that looked to be relatively soft. He had found his spot. The bear then took a swipe at Michael. He quickly jumped backwards and then threw the dagger directly at the nose of the creature. It penetrated a few inches into the right nostril of the bear. Once again, he roared loudly in pain.

Corbeau was just starting to gather himself as Michael ran toward him. "Come on," Michael said, pulling him aside.

The two knights ducked behind a nearby tree with a small bush to its side. They were safe for now. The men could see the bear rolling on the ground trying to remove the dagger from his nostril. Corbeau was the first to speak. He whispered, "What is this thing?"

"Not sure. I definitely haven't seen a bear quite like this."

Corbeau felt the back of his head and could see a little blood on his fingertips. "Hopefully this isn't a normal animal for Saison."

Michael continued to watch closely as he spoke, "No, something tells me this isn't typical at all."

Corbeau was relieved to hear this. "What do you say we do?"

Michael looked around the area by the bear. He saw a thick, dead tree leaning against another tree which apparently had stopped it from falling over. It wasn't far from where the bear lay at the moment. A plan formed in his mind. "Corbeau, do you see that tree over there?" Michael said, pointing forward to the left of the bear.

"Yes."

"If you can push off against that standing tree, I think it will have a clear path to fall. You'll have to push with all your strength. It's thick."

Corbeau knew what Michael was thinking. "I see. Do you think you can get the bear into position? He's quick."

"I'll see what I can do," Michael said. He then moved out to his right through the forest and back toward the bear. Corbeau followed the plan and went toward the tree.

As Michael approached the creature, he could see that the bear had finally been able to get the dagger out of his nostril. He roared loudly and looked straight at Michael.

Even though he was a bear, Michael could tell he had the look of revenge. He wanted to kill this man in front of him that had caused him this great pain. The bear moved on all fours toward Michael. The knight quickly pulled another dagger and threw it at the creature. It didn't penetrate, but the creature lost his focus for just a moment and Michael was able to move out of the way and into position. He faced the bear and pulled his small sword. The bear stood up again on his hind legs. Michael slowly backed up, hoping the bear would continue to follow.

Corbeau positioned himself to use his legs to push the dead tree. It wasn't holding on by much, but it was thick. He braced himself and pushed with all his might. Out of the corner of his eye, he saw Michael dodging swipes from the bear and leading him into the right position. Corbeau took a deep breath and pushed as hard as he could with his legs. Slowly the tree began to move. It tore through a few branches on the other tree. It started to fall and gain momentum.

Michael could see the tree starting to fall and he quickly realized the bear needed to be back another foot in order for their plan to work. He dodged one last swipe and then quickly thrust his sword into the belly of the creature. The sword only went in about six inches, but it did make the bear step backwards. With great speed Michael jumped to his side and rolled out of the way, leaving his sword in the belly of the beast. The bear wasn't able to react in time and the tree fell with great force on the bear's neck area, pinning him on his stomach against the ground. He was badly injured and unable to move. Also, the sword in his stomach was pushed further into his belly by the ground.

Michael yelled out to his fellow knight. "Corbeau, I need your sword."

With not a moment to lose, Corbeau tossed Michael one of his swords. Michael easily caught it as he climbed on top of the fallen tree. He rotated the blade in his hand and struck downward into the head of the bear. The sword only went in halfway. Michael applied more pressure and leaned on it with his body weight until the blade slid further into the head of the animal. It was just a moment later that the creature slowly stopped moving. This was its end.

Michael took a deep breath and climbed down from the fallen tree. He stepped a few feet away before sitting down comfortably beside a tree. He removed the black helmet he was wearing. Corbeau walked over and picked up the dagger the bear had pulled from his nostril. He brought it to Michael. "You may want to hang on to as many of these as you can," he said as he handed the chief knight his dagger.

"Thank you," Michael said in return. Grabbing the dagger, he could see that some of the bear's blood remained on the blade. It was the same dark greenish blood he had seen on the wolf's head in the Grimdolon castle. He wondered how the two were connected. Many questions filled his mind.

Both men sat in silence for a few minutes catching their breath and gathering their thoughts about the creature they had just fought. Being the summer section of Saison, the temperature was hot and both men were sweating. After a few minutes, Corbeau stood to his feet and made his way back to the bear, who was now lying motionless. He pulled his sword from the head of the animal; he knew he might be needing it if they met another vicious animal like this one. The knights then took a few minutes to clean their weapons before traveling on.

They were seated comfortably as Michael gave the orders, "I say we make our way up toward the autumn season and see what we can find."

"I agree. The temperature will be cooler. I would think that the settlers would be living there if they're still here."

Michael stood to his feet and held out his hand to help his fellow knight up. The men were about thirty yards from their horses. They had run off a little when the knights were battling the bear. Catching their horses, the men adjusted the saddles and were just about to mount when Michael caught sight of arrows around him. He quickly pulled a dagger and assessed how many men were around him. Seeing Michael out of the corner of his eye, Corbeau pulled his swords and looked at the men around them. There were seven men located to the east of them. They were dressed in the clothes of peasants and didn't appear to be skilled fighters. The men were a diverse group with various shades of skin tone.

Corbeau was the first to speak to them. "Are you sure you want to do this? We are trained knights of Mendolon. Drop your weapons and we will..."

"Corbeau," Michael said, interrupting his companion. He placed his dagger back in his belt. He then turned and addressed the group, "We mean no harm. We will surrender. Please, will you take us to your dwelling?"

CHAPTER 12

The men of Saison led the two knights of Mendolon toward the southeast of the forest which was the spring region. Their horses were also brought along. The forest men allowed the knights to keep their weapons if they agreed to keep them sheathed. Not much was said as the men continued to march through the forest. Occasionally Michael would catch a set of eyes watching him from various hiding places. As he locked eyes with them, they would disappear. The further east they traveled, the more hidden sets of eyes he saw.

It was the early evening when they arrived at the small village. Michael could see fifteen to twenty small tents spread out in the area along with small gardens positioned close to many of the structures. A few dozen people were among the tents doing various tasks. They looked to be of various ethnicities. Michael could also see a few children playing in an area north of the small village. Most of the people stopped what they were doing when they saw their men return with the two knights. It had been years since anyone new had been seen in the Forest of Saison. The fact that these two men were knights of Mendolon made this situation even more intriguing to them.

The two knights were marched into the center of the village. "Wait here," one of the men said as he walked toward the largest tent and entered it.

Corbeau whispered, "Michael, what should we do?"

"Let's just wait and see what develops." The men stood patiently as the people of the village walked toward them. Many of the children were fascinated—they had heard stories about the knights of Mendolon but had never seen them in person. Now before them stood two of the knights, both dressed in impressive armor; one blond hair and one dark brown hair, each having a different set of weapons attached to their armor, ready at their disposal.

It was just over a minute later that a woman exited the tent and approached the two knights. Her skin tone was light brown. She was thin and attractive, and she couldn't have been older than thirty years of age. She was dressed casually in a white blouse with brown pants and a pair of boots. The knights could tell she was a leader in this village. She was calm but spoke firmly as she met the knights, "Good evening. I'm Clara, the governess of this village. Please state your intention for being here."

"I'm Michael de Bolbec, and this is Corbeau de Lefevre. We're knights of Mendolon."

"Yes, that is apparent," Clara said, interrupting Michael before he could say anything else. "Please, I have a right to protect these people. I want to know why you're here."

"We're here looking for an escaped prisoner that is very dangerous. He's believed to be hiding in this forest."

A stern look formed on Clara's face. "Who sent you?"

Michael took a step toward the governess. "We came..." He stopped speaking for a moment as he noticed that the men quickly raised their arrows again. He started again, "We came on our own initiative. It is said that this escaped prisoner can produce immense power. He must be stopped."

Clara held up her hand, signaling that she didn't feel threatened. The men lowered their arrows. "Forgive me, men, but King Sebastian isn't well thought of here. We're quite skeptical of any ploy by his kingdom."

Corbeau spoke up, "I don't know how much news you receive in this area, but Mendolon is beginning to fall into disarray. Sebastian doesn't have any authority over us anymore."

A curious look formed on Clara's face. She then began to pace as she spoke, "Does this have anything to do with the discovery of the Grimdolon princess rescued by their king?"

Michael bit his lip as he looked off to his left. He tried to think of the right words to say. "It's not directly related, but it's a piece of a bigger story that is in play." Michael paused briefly before continuing, "Sebastian is out of control. He has grown power hungry, and he won't listen to reason any longer."

Clara's arms were crossed as she kept pacing. She thought hard about what this knight was saying. As governess, she was the main leader of this small village, and it was at times like this that she felt the weight of her leadership. She hoped these knights weren't lying about anything, but overall, she trusted them far more than she distrusted them. She issued a decree to the men who brought them, "See to it that these men get plenty of food and water and are well taken care of." She then turned toward the two knights. "Please take your time, but I'd like to see both of you in my tent before sunset."

Jean-Luc watched the land of Grimdolon from a high balcony of his castle. There were clear skies up above. People all around the kingdom were moving about, getting ready for the impending invasion of the soldiers of Mendolon. The king could see his citizens leaving their homes and moving to the southeast where there was an old Grimdolon fort. His father, the former king, had set it up for the kingdom's citizens to take refuge in the case of an invasion. Jean-Luc watched as families of beasts moved along with their children in hand. He felt burdened that they were having to go through this trial, but he knew it was a necessity to keep everyone safe. There was no guarantee that Grimdolon's warriors could completely stop the soldiers at their borders.

Etalon approached him from behind. "Sire."

"Yes?"

"The knight Gideon has moved to the southeastern ports with a troop of beasts. They should be in place by now."

"Good," Jean-Luc turned from the balcony. He was calm. "What of northwest?"

"The majority of the knights and our warriors are stationed there. I will be joining them, once I see to it that our citizens are safe."

"Very good. What about the mines?"

"Our guards will stay in place. If we sense Sebastian's forces are trying to approach them, our warriors are instructed to pull back to them."

"Very well," Jean-Luc was pleased to hear this. "If there's nothing else, then I will see to it the castle is in order before I join the others in the southeast."

"Yes, my king," Etalon responded before walking away.

Jean-Luc headed downstairs to the throne room of the castle. He walked slowly, passing warriors and various officials in the castle. Everyone was busy, occupied with specific tasks. It reminded Jean-Luc of an ant colony. Even though the armies of Mendolon weren't supposed to arrive until tomorrow morning, Jean-Luc wanted the kingdom and the castle ready by the early evening. He wanted to be prepared for any plan Sebastian might throw at them.

He entered the throne room and found Belle putting arrows into a quiver. She was dressed in her majestic knight armor and was in a hurry. Jean-Luc sighed as he approached the future queen. "My... my... my, how things have changed since last week at this time. The castle was preparing for our wedding, and now we're preparing for a war." Belle ignored Jean-Luc as she continued meticulously putting arrows into the quiver. He then went and sat comfortably on his throne. Jean-Luc adjusted his glasses as he spoke casually, "So, Belle... do you have a plan for those arrows?"

Belle smiled slightly at Jean-Luc's question. She didn't break her focus as she spoke. "Jean-Luc, please don't try to stop me. Before being a queen, I was a knight, and that will always be a part of me."

Jean-Luc leaned forward, resting his forearms on his legs. He wasn't in a hurry. "My love, where do you plan to join the battle?"

"In the northwest. That's where the bulk of the battle will be."

"Are you sure that's what you want to do? Etalon is perfectly capable of leading our forces."

Belle nodded her head. "Yes, I know, Etalon will do well. But more than anything I want the warriors of Grimdolon to see me with them. I don't want them to be confused in any way about which side I'm on. I also wonder if there is some way to prevent the soldiers from attacking. Maybe some of them will listen to their former princess." Belle stopped what she was doing for a moment. She looked straight at Jean-Luc before continuing. "Jean-Luc, I'm sorry, I know it's dangerous, but this is what I must do."

Jean-Luc rose to his feet. He straightened the top of his collar as he approached the princess. "Belle, my bride," he spoke with a smile. "I wouldn't have it any other way. I love this about you. You're loyal to your people, no matter who they are. No one is able to get between you and them." Jean-Luc gently placed his palm on her left cheek. The princess looked directly into his eyes. "The more I'm with you, the more I fall in love... I love you, Belle, just the way you are."

"Thank you, Jean-Luc, I love you too," she said placing her hand on his.

Jean-Luc pulled her close. He embraced her as he spoke quietly into her ear, "Just promise me this, that you will come back to me, and we will have a beautiful wedding."

Belle squeezed her future husband as tightly as she could. "I promise... nothing will come between us. One day we will have the wedding we were destined to have."

Michael and Corbeau were well taken care of by the people of the forest. They were fed wild game stew before having their small cuts and bruises cared for. Their horses were also fed and brushed. Once the forest people learned that the knights were not a threat, the mood around them became joyful. There was even a layer of excitement around the villagers concerning these men. The knights found the people extremely friendly. There were very few luxuries among these people, but they didn't mind. They were happy, content, and at peace with the world. Michael loved the atmosphere. Most of the older ones came to the forest twenty-five years ago with the first explorers, while others came from other kingdoms of the world in later years. They were a diverse group that truly formed one village.

Michael learned that the eyes of the forest were the small creatures called the Noe. They inhabited all parts of the forest, and they were the keepers of it. Rarely did they come out in the open. The creatures were a cross between a guinea pig and a small bear. They walked upright, and according to legend, their presence would bring healing and goodwill to anyone they crossed. Michael hoped he would see one while in the forest.

The sun was starting to set when Michael and Corbeau entered the large tent of the governess. She was sitting at a table along with two other men who also appeared to be leaders in this village. They were looking over plans regarding the wall around the border of Saison. Seeing the knights, Clara took notice. "Knights of Mendolon, please come in and have a seat."

"Thank you," Michael responded. Corbeau was just behind him. Both men sat down before introductions were quickly exchanged with the other officials.

Clara was courteous, but it was obvious that she wanted to keep things on the diplomatic level. "Please, I would like to hear more thoroughly the reason why you men are here."

Michael spoke, "About a year ago our kingdom was attacked from within. A criminal impersonated a beast and tried to throw our kingdom into chaos. This went on for six months. All would have been lost if it weren't for the help of the new king of Grimdolon, Jean-Luc."

"Yes, go on," Clara said, anxious for more information.

"While battling this criminal, he gained a following and was eventually able to break free all those held in Mendolon's prison. For the last six months, under the leadership of Knight Corbeau here, we were able to track down most of the escaped prisoners. But ... there is still one on the loose that must be found."

Clara interrupted him, "This is the one you're tracking? The one you say is extremely dangerous?"

"Exactly. We want to stop him before he strikes."

Clara brushed a strand of hair out of her eyes. She placed her elbows on the table and interlocked her fingers. She leaned forward, showing she was well engaged in the conversation. "Please, tell me more. Who is he?"

Michael continued, "He was in our prison for over twenty years. Before that he worked in the castle as a court jester, but it seems like that was all a ploy to steal secrets and formulas from our kingdom. There are only a handful of the people in the castle who even remember him."

All three of the officials looked at one another. The knights could tell there was something on their minds. Michael glanced over at Corbeau. It was obvious he was as dumbfounded as Michael in regard to what was transpiring among these officials. After a few seconds of silence, Michael spoke up again, "May I ask another question?" There was no response from the officials, but Michael spoke anyway, "I want to know what that bear creature was that we fought in the summer region of Saison." The three officials continued to sit in silence, not saying anything in response. Clara stood to her feet. She seemed to be deep in thought as she rubbed her chin and paced to the side of the large tent.

Michael grew impatient with the silence. "Is there nothing you can tell us? We want to locate this enemy before he..."

"We have him," Clara interrupted. She looked directly at Michael. "We captured him four months ago."

Both knights abruptly stood to their feet. Corbeau was particularly stunned—he had been chasing this villain for a few months now. To hear that he was now captured was shocking. He couldn't believe that these forest dwellers had apprehended this fiend. He spoke out, "Where is he? Can you take us to him?"

Clara held up her hand, trying to calm him. "He is located in one of our far tents. We created a holding cell for him. Guards watch him without break."

"How did you find him?" Michael asked, still shocked by this news.

Clara sat down calmly and began to explain the whole scenario of what had been occurring in the land of Saison. "About five months ago, we noticed a strange creature in our forest, close to the border between the autumn and summer regions. It was much like the bear you fought early today, except that it was a wolf. The creature was terribly vicious, and it took ten of our men to defeat it. One of our men even lost his life."

Both knights were locked into the conversation as Clara kept talking. "Over time our men noticed more of these vicious creatures appearing in the forest. At first it was a dozen of them, but now we fear it might be more. They began migrating south and taking over the summer area of the forest. We then urgently began constructing a wall around the outside of the summer section, hoping that none of the creatures had yet escaped."

"I see," said Corbeau. "The wall wasn't to keep others out, but rather to keep these creatures in."

"Exactly." Clara continued, "We put all able-bodied men on duty to construct the wall. We also had men constantly patrolling the line between the spring and summer section, hoping the creatures didn't come close to our village."

Michael and Corbeau found all this new information very enlightening, but they still wanted to know how the court jester was involved. "So, is that how you found the jester?" Michael asked.

"No," Clara said, shaking her head. "Four months ago, he came to our village in the middle of the day and turned himself in. He claimed responsibility for the creation of these new creatures, and said he didn't want to be around when they invaded the whole forest."

"What do you mean, claimed responsibility for the creatures?" Corbeau asked.

Clara took a deep breath before continuing. "Yes, he calls them his beauties. Somehow he has infected them, turning these animals into vicious, deranged killers."

A stern look formed on Michael's face. Even though the court jester was captured, it seemed as if other mysteries now lay before them. "Can you take us to him?" Michael asked.

Clara nodded and spoke quietly, "Yes... let's go immediately."

CHAPTER 13

Clara led the knights toward a tent located at the far end of the small village. The forest grew darker as the sun was setting. Strangely enough, this tent looked smaller than the others they had seen.

"You're keeping him in there?" Corbeau asked, pointing toward the tent.

Clara nodded as she responded, "It's actually an underground bunker. The first settlers dug it when they arrived. It used to be an emergency shelter."

The three arrived at the tent. A guard was standing at the entrance. He was armed with a spear and a small shield.

Clara spoke to him, "Luc, you can take leave for a while. We need to speak with the prisoner."

"Thank you," the guard responded as he walked away.

Clara lifted up the side of the tent and looked back at the knights. "Be careful on the steps. They're not well lit. There are two lanterns that will make things brighter once we get to the bottom." Corbeau started to step forward when she stopped them in their tracks to give them one more admonition. "Don't let him intimidate you. He'll try to provoke you to anger."

Entering the tent, the knights could see where a tunnel had been hollowed out in the ground. "Follow me," Clara said. The three descended slowly down the steps toward the lantern light. Though it felt much longer, they were fifteen feet underground when they reached an open room. It was a large area that went about fifteen yards back. Michael could see wooden bars in the middle of the room, sectioning off a prison for the jester. At first glance he couldn't be seen, but looking closely one could see the outline of a figure sitting at the back of the dungeon.

"Jester!" Clara called out. The three walked close to the bars. "Please, come forward."

All three looked closely in anticipation. At first nothing happened. Clara shouted louder, "Jester... I said come forward!" Slowly, the figure at the back of the prison began to move. He climbed to his feet and slowly approached the bars. As he came close to the bars, the knights of Mendolon were surprised by what they saw. He was wearing formal court jester attire like he was attending a ball. His coat was black with a red checkered pattern around the edge and around the collar. His shirt was white but dirty. His face looked as if it had been painted, but the paint was badly chipped and looked as if it had been running. On his head sat a traditional two-tailed court jester cap which was also ragged. The look on his face was what caught the everyone off guard. He was smirking, and looked to be filled with a devilish-joy upon seeing the knights.

"Well, well, well," he said calmly. "What do we have here?" Both knights thought his voice sounded sinister.

Clara spoke, "These are knights of Mendolon. They've been looking for you."

He started laughing hysterically and hitting his hand against the bars as he laughed. "I guess you've found me," he said through his laughter. The jester was extremely uncomfortable to be near. As he looked at them, it was as if his eyes were piercing through them, trying to determine what they were thinking, and more specifically what they were afraid of.

As the jester started to quiet down, Corbeau spoke up, "We've come to take you. You're one of the last of the escaped prisoners, and under the command…"

"Oh no, no, no… I'm not going anywhere with you. Not while those ghastly creatures are on the loose," he said with a facetious smile. "Have you met them yet? I know Clara has." Michael wondered what this statement meant. Glancing out the corner of his eye he saw Clara look to the ground. Her face looked to be a mixture of sadness and anger.

Corbeau was quickly losing his temper. "Yes, we've met one of them, and we want you to know that we put an end to him earlier today."

Jester stepped away from the bars and rubbed the bottom of his chin. He was trying hard not to laugh. He looked at Corbeau with piercing eyes. "So you think you've done a good deed, have you?"

Corbeau took a step closer to the bars. His anger was now on full display. "Yes, we have, and the next thing we're going to do is feed you to those evil creatures."

Michael remained calm. He remembered Jean-Luc's admonition to try to outsmart this adversary. This jester was truly intelligent and seemed like he was toying with them. Thinking it over, Michael decided a direct approach would be best. "Jester, our escaped prisoners spoke of a power you have. Is this that power? Creating these foul creatures?"

Jester stood silently for a moment as he stared at Michael. A smile came on his face and he thought about how to best respond. He took a few steps to his right, closer to a well-lit area. The jester spoke quietly, "Can you step further into the light?" Michael looked to his right, where the light shone more directly. Seeing no harm, he stepped over into it. Jester nodded his head as he got a good look at Michael. "You look like your father... did you know that?"

Michael found this statement very curious. A part of him wanted to pursue this question more, but he kept reminding himself what Jean-Luc had said, not to let the jester provoke him. He ignored the statement and question. "Listen, Jester, what is the hidden power that you have?"

Jester stepped back into the darkness, seeing that Michael hadn't taken the bait. Without taking his eyes off Michael, he licked the side of his mouth, wiping off a part of his face paint. He spoke quietly, "I have no power at all, Michael de Bolbec. But rather I am a man of science. I use formulas and experiments to get what I want." Jester stopped to wink before continuing, "This is why Hector had me arrested years ago. He knows my power. He knows my experiments far exceed anything he can create."

"How did you create the vicious creatures in the forest?"

"Through my experiments... I created a serum that changes them into the beauties you now see. It increases their strength, intelligence, aggression, and gives them a desire to dominate their prey." Jester stopped to clear his throat before adding, "But their greatest craving is for revenge."

Michael was confused. "Revenge? For what? Against whom?"

"Yes, Michael, my new friend, revenge against those who kill their brothers and sisters... those who kill their kind." The jester began laughing again as he finished his statement. "The bad news for you is that they are now coming for you."

It was obvious to all that the jester was enjoying this conversation. He was basking in this scheme he was developing. Michael didn't care. He was thankful the jester was giving him the information he wanted. "How many of these creatures did you infect with this... disease?"

The jester's eyes lit up. "Yes, my disease. I like that."
He paused again to laugh. "Altogether, I have created
nineteen of these beauties. This forest of Saison is good for
them as they enjoy feasting on the little Noe creatures. I
would imagine that by now the northwest section is free of
them, and my beauties are starting to migrate south."

Clara spoke out angrily, "So this is your plan. You
want to destroy the Noe creatures?"

"No...no. This is simply a fortunate consequence of
their existence."

"Then what is your plan?"

Jester bit hard on his tongue before his spoke. "I want
to infect this world with my disease," he said, pointing at
Michael when he used the word disease. He continued, "I
want to improve this world, make it like my world. It will be
stronger, more chaotic, more evil."

Michael paced slightly, thinking carefully about
everything Jester was saying. He rubbed his forehead as he
thought hard about what to ask next. "Will you do this
through infecting more animals?"

"No...no...no... I will enter the serum into the race of
men and the beasts."

"What will it do to man?"

"Oh, yes... a splendid thought. It will make him strong,
but its effects will take over his mind. The prospect of evil
will be before him in greater form. It will appeal to him, and
it will consume him."

"And what if man resists?"

Jester's smile widened again. "Only the strong will survive. Evil's pull on them will be too strong."

Michael felt himself reaching for the handle of his dagger. He knew the jester couldn't attack him through these bars, but he felt threatened. He kept going forward with his questions, "Will the effects be the same for the race of beast?"

The jester shook his head. "Sorry to say, my friend. It's very disappointing. It's simply fatal when the beasts are infected."

Michael pulled a dagger as he was beginning to lose control of his emotions. "Where did you make this disease?"

Jester stood still, looking at those in front of him. He didn't say a word nor make a sound. The knights wondered what was going on. It was a few moments later that he simply waved his hand, in order to say, *Back away*. He began stepping away from the bars and back into the shadows. "That will be all for now," he said calmly.

Michael squeezed the dagger in his hand. It took every bit of his self-control to stop him from throwing it.

It was late in the evening. Michael was still up as he sat comfortably around a fire that was slowly dying. Most of the villagers had gone to bed, and everything was quiet. He could see a few guards stationed on the western edge of the village. They were on watch in case any of the jester's creatures might try to venture into the village. Michael knew those men wouldn't be enough to fight one of those creatures, but at least the villagers could be warned.

222

Michael's thoughts went to the kingdom of Grimdolon. He wondered how things were progressing. He hoped that none of his instructions were short-sighted, and that he had mentioned all he could about the armies of Mendolon. After their talk earlier today with the court jester, he wondered if there was anything else that could be done here in Saison at the moment. The vicious creatures in the forest would need to be defeated, but it would take a much larger effort than just two knights and a handful of villagers. His best plan may be to head back to Grimdolon in the morning and help with the battle. After things were in order there, Michael could easily return and help in an effort to clear the forest of the vicious creatures. He would hate to leave these villagers, but for now he figured it may be the best course of action.

Michael was deep in thought when he was startled by a low-pitch whistling sound to the right of him. He turned and at first saw nothing, but after looking closely he saw two small eyes peeking from behind a tree. Michael smiled as the small Noe creature whistled again. He watched closely as the creature stepped from behind the tree and started approaching Michael. It was still in the shadows and its body couldn't be seen very well, only its eyes. They were locked with the knight's. Michael wondered if he should approach it, remembering the legends about them bringing feelings of peace and tranquility.

The knight was focused on the little creature when a voice interrupted him. "In all your travels, have you seen them before?"

Michael turned to see Clara approaching him. She took a seat beside him on the log where he was sitting. "No, no I haven't. From everything I've heard, they only live here."

Clara nodded. "Yes, I've heard the same. I believe that's why we've had so many settlers from different kingdoms."

Michael turned back to his right, but he could see that the eyes were now gone. A feeling of disappointment engulfed him. Clara spoke up, "Oh, I see that you're taking a liking to them too... don't worry, one might come back if you wait long enough."

Michael turned back and looked toward Clara, realizing that she sensed his disappointment. He smiled slightly at Clara's comment. He decided to change the subject. "How long have you been here in Saison?"

"Close to sixteen years ago, I came with my family," Clara spoke comfortably, reminiscing on the past. "My father heard of a better life, a simpler life in this forest. It turned out to be true. Things have been pleasant and peaceful the whole time... that is until the creatures started showing up five months ago."

Michael nodded as he took in the information. "Where did your family migrate from?"

"The southern region of the empire. It was at a time when work was hard to find, and large numbers of people were moving to the capital city. My father wasn't one to just follow the crowd, so we decided to explore Saison. He heard about the few settlers that were here."

"Do your parents still live here?"

"Yes, their tent is right over there." Clara pointed to a tent on the western side of the village. "They're quiet folks, close to seventy years old now. I was the youngest of their five children—the only one who followed them here to the forest."

Michael found her story interesting. Before today, everything he had ever known about the Forest of Saison was from rumors and legends. He found it fascinating how simple the lives of the villagers were. These villagers would surely find humorous some of the stories and theories that citizens of Mendolon told about them. Their lives reminded him of the simple pleasures of a quiet life. The life he had experienced the last few months while working on the farm.

Changing the subject, he turned to Clara, "What did the jester mean earlier when he mentioned you meeting his creatures?"

Clara looked at the ground and nodded, knowing the question was coming. She waited a few moments before speaking. "About five months ago, a father and a son were hiking through the fall section of our forest. They spotted a strange creature in the forest but were able to hide from it. They came back to the village and reported that they had seen something mysterious. A team of ten men were sent out. The men were ambushed by a wolf as they crossed into the fall section. They were able to defeat him, but there were others. None would've escaped if it wasn't for the governor distracting the other creatures and leading them away from our men. He sacrificed himself to save the whole troop."

Clara stared deeply into the fire. There was much on her mind. She continued with the account. "It was about four weeks later that Jester showed up at our village and turned himself in. He admitted that he had a hideout where he was working, somewhere in the fall region. We haven't been able to locate it yet."

Michael had a number of questions, but mainly he wanted to hear more about the day the governor died. "That must have been a hard day when the company returned."

"It was." Clara wiped a tear from her eyes. "From what we know, the governor was the first person ever killed in this forest. In this place of peace and tranquility, death found us."

"I'm sorry," Michael said as he put his hand on her shoulder. "He sounds like a good man."

"His name was Roland." Clara stopped to catch her breath. "And he was my husband." Michael didn't know what to say. As she was telling the story, he had begun piecing everything together. This was a personal battle for her. The jester was responsible for the death of her husband. In light of this, Michael found it very impressive how Clara had kept her poise earlier in the day when they were talking with the jester.

Clara continued, "Roland and I met here in Saison, and we were married for ten years. I miss him every day, and I still wonder how I'm going to go on without him. I have a young daughter, and I keep telling myself to be strong for her, and strong for the village."

Michael was surprised to hear she had a daughter. Clara projected herself as such a focused leader. He was impressed by how much she was balancing in her life. "I'm sure you're doing a great job. From what I can see, the people seem to have great respect for you," Michael said quietly.

"They do. When governors are elected they're elected as a family. After my husband passed, I had to balance my mourning with my leadership as governor. It's been difficult."

"I can't imagine."

Clara wiped her eyes as she tried to gather herself. She stood to her feet and put a few large sticks on the fire that was in front of them. The fire quickly picked up before she sat back down beside Michael. "Please, I hope you didn't get the wrong idea from earlier today, but I'm really glad you're here. I'm hoping there is some way you and Corbeau can help us."

"Thanks," Michael paused a moment before continuing, "I've been thinking about it. I keep going over Jester's words from earlier. I wonder if there was something he said that we could use to defeat these creatures."

Clara nodded, "Yes, and honestly I'm a little afraid for you too. The idea that these creatures seek revenge sounds frightful."

Michael turned sharply and stared at Clara. Her last statement stood out to him. An idea came to mind. He spoke with a hint of excitement in his voice, "Yes, but maybe this can be used against them."

Clara was a little confused. "What? What can be used against them?"

Michael stood to his feet as a plan was quickly forming. He rubbed his fist in the palm of his other hand as he spoke. "Revenge... use their desire for revenge against them."

CHAPTER 14

Corbeau sat alone by candlelight in a small tent. It was still dark out, as it was another half hour before sunrise. Michael had devised a plan for battling Jester's creatures, and late last night he stayed up late thoroughly explaining it to both him and Clara. Everything would have to be executed in exact precision, and Corbeau was already prepared for his specific tasks. He was dressed in his armor with his swords cleaned and ready for use.

Currently, Corbeau had a feather pen in his hand with a sheet of paper in front of him. He had brought them with him from Mendolon along with a small jar of ink. Even though it upset him at first, his conversation with Michael the day before had motivated him to keep writing to his wife, and to keep trying to reconcile with her. For the last three months he had written to her every two weeks, hoping he could somehow win her back.

Corbeau's relationship with his wife had been strained since he became a knight. Usually when one became a knight, the pledge of fighting for the ideals of justice and honor brought out the finer characteristics of the men and women who attained the status. The knights would also keep each other accountable on their ideals, thus strengthening the company. Ironically for Corbeau, becoming a knight did the opposite for him. Being one of the youngest men ever to achieve knighthood brought arrogance and pride into his life. The more fame he gained throughout Mendolon, the more difficult he became to live with.

His wife, Renée, would say everything came to terrible culmination when Michael de Bolbec became the chief knight of Mendolon. The fame of Corbeau became an afterthought among the kingdom's citizens. For now, they had a new hero, by far the youngest chief knight ever, Michael de Bolbec, son of the legendary knight, Albert de Bolbec. Corbeau became angry and extremely jealous of Michael. He felt cheated by King Sebastian and all the other knights for passing over him in this decision. Corbeau didn't know how to deal with the emotions inside of him that welled up, and he began to medicate himself and ease his problems through the companionship of a mistress. He knew it was wrong, and not long into this new relationship, his wife found out and left him. The mistress was now just a memory, and he was left missing his wife.

The words came easily for Corbeau as he wrote the letter. He pictured his wife reading it. With this new turmoil in Mendolon, he wondered how he would get this letter to Renée or when he would see her again. Hope kept him going. Hope that somehow and in some way, he could get this letter to her. And hope that somehow, he would be able to reconcile their marriage.

Etalon was on horseback, watching the northern section of Dragon Waste through a monocular. It was a foggy morning and he couldn't see very well. Belle was beside him on her horse. Many of the knights of Mendolon, along with a few hundred warrior beasts, were behind them. They were waiting for the soldiers of Mendolon. Two hours ago, a lone scout had reported to Etalon that he had spotted about eight hundred soldiers coming their way. Even though Grimdolon's forces were smaller in number, they knew their abilities were superior and their chances of victory were at least plausible. Overall, their main hope was that there would be no loss of life. Belle especially hoped that through reason and diplomacy they could get the soldiers to turn back and help the knights call for a vote of no confidence against King Sebastian. But even if they did have to fight, they were looking for ways to preserve the lives of their enemies as much as possible.

"Etalon, do you see anyone coming?" Belle asked.

"No, not yet, my queen, but it shouldn't be too much longer."

Belle looked behind her to see the Mendolon's knights and Grimdolon's warriors standing in formation, ready for the battle. Everyone was quiet as they awaited instruction from their leaders. She saw Bernard standing near the front. Out of all the group, he was the only one who looked nervous. He was very skilled in swordsmanship but lacked confidence at times. Looking right at him, Belle gave a small wave to her friend. He smiled nervously as he waved back.

"Your highness," Etalon spoke out.

"Yes."

"Mendolon's soldiers are starting to come into view."

Etalon held out the monocular for her to see. She took it and looked far into the distance. She could see hundreds of soldiers emerge from the fog. It felt strange seeing them approach her and thinking that she might have to do battle with them. More than ever, she hoped that a peaceful solution could be reached.

"Do you see any threat of arrows?" Etalon asked.

"No, but have the warriors raise their shields, just in case."

"Shields up!" Etalon called out to the warriors behind them. They promptly responded by raising their shields.

As the soldiers kept approaching, they could see them more clearly. Something Belle found fascinating was the look of anxiety on the face of the soldier in front. She recognized him but didn't know his name. She wondered why Sebastian would have him lead this charge. This soldier didn't look composed at all. She wondered if this could be used to their advantage in negotiations.

The soldiers came within a hundred yards of Belle. The knights and the beast warriors could now easily see the army approach them. The warriors stood in battle stance and gripped their swords and shields tightly. They were prepared just in case the soldiers charged forward.

As soon as he was sure the soldiers could hear him, Etalon called out to them, "Soldiers of Mendolon! I would ask you to stop!" The lead soldier held out his hand to stop his men. They were fifty yards away at this point.

The lead soldier turned and spoke to those in the front of the army. He then turned and began walking by himself toward the forces of Grimdolon. "It looks like he wants to meet," Belle said to Etalon.

"It appears so," Etalon responded. The two of them dismounted their horses and approached the soldier.

As they met in the middle of the open area, Belle could see that the soldier was visibly shaking and extremely nervous. He looked to be in his mid-twenties and in no way should he have been the one leading this army. "Greetings," Belle said as tenderly as she could.

"Your highness," the soldier said with trembling in his voice.

Etalon spoke harshly, "What is the meaning of this invasion?"

"Yes, we've come…" the soldier paused for a moment to draw upon his memory the speech he was supposed to say. "We've come on behalf of his imperial majesty, King Sebastian, ruler of the triumphant and prosperous land of Mendolon, to ask for the surrender of your territory and your mines. All those who refuse will be subject..."

Etalon abruptly interrupted, "We will do no such thing! Sebastian has no right to invade our sovereign kingdom. We've made no threat against him. He's fortunate we haven't come against him with our forces."

Belle put her hand on Etalon's arm, trying to keep him calm. She spoke sincerely to the soldier, "Please, will you reconsider? Etalon, here, is correct. Sebastian has no right to invade our land. We would desperately plead with you not to do this."

The soldier was silent. He didn't know what to say. He looked back at the soldiers of Mendolon. It was obvious that he wasn't supposed to negotiate, but rather to try to force Grimdolon into surrendering. Belle could tell his anxiety was spilling over, as he was breathing heavily and seemed to be on the verge of hyperventilating. Belle looked right into the nervous soldier's eyes as she continued, "Listen to me, you don't have to do this. Join us, and the knights can lead a vote of no confidence against the king. The citizens of Mendolon would easily support this effort."

The solider did not respond but rubbed the back of his head as he thought about what to do next. Belle looked behind her at the knights and warriors. They were focused and hadn't broken formation or their concentration. Across the field, the Mendolon soldiers stood steady and their weapons were held at their sides. They looked to be waiting anxiously for word to return from their leader as to what to do next.

Etalon began growing impatient. "Well, what will it be? Will you, indeed, lead us into a war?" He was close to shouting at this point.

The soldier shook his head. He seemed on the verge of tears as he spoke, "Sebastian's threatening us. He says he has the power of the Great Dragon."

"We've heard," Belle said.

"King Sebastian says that whoever won't fight will be eaten or burned alive by a dragon."

"How do you know he has this power?"

"He admitted that he led the small dragon into Dragon Waste years ago. He even showed us the books written about it. You, Princess, out of all people, should know that he manipulated or controlled this dragon."

Belle and Etalon looked at one another. Etalon held out his hand as if to say to Belle, *Go ahead and keep trying to persuade him.* She turned toward the soldier as she continued, "If Sebastian truly has this power, then we will help fight against any dragon. We all know that over a year ago a group of us knights took on that dragon and defeated him. And this time, not just the knights, but Grimdolon's warriors will help you against any dragon that threatens you or the citizens of Mendolon."

The soldier nodded his head as he thought about what Belle had said. He was truly under-qualified to handle any situation like this. He stuttered as he spoke quietly, "Let me... let me, please, speak with some of the others."

"Thank you... very gracious of you," Belle responded kindly.

Belle and Etalon watched as he retreated to his men. They watched him join the other soldiers of Mendolon before they began walking back to their respective side. Etalon was the first to speak in his deep billowing voice, "Do you think they will take our offer?"

Belle shrugged her shoulders, and brushed a strand of her brown hair out of her eyes. "We can only hope."

Jean-Luc and Gideon waited at the ports on the southeast side of Grimdolon. They were standing behind a stone wall along with a handful of Grimdolon warriors. Sebastian's strategy for conquering usually included spreading out the troops in two different areas of the land. This way an opposing army would be stretched thin, having to divide its forces between two different areas.

Grimdolon's coastline was very dangerous because of the many large rocks that lined the coast. Many boats had crashed there over the years. This southeast corner of the kingdom provided the only safe place where boats could come to land. Jean-Luc knew that if Sebastian was coming at them with any type of boats, this would have to be the area where they landed.

Gideon gently stroked his mustache as he waited for the ships to arrive. He looked over at Jean-Luc who was slicing the peel of a Grimdolon apple as he waited patiently. Jean-Luc cut a slice and held it out. "Would you like a slice, my friend?"

"Thanks," Gideon said quietly, grabbing it from Jean-Luc's hand. He had once tasted a Grimdolon apple many years ago. As he took a bite, his memories of its delicate taste came flooding back. It was by far the best apple he ever had. "It's very good," he said to Jean-Luc.

"I presume you've had one before?"

"Yes," Gideon said as he took another bite. After swallowing, he continued, "Before Dragon Waste was established, there were residents that would find them in the forest close to your border. These residents would often charge a high price for the apples, but as a knight occasionally I would get them as gifts when I had to travel in our kingdom."

"Have you ever tasted anything quite like it?"

"Well... nothing quite as good as this, but there are some kingdoms in the north that have their own unique fruits. They are delicious in their own way."

Jean-Luc simply nodded in return. Gideon was thankful for this casual banter. It tended to keep him focused.

It was just a few minutes later that the men began to see three ships side by side coming toward the shore. They were standard war boats with large sails. Each probably carried around a hundred men. Jean-Luc turned to a beast behind him. "Blow the horn," he said to one of the warrior beasts. Instantly, one of the beasts started blowing a trumpet. He hoped that it would be a signal to those on the ships that they were about to be fired upon and needed to retreat immediately.

After the horn was blown loudly, Jean-Luc and Gideon watched to see what the boats would do. They waited for another minute and the boats did not alter their course. "Blow it again," Jean-Luc commanded. Once again, the warrior beast blew the horn as loud as he could, but still they could see no change in the course of the boats.

Gideon was the first to speak. "I think we have no choice."

"Sadly, I think you're right. Command the beasts as you see fit."

"Yes, your majesty," Gideon said to Jean-Luc. He then shouted to the orders to the beasts behind him. "Arrows up!" Around sixty beasts lifted their arrows. "Bring out the torches!" Five torches were brought out, and quickly the ends of the arrows were lit.

Gideon continued to watch the ships as they progressed toward the shore. The plan was for the arrows to light the ships on fire and thus force the soldiers to jump overboard and consequentially swim to shore. By the time they would arrive, they would be tired, wet, and cornered. Hopefully they would see they were outmatched by the warriors of Grimdolon and surrender.

The ships were now within seventy-five yards. Gideon took one last look at the warriors who stood with bow strings pulled and arrowheads on fire. He took a deep breath. He knew there was no turning back, "Fire!" The warriors of Grimdolon let their arrows fly through the air and stick into the wooden boats. Very few missed. The fire of the arrows transferred to the boats and the sides of the vessels quickly lit up in flames.

Jean-Luc watched through a monocular to see what would transpire. The boats continued moving forward. He looked from boat to boat, and could tell something was wrong. He expected to see soldiers abandoning ship, but instead he saw... no one. "Something's not right," he said to Gideon.

"What's wrong?"

"The men aren't jumping ship."

Gideon was puzzled. "Do you think we should fire another round of arrows?"

Jean-Luc didn't respond but rather continued to examine each of the boats. Focusing on the one that was a little closer than the others, he inspected the deck. He saw something odd. He could barely see it in between the smoke of the fire, but he knew what he saw. It was a man tied to the mast of the boat. Instantly, the thought came to mind— Sebastian knew Grimdolon traditionally shot arrows of fire against intruding boats. He must have had these boats filled with soldiers who were against him and his plans. Soldiers he wanted dead.

Jean-Luc cried out to the others, "There are prisoners on these boats! Quick, grab the ropes! We must save them!"

The warriors didn't question Jean-Luc. They quickly grabbed their collection of large ropes with grappling hooks on the end. These ropes were brought in case they needed to climb aboard the boats, like they needed to now. Those carrying the ropes hopped in rowboats situated along the shore. Others simply dropped their weapons and swam toward the boats. Jean-Luc and Gideon were in separate rowboats. Those paddling the small boats were moving as fast as they could. They could feel the heat of the fires as they continued to spread.

"Head to the back of the ships!" Gideon called out as they were getting close. The fire hadn't yet spread to the stern of the ship. The beasts moved efficiently as the rowboats got into position and the grappling hooks were thrown. Two ropes went up for each of the ships. The ropes held tight and Jean-Luc was the first to climb up the ship closest to him. He didn't even think about the twenty-five feet needed to climb to the top. Hand over hand, without fear, he pulled himself up the rope as quickly as he could.

Reaching the top of the boat, he climbed over the railing and landed on the deck. He saw dozens of soldiers sprawled on the deck of the ship, their hands and feet tied. Along the bow, the fires were within three feet of the men. Seeing Jean-Luc, many of the men screamed for help. By this time, other beasts were starting to reach the deck. Jean-Luc pulled a knife and called out orders. "Start at the front of the ship! Cut their ropes and tell them to abandon ship! Hurry!"

The scene was chaotic as the fires kept spreading and the soldiers called out for help. The warrior beasts cut the soldiers' bonds as quickly as they could. Some of the soldiers stayed and helped their fellow soldiers while others simply jumped overboard. A few of the men at the front of the ship were on fire, and for those men the beasts just cut their hand bonds before throwing them overboard. Jean-Luc glanced across to the other ships and could see those soldiers being rescued in the same manner.

A dozen of the warrior beasts, along with Jean-Luc, moved to the lower levels of the ship. It was much hotter and they could see around thirty men, some of whom were unconscious. The smoke was heavier on this lower level and Jean-Luc started to cough. The beasts quickly got to work cutting the men's bonds. The warrior beasts quickly picked up those who were unconscious and carried them out. The warriors seemed to be working even faster with the added threat of the smoke.

There were only a few men still in their bonds when Jean-Luc heard a terrible creaking sound. He paused for just a moment as he realized the boat was beginning to fall apart. He knew they didn't have much time. "Quick! Grab the soldiers, we must get out of here, now!" The beast warriors easily picked up the men and flung them over their shoulders before heading to the upper deck.

Jean-Luc heard a cry on the far end of the ship. "Help... don't leave me!" Jean-Luc couldn't see the man, but he ran toward the voice in the smoke.

"Where are you?" Jean-Luc called out as he ducked low, trying to avoid the smoke.

"Here... over here!" the soldier shouted. Jean-Luc ran toward the sound of the voice and found the man. "Thank God," the man said, exhausted.

Jean-Luc wasn't as strong as the warriors and wouldn't be able to fully carry him out. Using his knife, he cut the soldier's bonds. "Let's move quickly," Jean-Luc said.

They were both about to move when they heard a terrible sound. The creaking grew louder. The boat was crumbling. It would only be a matter of seconds before the boat would sink into the water. They would not make it. "No... No!" the soldier cried out in terror, sensing that this was the end.

Jean-Luc remained calm as he tried to quickly think of something. It was just a second later that he saw a large piece of this boat's wall fall from the side, revealing the light from the outside. Smoke instantly went out the boat's hole. He knew what he had to do. "Follow me!" he said to the soldier. Jean-Luc stood tall, his head covered in the smoke. He ran as quickly as he could toward the opening. The soldier was behind him. As he reached the wall, Jean-Luc flung his body into it, breaking through to the outside. His plan had worked. The outer wall of the boat had grown fragile from being burned. It easily broke with Jean-Luc's force ramming against it. The soldier jumped after him and both men went crashing down into the sea.

As Jean-Luc and the soldier came up from the water, they could see the boat crumble into the water. "Quick, swim!" Jean-Luc yelled. Both swam away as fast as they could. Small pieces of the boat floated around them. Thankfully they were able to escape without being seriously injured. Jean-Luc could see a few hundred soldiers, along with the beasts, swimming up to the shore. From what he could see, it looked like their rescue mission had been successful.

Gideon approached Jean-Luc as he made it to the shore. The young king was tired, wet, and had lost his glasses when he jumped into the sea. Gideon spoke, "Sire, these soldiers are confirming our suspicions. They were not in favor of Sebastian's invasion, so he had them captured and bound on these ships. There was a small crew steering these vessels, but they abandoned the vessels right before we fired on them."

Jean-Luc reached up and felt the side of his neck. He had a large cut from breaking through the ship's wall. He took a deep breath in frustration before speaking, "Of course." He brushed his fingers through his mane, trying to dry it. "Sebastian anticipated our attack. He thought it would be an easy way to get rid of his opposition. I should've seen it coming."

"And listen to this," Gideon added. "The soldiers who are approaching the northwest doubt the king's plans as well. They are only marching to battle because they feel threatened by Sebastian's power. He knows they are no match for the beasts and the knights in the northwest."

The castle servant, Jonas, approached Jean-Luc with a new pair of glasses. "Thank you," Jean-Luc said as he slipped them on. He then turned to Gideon. "Well then... I would say we need to make for the northwest. There's not a moment to lose."

CHAPTER 15

Michael and Corbeau stood on the outskirts of the forest village. Clara was with them along with ten men from the village. Michael's horse was close by, and he was tightening the saddle. He had been giving instructions about their exact plan of attack against the jester's creatures. The mission was dangerous, but he knew it was their only hope for eradicating these animals that posed such a threat. Everything was in place, and Michael was ready to mount his horse.

"Are you sure about this?" Clara asked.

"No, but all we can do is try." Michael didn't stop working. "This is the best plan available. We can't have these creatures multiplying and destroying the forest, and they won't stop here."

Clara sighed as she looked back at her people gathered to watch the men leave. Many of the villagers looked to be at peace, not knowing the true threat against them. If this plan didn't work, they would have to leave the forest and their homes. A part of her wished she could go with these men to help with this plan, but as the leader of the village, she knew that she needed to stay. The people needed her.

At that moment a young girl ran toward Clara. "Momma," she cried, embracing her with a tight hug. It was still early in the morning and her daughter had just awakened for the day. She looked to be about five years old. She favored her mother strongly.

"Good morning, my love," Clara said. Michael stopped what he was doing as he observed this beautiful scene. The love between this mother and daughter was evident. He couldn't imagine what it had been like when they heard that this girl's father had been taken from them. To have such a lovely family, Michael knew he must have been a great man. He hated that these creatures had taken him from them. As he mounted his horse, he felt an even greater resolve to put an end to these vicious creatures.

Michael addressed the others, "Men, plan to move out immediately. Knight Corbeau will give instructions should anything not go as planned." Corbeau nodded in agreement. The chief knight turned to his horse, ready to begin the mission. Out of habit, he checked his daggers one last time, knowing he was going to battle. He addressed the men once more, "I shouldn't be long... be ready!"

"Michael," Clara spoke up, stopping him. She was still holding tight to her daughter.

"Yes?"

Clara looked right at him and spoke sincerely, "Please... do be careful."

Michael smiled just a little as he looked back at the governess. He was glad he was able to get to know her a little the day before. She was truly a person to be admired. "I will. Goodbye."

✎❧

Michael de Bolbec journeyed through the summer section of Saison. Even though it was early in the day, it was still hot in this area. It had been an hour since he left the forest village. Currently, everything was quiet in this section of the forest. He hadn't seen any of the eyes of the Noe either. It was obvious to him what was occurring. Many of the Noe and the ordinary animals of this section had migrated because of the jester's creatures. Eventually this area would be completely cleared and they would move into the spring quadrant.

The fallen tree from the day before came into sight. The vicious bear was still underneath. Michael could see that his eyes were sunken in, and strangely enough the creature looked even more unnerving as a corpse. Michael checked his bearings before climbing off his horse. Everything was silent. He grabbed the black helmet off his horse and placed it on his head. He felt fear rising inside him. It would have to be suppressed. A lot was depending on the next few minutes going according to plan. He pulled two daggers from his belt as he knew the creatures would be coming soon.

The chief knight climbed on top of the tree over the bear's neck. He looked around one last time before shouting as loud as he could. "I killed this creature!" He waited, but there was no response. He continued, "This is my doing! My work! I killed him! Do you hear me? It's me you want!"

There was a small rustling about forty yards away. Michael turned and saw a small creature rising up. It was a fox. Its fur was dark brown and on its face was the same evil expression as the bear he fought the day before. Michael threw a dagger toward him. The fox easily moved to the side, missing the flying object. Michael shouted again, "Come and get me, you fiend!"

He was surprised as another creature started rising up from his right. He could tell it was some type of boar, but Michael didn't stop to stare at it as it was much closer than the fox. He simply ran and jumped on his horse. "Let's go," he said, giving his horse a strong kick. It was as if the horse felt the danger of the creatures as it immediately started running without caution. They were moving toward the south.

As they rode along, Michael saw from the corner of his eyes two more creatures rise up, a deer and another bear. He knew they were all coming for him. The jester was telling the truth. The spirit of revenge was in them, and they ran to attack this man who had killed their fellow bear. Michael knew they wouldn't stop until he was dead.

The horse was running at full speed, dodging trees and bushes along the way. Michael looked up ahead and saw a wolf in the woods to the right of the path. It was another of the jester's creatures. As the chief knight passed the wolf, it joined the pack chasing him. Other creatures had also joined. Michael could hear their growls and snarls behind him. He wondered how many there were, but he dared not look back. He kept his eyes forward, hoping he would reach the edge of the forest soon.

Corbeau was high in a tree close to the border wall. This was all according to plan; he was the lookout man for this mission. He could hear the sound of the creatures moving closer. The village men were outside the wall. He called out to the men, "Open the wall. They're coming." He watched closely for the chief knight. Corbeau hoped Michael de Bolbec would be the first thing he saw.

From the outside of the village, men pulled on twelve of the logs in the wall. They had cut the ropes that bound them. After struggling for just a moment, the logs began to fall. The men ran out of the way as the logs came crashing down with a loud thump. According to the plan, the men then scattered and then found places to hide far from this opening.

Corbeau saw Michael come into view on horseback. One of the jester's wolves was only a few feet behind him. Corbeau quickly reached behind him for the bow he brought with him. He pulled an arrow back and let it fly. The arrow hit the wolf's neck. The wolf cried out as he slowed down. Michael was then able to gain close to twenty feet on this creature. Corbeau watched as about a dozen other creatures overtook the wolf and kept chasing the chief knight of Mendolon. He pulled another arrow and let it fly, hoping to distract the next creature in front.

Michael's horse kept moving at full speed toward the opening in the wall. So far, the plan was working; the wall was open in this spot and the creatures were following him. Corbeau kept shooting arrows. They were slowing the vicious animals down just enough for Michael to gain some distance on them before they reached the outside. Michael would have to stay focused. There would be no margin for error once he made it outside the forest.

As the horse passed through the opening in the wall, it jumped over a few of the logs that lay on the ground. Michael was twenty yards past the opening when the creatures attempted to pass through. They became log jammed as six of them tried to pass through all at once. Michael turned and looked through the eyes of his dark helmet into the eyes of the creatures. The creatures growled in a murderous rage as they looked back at the knight. Their evil red eyes were fixed directly on him. Michael could clearly see their sharp teeth and saliva dripping from their mouths. He knew they would show no mercy if they caught him.

Michael grabbed a dagger from his belt and threw it toward the one of the wolves. It stuck at the bottom of its left ear. The wolf let out a terrible cry of pain. It drew back from the opening with its head toward the ground. The other creatures seemed to take notice, and this made them even more angry. Michael smiled to himself as things were falling into place. He was their target, no doubt about it. He turned his horse, and galloped away from the forest.

Belle and Etalon waited anxiously for a reply from the soldiers of Mendolon. A few hours had passed since they'd spoken with the top official. It was now just passed the noon hour, and the warriors of Grimdolon were growing restless. The morning fog had cleared and there wasn't a cloud in the sky. The sun was shining brightly. From where they stood, Belle and Etalon could see the top officials of the army deliberating, and sometimes their discussions looked quite intense.

"What's taking them so long?" Etalon said with clear frustration in his voice. Belle didn't respond to the beast, but rather watched through a monocular at the soldiers discussing their plans. Etalon continued, "These soldiers should know their best options are retreat or surrender. This is only going to lead to unnecessary bloodshed. Especially with how nervous they are, they can't possibly think they can defeat us."

Belle spoke, not taking her sight off the men. "I'm hoping this long delay is good news for us. Surely at the very least they must be considering a truce of some sort."

"Well, I hope they come to a conclusion soon."

Belle continued to watch the soldiers discuss their plans. Her mind occasionally went to Jean-Luc and Gideon in the southeast. The boats would've arrived by now on the shores of Grimdolon. She wondered how many men were on board the ships, and if a battle had broken out on the shore. She could only hope that everything was going well and her fiancée was safe.

Things began to change as the lead soldier approached the open area between the armies. "Etalon, they've reached a solution." Etalon and Belle went forward on horseback to meet the young soldier coming toward him. They could see he was shaking and sweating as he rode his horse forward. Belle felt sorry for this soldier. He was obviously a young recruit and shouldn't have been placed in this situation.

As they met, Etalon was the first to speak. "Well, have you come to a conclusion?"

The soldier swallowed hard as he nodded his head. He looked on the verge of tears. "Y... yes, we... we have," he was stuttering. "We regret to inform you that.... that we have no... no other choice. We must go to war."

Belle's face dropped. "No, please," she pleaded.

"Are you crazy?" Etalon shouted. "Sebastian is going to lead you to your doom!"

"I'm... I'm sorry. There's nothing we can do. He will feed us and our families to the dragons."

Etalon pulled his hair in frustration. "This is madness."

"I'm sorry... I'm so sorry," the soldier said once more before turning his horse and going back to his people.

"War it is then," Etalon said as he pulled his sword.

251

Belle and Etalon rode back quickly to the knights and warriors. Arriving back, they dismounted their horses. Bernard spoke up, "What did they say?"

"Fools," was all Etalon could say.

"Sebastian has them completely terrified," Belle said, "They're choosing to fight."

"What? God, help us all," Bernard cried out.

Etalon, knowing what he now must do, addressed their army as loud as he could. "Warriors of Grimdolon, we're moving to battle. Shields up. Swords ready."

The Grimdolon army, along with the knights, moved forward as the army of Mendolon began to move toward them. Everyone was quiet, ready to charge. Belle felt a bead of sweat slide down her forehead as the armies got closer. She could only hope that as they got closer the soldiers of Mendolon would see their forces and reconsider. A thought of guilt came to mind. Maybe somehow this was her fault. If she was still in Mendolon, maybe she could've talked Sebastian out of all this. Or maybe she could've helped Michael raise a vote of no confidence against the king. Somehow, some way, maybe she could have prevented this.

Swords were raised as the armies were within twenty yards of each other. Everything was quiet as the armies were at the point of no return. Belle wondered what the first move would be. Things had progressed too quickly. Just a few minutes ago there was hope that somehow all this could've been prevented, but now they were on the verge of war. Many would be injured. Many would lose their lives.

Still trembling, the young leader of Mendolon raised his arm to signal to the soldiers to move forward. The Grimdolon forces waited quietly as they didn't want to be the ones to make the first move. Mendolon was the aggressor, and Grimdolon would not fight until they absolutely had to. The young leader tried to speak, but no words would come out of his mouth. In that moment it was as if he felt the weight of what he was about to do. He was going to be the one to start this battle. The one to initiate all the bloodshed.

The young soldier mustered up all the courage he could find and was just about to bring his arm down to charge when he heard someone shouting to the north. He turned his head and there he saw the chief knight of Mendolon, Michael de Bolbec. He was dressed in his battle armor and was riding straight toward the armies. He could clearly be seen and even though he was wearing his helmet, he was recognized by most.

"It's Michael," Belle announced with great joy in her voice.

As the knight got closer, they could tell what he was shouting. "Take up arms. An enemy is coming!" Both groups were stunned as they wondered what was transpiring. Michael rode directly between the two groups as he kept yelling, "Turn to the north! An enemy is coming, riding over the hills!"

Michael pointed to the north and both armies could see the horde of vicious animals coming over the hilltop toward their armies. There were over a dozen of the creatures. In their evil rage, they had followed Michael all the way from the Forest of Saison, and now they were running toward the two armies. Etalon knew of these creatures because he had battled one before. He shouted to both armies, "Warriors and soldiers, we must fight this evil. Quick!" He turned his horse as he led the warriors toward the creatures. The soldiers of Mendolon followed behind.

The creatures met the armies in an epic clash. Man fought alongside beast as all attention was now focused on these creatures from Saison. Arrows were initially fired at the animals, but the beasts and soldiers found that the arrows did minimal damage to the creatures' thick outer skin. Swords, battle axes, spears, and maces proved to be more effective as the fight transpired.

Etalon ran toward one of the wolves since he had fought one before. The creature attempted to bite him, but he was quick with his sword to block any bite against him. With the creature engaged and distracted by Etalon, the soldiers and warriors attacked the body of the wolf. The animal would then turn to face those behind him, but that would leave Etalon free to attack him. The wolf was simply outnumbered, and the soldiers and warriors were eventually able to penetrate the thick skin of the wolf and put him to death.

The fox was moving rapidly among the soldiers, biting whoever he could. Currently he was latched onto the shoulder of a man who screamed wildly in agony. The man fell to the ground and tried frantically to pull the fox off. "Help me! Help me!" he yelled.

Bernard was close by. He lifted his sword and brought it down swiftly against the tail of the fox. The sword sliced through the tail and severed the last fourth of it. The fox let go and turned toward Bernard. The murderous look on the creature's face was easily seen. His evil red eyes focused directly on Bernard as he growled.

"Oh no," Bernard said under his breath. He gripped his sword tightly as he tried to think of how to best beat this fox. Without warning, the creature leaped toward the knight. He was expecting Bernard to run like the others, but Bernard did no such thing. Almost without thinking, Bernard lunged forward with his sword and thrust it into the mouth of the creature. The blade of the sword went through the roof of the creature's mouth and the top of his head. With the fox stuck on the end of his sword, Bernard released it as the fox fell to the ground. A group of men and beasts then attacked the body of the fox. It wasn't long before this vicious creature was dead.

The battle against these creatures continued to rage as knights, soldiers, and warriors fought them. Michael and Belle were fighting a bear that was in their midst. The animal had already gravely injured one of the warrior beasts and two of the soldiers. He was the strongest creature in the group and they knew he shouldn't be dealt with lightly. Currently Michael was trying to keep the creature's attention focused on him. With each swipe from the bear's claw, he jumped back a little further. He would have to think of something drastic to destroy this evil fiend. The bear swiped again, and Michael blocked it with his dagger, but the force of the bear's paw knocked Michael backwards in the process.

Belle shot an arrow at the bear, distracting it briefly. The chief knight had an idea. "Belle, get ready."

Michael continued to watch the bear closely as he called out to a group of knights, "Attack him from behind!" Five knights and three soldiers ran toward the creature and stabbed him in his back with their swords and spears. The majority of them left their weapons in his back. The bear looked toward the sky and growled angrily. He then turned to face his enemies behind him. Seeing the animal's face, the knights and soldiers jumped back in fear.

Michael knew this was his chance. He quickly climbed on the bear's back, using the weapons as a ladder. The bear turned back around frantically as he felt someone on his back. Before the creature could react, Michael pulled one of his daggers and jammed it into one of the bear's eyes. The creature growled terribly from his pain. He reached up with a paw and grabbed Michael, throwing him to the side. The dagger was still in his hand, and the eye was on its end. The bear's empty socket was bleeding and a terrible smell was coming from the dark blood that flowed.

Landing on the ground, Michael looked over at Belle who was holding an arrow. "Aim toward the eye!" he called out.

Belle watched as the bear's face looked toward the ground. She pulled back an arrow and watched closely. The bear slowly looked up. He was angry, looking for revenge. Belle knew this was her moment. She let the arrow fly. It flew through the air and struck perfectly into the hole Michael made with his dagger. The arrow penetrated through his head and into the brain of the creature.

The bear growled one last time before crashing to the ground. He was still moving but was slowing down. The warriors, soldiers, and knights then moved in and were able to completely defeat the bear. The main threat of the creatures was now vanquished. Michael looked around the battlefield and could see the other creatures had also been killed. He took off his helmet and laid down on the ground. Between the long ride and the fight, he was tired. The threat of the jester's creatures was no more. Michael felt he could now rest peacefully.

CHAPTER 16

Michael was seated comfortably on the ground of the battlefield. His armor was off and lying beside him. He casually drank from a water skin as he attempted to gain back his strength. The jester's creatures had been defeated. The Grimdolon warriors, Mendolon soldiers, and the knights were now helping one another take care of those who were injured. It was unfortunate to see that these creatures had taken the lives of a dozen soldiers and two Grimdolon warriors.

The battle had been short but intense. Michael's actions had gone according to plan. The creatures were provoked by their anger and their hunger for revenge, and they followed him for miles to Grimdolon. The journey from Saison had been strenuous because the jester's creatures were fast. Michael had to occasionally turn and throw a dagger toward the one that was in the front of the pack. He found this beneficial also since it kept the creatures angry and focused on him. He wanted to be sure they were led all the way to Grimdolon without distraction.

Michael continued to watch as the bodies of those killed were respectfully covered and carried away. He was thankful he had arrived at this battle when he had. Even though there was loss of life, it was greatly less than anything that would have occurred if these forces of Mendolon and Grimdolon collided. At the moment it was also amazing to see the harmony between the two kingdoms.

Belle walked over to where Michael was seated. "You okay?"

Michael looked off to the distance. "Yeah, I'm glad it's over."

Belle sat down beside him, "Yes, me too." She took a deep breath before continuing, "But in honesty, Michael, I'd face those vicious animals all over again as opposed to going to war against Mendolon."

"So they wouldn't take your proposal of a truce?"

"No," Belle said, shaking her head. "I'm glad you showed up when you did."

A tired grin formed on Michael's face as he looked at Belle. "It feels like old times again, me and you fighting together."

"It does, but I don't think we've ever battled anything quite like those creatures."

"I think you're right, and let's hope we never have to again."

Those on the battlefield began to stir as Jean-Luc and Gideon rode onto the scene. A handful of Grimdolon warriors were on horseback behind them. The warriors and knights were anxious for word of what had happened in the southeast. Belle rose to her feet as Jean-Luc and Gideon rode within fifty feet of where they were seated. They quickly dismounted. Belle ran to her fiancé and embraced him before asking, "What happened in the southeast?"

There was a clear look of disappointment on Jean-Luc's face. "It was a ploy of deception by the devious king. Ships arrived at our ports with soldiers bound and stranded on them."

"What?" Belle was curious. "This doesn't make sense. Why were they bound?"

Jean-Luc adjusted his glasses. "Apparently, they were the soldiers who weren't approving of Sebastian's actions. He had them confined on three wooden ships knowing we would fire on them with burning arrows."

"Oh no!" Belle put her hands over her mouth. "Do you know how many men went down with the ships?"

"Well... it's hard to determine exactly, but I do believe most, if not all, of the men were saved."

"What? How?"

Jean-Luc continued, "After observing the captured soldiers on board, we knew this was a trick from Sebastian.

Our warriors acted quickly and climbed aboard the burning ships, cutting the bonds of all the men they could."

"Where are they now?"

"They're being questioned by some of our warriors. We're trying to figure out what is Sebastian's next plan of attack."

Belle was pleasantly surprised by all she heard. She was sad to hear that the soldiers were used as pawns, but she was greatly pleased that the loss of life was a lot less than it could have been. This attack against Grimdolon by Sebastian had greatly turned in their favor.

Jean-Luc scanned the battlefield that lay before them. He saw the body of the dead bear close by. He instantly recognized it as the same type of creature that tried to attack his warriors a few days ago. He took note of the other animal bodies that were spread abroad across the battlefield. There were numerous swords and arrows left in the body of each creature. "Looks like you've had an interesting morning yourself, my love," he said, addressing Belle.

"Yes, Michael led these animals from Saison. There were fourteen in all. They were difficult to kill, but our numbers were too great for them."

Jean-Luc rubbed the bottom of his chin as he took in all this information. "Well... I guess we've found the solution to bringing man and beast together."

"Ironically, I think we have. Etalon led both armies to battle the creatures as they followed Michael into our midst."

Jean-Luc peeked around Belle and saw Michael sitting comfortably on the ground, gathering himself. He was drinking casually from a water skin and eating a small serving of bread. "Maybe I should have a word with the old boy," Jean-Luc said as he stepped from Belle to approach Michael.

Walking past the bear, Jean-Luc couldn't help but notice the expression on the creature's face. Its teeth were sharp and looked as if they could kill with one bite. One of the bear's eyes was gone and an arrow was in its place. In the other eye shown a faint red glow that was fading. Jean-Luc stepped close to the creature and noticed the scales on its neck, similar to the creature he had observed in the castle study. He touched them and found the texture similar as well. He raised his eyebrows as he turned from the bear and continued toward Michael.

Michael saw Jean-Luc approaching and quickly took notice. "Nice of you to show up," he said, joking.

Jean-Luc smiled. "Well, I would've greeted you properly if I knew you were coming back so soon and bringing friends."

"How did it go by the ports?"

"It was quite eventful," Jean-Luc replied. He then explained in great detail the account of firing on the ships and then having to rescue the men onboard. Michael just shook his head through most of the account. He knew Sebastian was diabolical, but he never figured that he would stoop this low. But overall, like the others, Michael was thankful that there were more soldiers rebelling against the king's wishes than they expected.

Michael took another sip of his water and then stood to his feet. The warriors and soldiers continued to minister to those injured on the battlefield. "Did Belle tell you what happened here?"

"She did. Very clever of you, Michael. How did you know the creatures would follow you?"

"The jester. We found him in the forest of Saison. He told us how the creatures would react."

Jean-Luc eyes grew wide. "Where was he?"

"Captured. Those who dwell in the forest had him imprisoned in the spring region."

"Interesting... and I deduce that he created these monsters that our armies defeated."

"That's correct. He created a powerful serum and injected it into these animals. He was hoping they would take over the forest before spreading to other regions."

Jean-Luc was puzzled by some of the information Michael was giving him. A curious look formed on his face. He rubbed his mane as he thought through everything. He had more questions. "Do you know how many more of these creatures there are?"

Michael nodded his head. "I think we killed them all. The jester said he created nineteen of them."

Jean-Luc didn't say a word. He rather turned and observed the battlefield around him. He stepped to the side and counted the dead bodies of the animals. More questions arose. He turned again to face Michael. "I counted fourteen, the same figure Belle told me. Of course, there was also the severed head our warriors brought in, so that would leave four of these creatures still alive."

"Hmm... two others were killed in Saison." Michael recounted the others in his mind. Clara had said one was killed by the men of Saison months ago, and then he and Corbeau had killed the bear the day before. That left two that were unaccounted for.

Michael began to worry that there were creatures still in Saison. Even though it was a long ride to Grimdolon, he was sure that none of the animals left the pack as they followed him. He thought out loud, "Maybe the last two are still in Saison... but surely they would've heard the others when they chased after me." He paused for a moment before continuing, "And I feel certain I didn't lose any during the pursuit."

Jean-Luc took off his glasses and spoke with urgency in his voice, "Michael, I'm afraid somehow this is a ploy of the jester. It's very curious that he seemingly told you the truth in everything. It's sounds like he is toying with you."

Michael bit his lip as he knew Jean-Luc's assessment was correct. He quickly picked up his armor and put it back on. He knew what he needed to do. "I've got to get back to Saison right away."

Thunder rumbled in the distance as Michael crossed back into the forest. He was tired, but the urgency of the mission made him forget about any fatigue he had. He was anxious to question this jester, figure out if there were other creatures on the loose, and then try to decipher if there was a greater plan brewing. Jean-Luc was right; it was curious that he seemingly told the truth about his plans.

It was evening by the time Michael made it to the village. There were a few people walking about, but for the most part, everything was quiet. Michael rode close to the large tent where he had met with Clara the day before. A light rain began to sprinkle from above. He dismounted his horse and quickly walked toward the small tent where Jester was held.

Hearing a horse ride in, Clara looked outside and saw the chief knight. "Michael!" She ran toward him. She was excited to see him since she hadn't known when or if he was going to return. There was always the prospect too that he wouldn't make it back alive. He stopped to face her. She continued, anxious for information, "What happened to the jester's creatures? Did they follow you to Grimdolon?"

"They did. Everything went according to plan. The Mendolon soldiers abandoned their plan of invasion and helped destroy them."

Clara was curious about Michael's response. She could tell he was distracted in his answer. "That's great... but is everything well?"

"I don't know for sure. King Jean-Luc of Grimdolon had a lot of questions concerning the jester, and it appears there may be two more creatures on the loose."

She was a little confused. "Is there anything else?"

Michael didn't know quite how to answer. He shook his head as he spoke, "Like I said, I'm not sure, but we fear this jester may be toying with us." Clara just stared at

Michael as she took in what he was saying. She knew there was at least some truth to what Michael was telling her. Michael continued, "I'm going to question him right away."

Clara now understood his concerns. "Okay," she simply said, following him toward the tent. They quickly entered and descended the steps. Like last time, the torches helped light the way. This time Jester sat off to the side in the torch light. He didn't say anything as he watched the governess and the knight descend the steps. He was still dressed like a court jester including his two-tailed hat and fading face paint.

Michael was the first to speak, "Jester, I need to speak with you."

The court jester groaned as he stood slowly. He approached the bars. "Welcome back."

"What you told me was the truth. The creatures were full of anger and revenge. I provoked them and they followed me all the way back to Grimdolon. There was an army waiting for them, and they were killed."

"Very good," the jester said with amazement in his voice. "I had my doubts, Michael de Bolbec, but impressive nonetheless."

"Why did you tell me the truth? Were you trying to scare me?"

The jester smiled facetiously. "I wasn't telling *you* the truth."

Michael tried to stay focused. He was stern as he spoke, "Are there more diseased animals out there? You told me you created nineteen creatures. Seventeen have been killed. Was that a lie?"

The jester laughed. "You need to listen more carefully to what I say. I'm not lying to you. I'm telling you the truth. I only created nineteen."

Michael's voice was rising with each question. "Then where are the last two?"

The jester waved his hand in a dismissing manner. "No need to worry about them. They're far away. No threat to you. I created them long ago, before my imprisonment in Mendolon."

The chief knight turned away from the cell. He was puzzled by everything unfolding. He wondered what direction he should now take in his questioning. He turned back to face the jester. The prisoner looked straight at the chief knight. He continued to smile viciously as if he was hiding something.

Michael continued, "Why did you tell me about the creatures' hunger for revenge if you knew there was a possibility I could destroy them? They can no longer be a threat to this forest."

The jester laughed again. "Do you think that is what I want? This small forest was just an experiment. I will still achieve the chaos I desire. I will turn this world more like mine."

Michael pulled a dagger. The jester didn't seem intimidated. The chief knight was shouting at this point. "Jester, is this a lie too? There's no point in talking to you if I don't know when you are telling the truth and when you're lying!" Clara reached up and grabbed Michael's arm in a simple attempt to calm him.

Jester shook his head. "Michael, Michael, Michael... you're not listening carefully. I was not lying. I was not telling the truth to *you*."

"What are you talking about?"

The jester licked his lips. He leaned forward against the bars. "Fine, I tell you this." The jester's voice was lower at this point. "The last two creatures you asked about live in Mendolon."

Michael was shocked. "What? Where?"

"Well, one lives in a swamp... it was a snake and believe it or not, your fellow knight has met him before, and was even bitten by him."

"Corbeau?"

"Yes, precisely. I could tell by the look in his eyes that he had tasted of the power I spoke of. In his heart of hearts, there is a small place inside him that desires it. So, that's why I said I wasn't telling *you* the truth... I was telling *him* the truth."

Michael didn't care to play these semantic games any longer. "Where is he?"

"He came to me earlier today, when no one was watching. I sent him away to my lab. It's in the northern part of Saison in the fall region close to the winter line." The jester laughed slightly before continuing, "But you better hurry. He thinks he is going to foil my plans; but in reality, this power of my disease will grip his heart."

Michael quickly turned to leave. He was on the first step when the jester shouted out, "Oh, and Michael!"

The knight stopped and looked back over his shoulder toward the prisoner. The jester just looked at him and smiled for a few seconds. Michael grew impatient. "Yes, I'm waiting!" he shouted.

The jester cleared his throat before speaking, "You're in for a bit of a surprise also as you come close to my lab. There you will see my main ingredient for my disease. I think you will find it quite ironic."

Michael didn't know what to say to this last statement. He simply looked over at Clara and nodded, as if to say he was going after Corbeau.

"Go," was all she said in reply.

Many years ago...

Mamour walked the halls of the castle of Mendolon. He was disappointed. After three years of trying, it looked like his desire to become a knight of Mendolon was fading. He was too small, not fast enough, and nowhere near as skilled with a sword as he needed to be. The chief knight was gracious and affirmed his character, but was honest and told him that it would most likely never happen. In fact, Mamour's abilities wouldn't even qualify for a soldier.

Three years before, he had acquired a job in the castle while he stayed focused on his training for knighthood. His plan had been to get to know people close to the knights and learn as much as he could about the training he needed. He would have an opportunity to get to know the chief knight, let him see his character and his strong desire to be a knight of Mendolon. Still to this day, Mamour would say it was a good plan, but unfortunately his small stature and skills didn't measure up.

He kept his head down as he passed a number of people in the castle hallway. He went straight toward his study. Even though his head was down, Mamour was easily recognizable with his almost white blond hair. No one said a word to him as he kept from making eye contact. He fought back the tears that started to well in his eyes. Emotions of anger, sadness, and uncertainty filled his mind.

Reaching the door to the study, Mamour grabbed the door handle. He paused briefly, looking down at his hand. He opened his palm and saw the star necklace in his hand that his mother had given him before leaving for Mendolon. He felt like he had disappointed her. He didn't know how he would ever tell her that his dream of becoming a knight was over. While he knew there was disappointment and anger in his heart, he remembered his mother's final words: "Choose good, choose good."

Mamour just shook his head as he opened the door to the study. Stepping inside he was taken aback as he found it disheveled. Papers and various objects were scattered about on the floor. He was a little scared. Slowly he stepped further into the room. It looked like there had been a fight as some of the furniture was broken and books had been knocked off the shelf.

He stepped closer to a desk at the far end and peeked around it. He gasped as he saw the body of his superior—dead on the floor. He stumbled backward into a bookshelf. A few books fell to the ground. Mamour felt lightheaded, dizzy. He was breathing heavily and was close to hyperventilating. He crawled a few yards before standing to his feet. His vision was fuzzy, but he could easily see the light coming from outside the door as the hallway was brighter.

Reaching the doorway, Mamour stopped to take a breath, and he leaned his hands against the sides of the door frame. He continued to breathe deeply. He tried to think clearly about what to do next. Mamour had just met with the chief knight, so hopefully he was still in the castle. His foot went forward as he knew he had to keep moving so that he wouldn't faint.

Before taking another step, Mamour felt a strange pain surge through his arm. He screamed as he fell to the ground. He looked over at his arm and saw a small knife. His vision continued to blur and he was starting to lose consciousness... but before the world went dark, he was able to see the boot of his attacker step over him and run down the hallway.

CHAPTER 17

Michael entered the autumn region of Saison. He had traveled a route through the summer area and was now headed in a more northern direction toward the area the court jester had told him about. It was starting to get dark as it was dusk, and the rain was lightly falling. Leaves of various colors covered the ground. If it had been a different time, Michael would have gone slowly and reflected on the beauty of this region, but for now Michael was anxious to find the jester's lair and more specifically, find his fellow knight, Corbeau.

As Michael continued through the autumn region, he noticed the eyes of the Noe were no longer around. It made him sad since he had come to appreciate and love these creatures of the forest. He also thought about the jester's creatures clearing them from this area. That thought saddened him even more. This forest of Saison was their natural habitat. They were creatures of beauty and this was their only known dwelling. Michael hoped that one day this section would again be filled with the Noe.

One thing the jester said kept passing through his mind. It was the statements about his father. He knew this had been a tactic against him to get him thrown off course, but still he couldn't help but think about his father. He had been lost in a battle when Michael was young. Now that he was a knight himself, Michael would've loved to talk with him about his adventures and experiences being the chief knight. Michael wondered particularly if his father had ever traveled through this area.

Michael was approaching the northern section of Saison that was close to the winter line. He stopped his horse suddenly as he saw something unusual. It was a very large dead creature. It smelled terrible. He stopped and put on his black helmet. He couldn't tell what it was since much of the skin of the creature was peeled off and many of its organs were missing. Some had apparently been half eaten by other animals. The creature's skeleton was still in place and some of the dark red skin still remained. Overall it was obvious that this creature had been here a few months.

As the chief knight stepped closer, he noticed the long tail and the long neck of the creature. Even though a large portion of this creature was missing, Michael now knew it was a dragon. He thought it very odd that the body of this creature lay here. Dead dragon bodies were usually disposed of by their own, unless they were killed in battle. *Could the jester have killed this creature?* Michael thought to himself. This seemed odd. The jester didn't appear to be a warrior in the least. More than likely he wouldn't be able to defeat a creature like this on his own.

Michael stepped around the head of the creature and beheld the creature's face. Both his eyes were missing as they had obviously decomposed. Even still, it looked like an evil creature. Michael noticed a weapon on the ground under the head. He slowly reached down and picked it up. He couldn't believe what he saw. It was a dagger... his dagger. He inspected it from every side and it was obvious that this was his weapon. He looked back at the face of the dragon, and he could see that this was the dragon of Mendolon that had dwelt in Dragon Waste for years. Apparently after the knights defeated him, he flew north and stopped in this area of Saison. It looked as if he had died slowly, bleeding from the wounds sustained in the battle against the knights.

Michael was mesmerized, looking at the dagger, when a voice interrupted his thoughts. "Strange... isn't it?"

Michael turned and saw his fellow knight. "Corbeau!" he shouted out.

Corbeau was a few feet away leaning against a tree. He was holding his stomach as he looked sick, his face pale. "It looks like the disease the jester created uses dragon's blood as the main ingredient. He was creating a 'dragon's disease.'"

Michael looked back at the dragon and then looked back at Corbeau. He wasn't sure what to ask first. He said the first thing that came to mind. "How do you know this?"

Corbeau snickered. "He has a few vials of it, not far from here in a small shelter. It was obviously used as his lab. He has a wide range of chemicals in there."

Michael noticed Corbeau's voice was a little different and his hair looked darker. "What's... what's wrong with you, Corbeau?"

Corbeau fell to one knee. "What's wrong with me?" He repeated, mocking Michael. "Nothing actually... I'm getting stronger."

Michael spoke quietly, "What did you do?"

"I drank a vial of the serum." Corbeau stopped and grabbed his stomach tighter. He winced in pain. "I can now feel it moving through my body."

Michael was angry and a little confused. "Why would you do this?"

"Michael... Michael... we've seen this power on display. We need this. I need this."

Michael shook his head. He noticed Corbeau's complexion starting to change further. Corbeau groaned as he completely fell to the ground. Michael took a step closer to him. He wondered if his fellow knight was dying. "Corbeau?" he asked, concerned.

It was just a moment later that Corbeau began to rise to his feet. The pain was leaving. He looked directly at Michael. His eyes were now red and there was evil in them. He slowly looked down at his hands before flexing his bicep.

He was suddenly feeling stronger. A devilish smile formed on his face as he addressed his fellow knight. "I'm stronger now, Michael, and I will defeat any enemy that is in my path."

Michael's hand went toward the handle of one of his daggers. "It's taken ahold of your mind, Corbeau. Evil is infesting you."

With clinched teeth Corbeau pulled both of his swords. He then spoke softly. "I should've been chief knight... not you." His words were methodical as if he'd been thinking about them for a long time.

"Stand down, Corbeau!" Michael ordered.

"The only reason you're the chief knight is because of your father. We all know the position was mine. My skills as a blacksmith are unrivaled. I have more experience than you, and I am older and wiser... and now, I will show you that I am the better swordsman."

Corbeau sprang toward Michael. The chief knight quickly pulled two daggers and blocked Corbeau's swords. As their weapons were locked, Michael kicked him in the stomach, pushing him backwards. Corbeau snarled in anger. Michael quickly put one of his daggers back in his belt and pulled a new sword he had received from Jean-Luc. Corbeau came back at Michael with a strong swipe of his sword. Michael blocked the sword and then pivoted to block Corbeau's other sword. He then stepped back and blocked another swipe from his opponent.

Michael kept moving backwards rapidly, blocking his fellow knight's every swipe. His back then rubbed against a tree. He rolled off to the side as another swipe came toward him. Corbeau's sword hit the tree and was planted firmly in the bark. Michael moved a few feet away and caught his breath. He held his sword in a defensive position. He knew he had just a moment to gather himself before Corbeau approached again. It was easy to notice that because of the serum, Corbeau was now faster and stronger. Michael wondered how he would win this fight. He didn't want to hurt his friend, but at the moment he knew the rage inside Corbeau couldn't be reasoned with.

With his sword out of the tree, Corbeau turned toward Michael. The chief knight pulled a dagger and threw it at Corbeau. As Michael expected, Corbeau easily used one of his swords to deflect the dagger. "Get ahold of yourself!" Michael shouted.

Corbeau growled at Michael angrily. He jumped forward at Michael with his swords. Michael blocked one but the other caught him in the lower shoulder between two plates of armor. The blade only went slightly into his flesh, but it was firmly stuck between the armor. With his free hand, Michael grabbed Corbeau's wrist and squeezed. He could feel the wound in his shoulder opening up more with each move of his arm. Michael then shifted his body and pulled the sword from Corbeau's hand. He then had to think quickly as Corbeau took another swipe with his other sword. Michael blocked again.

Corbeau quickly punched Michael in the side of his head. Michael spun and fell backwards. He heard Corbeau approaching and threw himself to his left. Corbeau swiped his sword and missed Michael, striking it against the ground.

As Michael rolled on the ground, he felt the sword stuck in his armor dislodge. He wasn't sure where the sword was now, but he knew he couldn't let his adversary get it. His best plan was now to go on the offensive. He took another dagger and threw it at Corbeau. It hit the center of his armor and easily fell to the ground. Corbeau was only mildly distracted, but it was just enough for Michael to lunge forward and tackle his opponent. Corbeau landed on the ground and dropped his sword as he was unprepared for this move by Michael. His sword landed a few feet away.

As both men were on the ground, Michael rose up and delivered a quick punch to the side of Corbeau's head. Using his new-found strength, Corbeau then grabbed ahold of Michael and flipped him over his head. As Michael's body hit the ground, he was able to move into a quick roll and was able to get back to his feet. Unfortunately, two daggers fell off his belt in the process, leaving only one. Michael sprang toward his fellow knight as he also was getting to his feet. Michael knew he couldn't let Corbeau find his swords. Michael threw a punch with his left hand. It was blocked. Corbeau tried to kick Michael, but that was blocked. Michael quickly threw another punch, but it was also blocked. On and on the men continued, throwing kicks and punches and blocking each other's attempts. Their training was similar, and with Corbeau's new power, their skills were close to equal. As they were fighting, Michael noticed the red eyes of Corbeau. Like the jester's creatures, he saw the vengeance in them.

After a solid minute of hand-to-hand combat, Michael stumbled slightly on a fallen branch. It was all Corbeau needed to gain an advantage. He landed a punch square to the chin of Michael. It stunned him, and Corbeau was able to grab ahold of Michael and throw him into the dilapidated body of the dragon. Michael landed against the upper section of the body and rolled down. His back hurt as it hit one of the dragon's back spines.

Corbeau ran toward Michael. He noticed one of the dragon's small bones that had fallen to the side. It was only a foot in length. He quickly picked it up and swung it against Michael's head. Even though Michael was wearing his helmet, the hit still hurt profusely. Michael fell to the side against another section of the dragon's bones. He felt a little bit of blood begin to run down the inside of his helmet. It made him dizzy.

"And now, Michael," Corbeau was smiling as he spoke. "Nothing will stand in my way. I will be chief knight and maybe even king someday. My power will be matched by no one."

Michael sat up with his back against the dragon's body. He wondered if this was his end. He glanced to his left and saw something hard beside him, buried under fallen leaves. It felt like metal. He glanced at it and could see the handle of a very familiar sword. This was Belle's sword. The one used to stab this dragon. As the dragon's body deteriorated, the sword must have fallen to the ground.

Corbeau lifted the bone into the air to continue beating Michael. But before he could strike, Michael grabbed the sword and turned his body toward his fellow knight. He swung the sword and sliced into the hand of Corbeau, cutting it off just above the thumb. Corbeau screamed in pain before falling to his knees and grabbing his injured hand. A dark brownish-green blood leaked from it.

Michael slowly stood to his feet. He unstrapped his helmet and tossed it to the ground. He took a deep breath as he watched Corbeau struggling with his pain. He hated that it had come to this. Michael spoke compassionately, but also with a bit of sorrow, "Corbeau, my friend, please come back to Grimdolon with me. Let's try to find some way to cure you of this."

Corbeau was shaking as he tightly held his hand. A few strands of his dark hair fell over his face as he looked up at Michael. "You will die for this, Michael de Bolbec!" He seemed to struggle with each word as he was in agony. "This dragon's power will continue to make me stronger. I'll be the most powerful knight that ever lived."

Michael shook his head before pleading with his friend. "Please, listen to me. You're not thinking clearly. This dragon's disease is turning you evil. You don't have a choice."

"No, No!" Corbeau yelled. "This is what I want. I chose this. Unlike you, I will do whatever it takes. I will sacrifice anything to be the best. I will have the most power."

The chief knight bit his lip. He knew Corbeau was right. His obsession had gotten the best of him. The bitterness, the anger, and the jealousy were left unfettered and continued to grow for too long. When he heard from the court jester about this dragon's disease and the power it gave, he couldn't resist. It wasn't the disease that made him evil, it was the choice to bring in the evil... that was truly his sin.

Michael threw down the sword. He wanted to show his friend that he didn't want to fight any longer and that he cared for him. Maybe there was some way that he could break through to him. "Listen to me. This obsession is killing you. With this dragon's disease in you, it's only going to get worse. You'll never have the power you desire. There will only be death and destruction in your future."

It was as if something Michael said made Corbeau furious. He sprang toward Michael, growling as he approached him. Michael knew what he had to do. He quickly pulled his last dagger and slashed it upward against the right side of Corbeau's face. Michael then quickly spun into a kick that struck the left side of his head. Corbeau's body twisted and his face hit hard against the ground.

Corbeau lifted his head off the ground and looked at Michael. The wound on his face was bleeding. He spoke through clinched teeth. "You're not man enough to finish me off."

Michael took a deep breath as he spoke quietly. "I've heard that phrase before... just not from you." He turned his back to Corbeau and walked a few feet away from him and the dragon's body. He calmly looked to the east toward the winter territory, trying to quiet his mind. He didn't feel threatened by his fellow knight at the moment. There was a downward slope in front of him, and he could feel the cold air of the winter section that was only a few feet away.

Michael felt tears beginning to well up in his eyes. He was the chief knight and felt responsible for those in his command. He hated that Corbeau had destroyed himself and brought this fracture to the company of knights. The knights all swore an oath to strive for ideals such as truth, hope, and justice. He wondered how the others would respond to the news of one of their own falling prey to his own bitterness and obsession.

Michael wiped his eyes with his fingers and was about to turn around when he felt a hard strike against the wound on the side of his head. He fell forward and rolled down the slope in front of him. His body picked up momentum as it continued downward. His head and body hit branches and other rocks as it continued down the fifty-foot slope. When his body stopped, it landed in a half foot of snow in the winter territory. He closed his eyes as he fell unconscious.

Sebastian's aged assassin watched as Michael's body rested at the bottom of the slope. He was standing a few feet away when he threw a stone directly into the wound on the side of Michael's head. The assassin had followed Michael and Corbeau all this time and had waited for the right time to attack. He laughed to himself—his patience had paid off. He turned and walked aside to the small wooden shack the jester had been using for a lab. Sebastian had ordered him to follow the knights and see if he could find the source of this dragon's disease. The assassin entered in and collected the six remaining vials of dragon's disease. It was easily recognizable since it was a green substance that was thick.

He then put them in a bag that was on his side and quickly walked out.

Walking close to Corbeau, he spoke out mockingly, "Goodbye, Corbeau de Lefevre."

"Wait," Corbeau called out while still lying on the ground. "Take me with you."

The assassin laughed a little before speaking, "And why should I do that?"

Corbeau struggled as he spoke. "Because the dragon's disease is running through me. You only have six vials of it. The effect the serum has on me can be studied, and, listen to me, my blood can help you make more!"

He rubbed his white beard as he considered Corbeau's offer. "Sorry... it's tempting, but we will study it just fine once it's used in others." The assassin turned to walk away, thinking he would leave Corbeau to die.

Corbeau shouted out one last time. "Listen to me! I will serve King Sebastian. I will help him spread this disease and bring power to the kingdom of Mendolon."

The aged assassin stopped in his tracks. He slowly turned and looked at Corbeau, as if he was in deep thought. He then took a step closer to the fallen knight. Corbeau was still holding his injured hand. He was still in pain, and the assassin knew that this knight would be at his mercy. "How do I know we can trust you?"

Corbeau growled, angry at the question. "I just battled Michael de Bolbec and tried to kill him. He did this to me. This is his fault." He slowly stood up, stumbling a little before continuing. "I will be the new chief knight of Mendolon. I will stand for power, vengeance, and victory."

The assassin nodded his head and smiled. "Yes." He liked what Corbeau was suggesting, and he thought it was at least worth a try to bring him before Sebastian. It might gain him some favor with the king. "I will bring you back to Mendolon, and you can make your offer to the king yourself."

"Thank you." Corbeau slowly began walking toward the assassin. He was hurting badly, but his anger motivated him and kept him moving forward.

As he approached the assassin, he noticed something to the right of him. He stepped to the side and picked it up with his uninjured hand. Seeing what he was doing, the assassin spoke quietly in agreement, "Hmm... yes, I think you can put that helmet to use."

Corbeau snarled one last time before placing Michael's black helmet over his head.

CHAPTER 18

Hector leaned against the bars of his prison cell. He had been in this cell for close to a week. Anxiety and boredom were at their peak. He wondered how much longer he would be in here. Sebastian had a servant come once a day to bring him food. That was his only interaction with the outside world. Thankfully, the servant would give him any information he knew concerning the comings and goings of the kingdom.

A fellow prisoner moaned in a distant cell. This was a daily occurrence and usually happened about the same time. Hector didn't want to listen to this today. He walked toward his bed and sat comfortably on the edge. He wondered how he had come to this point in his life. As the king's advisor, he should have persuaded the king to stay away from dragons and to have no dealings with them. He could now clearly see how they were grabbing ahold of his heart.

Hector reached into his pocket and pulled out the item that brought him the most comfort in life. It was the star necklace, given to him by his mother. It reminded him of his previous life before coming to Mendolon. His life before being stabbed by the court jester. The life where he was known by his mother's term of endearment, Mamour, meaning "my love."

He would never forget that fateful day when he found his superior lying on the floor dead in the study. Though he felt faint, he had been trying to escape and warn the castle officials about the murder. But as he was in the doorway of the study, the court jester sprang from the shadows and stabbed him with a knife dipped in the serum of the Dragon's Disease. The jester then ran from the castle and hid in the swamp. It was there that he experimented with a snake. Hector eventually had him hunted down and arrested. But for Hector, personally, it was too late. He was the jester's first creature.

The disease took over Hector's life. He continued working in the castle in the area of chemistry and medicines. It wasn't long before King Sebastian recognized his exceptional work, along with his propensity toward evil and hatred for the race of beast. He had him promoted to the role of advisor, and it was there that he served for nearly twenty years.

The man in the prison continued to wail and moan. It irritated Hector. Angrily Hector arose and walked back to the prison bars. He would give this prisoner a piece of his mind. He opened his mouth to yell out toward the man, but in the last moment he stopped himself. Suddenly he felt pity for the fellow prisoner. Maybe it was the necklace in his hand or the thought of his mother that brought these sudden emotions. He put his fist to his forehead and shook his head. The prison was truly taking its toll on him. He turned and slowly walked back toward his bed. His mother's words flowed through his mind: *Choose good. Choose good.*

After a few steps, Hector caught sight of himself in a mirror to his left. He paused for a moment before stepping closer to his reflection. The mirror was a small square, a foot and a half on all sides. It had been left on the wall from the time Jean-Luc occupied this cell.

Hector stared at his reflection in the mirror. For the most part his reflection looked the same. His hair was black. His complexion was pale, and his eyes had a palpable look of hatred and evil, all an effect of the jester's Dragon Disease. He put his face even closer to the mirror—something looked out of place. It was his hair, or rather a few strands of it. He grabbed them with his hand and held them closer to the mirror. He couldn't believe it. They were blond, just like his hair used to be. He examined the strands further and, sure enough, there was no mistaking that the color of these hairs had changed.

Hector turned and headed back to his bed. Thoughts entered his mind that he never thought he would think, *The dragon's blood is beginning to fade.*

৵৬

Michael slowly opened his eyes in the morning light. Everything was quiet. He felt cold as he had been lying there in the winter region all through the night. *How did I survive this?* he thought to himself. He touched the side of his head. There was still dried blood from the assassin's hit, but the wound was closed. He could feel some type of paste on the side of his head, closing the wound. Strangely enough, Michael also noticed that he was lying on a blanket made from animal skin. He sat up and looked around the forest. Snow was lightly falling, and there was a beautiful terrain of rocks and trees before him covered in snow. It looked like a land of purity.

Continuing to examine his surroundings, he noticed something quite curious. There was a row of Noe creatures standing in front of him. There were seven of them, and they stared at the chief knight as if they were concerned for him. It was obvious that they were the ones who took care of him during the night. They kept him alive. "Thank you," Michael mumbled under his breath, a little stunned. His body was sore and most likely one of his ribs was broken, but, all things considered, he was amazed at how well he felt. The little creatures watched intently as he stood to his feet. They spoke with quiet pigeon-like sounds.

Michael brushed the snow off himself as he looked around. He then turned and saw the large hill from which he had rolled down. It was steep and he knew that in his present condition, he would not be able to ascend it. He figured that last strike against his head was the work of Sebastian's assassin. Currently, Michael wondered if Corbeau was still at the top, or if he had been captured or killed by Sebastian's assassin. Michael felt for his friend, but he knew there was nothing he could do at the moment.

He took a deep breath and then looked back at the little creatures. "Well... you fellows wouldn't know the way back, would you?"

The Noe creatures looked at one another intently as if they were communicating. They then turned and began slowly walking away from Michael. Their walk reminded Michael of a small penguin waddle. After they had taken a few steps, three or four of them turned to see if Michael was following. It was clear they were now leading him. "Okay," he mumbled as he began to follow.

The journey was difficult as they walked through the winter section. Snow was blowing, and Michael was already cold from spending the night in this territory. The Noe moved slowly as they walked along. Michael thought about running ahead, but he decided otherwise. These creatures had kept him alive during the night. He felt as if he owed it to them to let them lead. Occasionally, Michael would catch sight of other Noe creatures watching them. He was thankful to see they hadn't been eliminated in this region. Their presence was comforting.

After walking for an hour and a half, they passed over the line into the autumn region. They were still moving south, but they were now in the section of autumn which was warmer. Occasionally the winds from the winter section would blow over into their area, but for the most part, this part of the journey was much more pleasant. A few birds chirped and leaves fell into his path. The only disappointment was the reminder that the Noe had been killed in this section. He hoped it wouldn't be long before this region was again filled with these little creatures.

As Michael continued walking south, a thought crossed his mind. *What is the center of the forest like?* He wondered if they would pass by it and see where the four seasons converged. He wondered, if in any way, he would gain a greater sense of how the environment of this forest truly worked. These thoughts would have to wait for another day because at present, the Noe were working their way back to the path from which Michael came. They were leading him back to the village.

It was early in the afternoon when they reached the line where autumn fades into summer. The Noe stopped, and Michael walked in front of them a few feet into the region. He knew his way back from here. Looking around the area, he found that it was quiet. He then turned and looked back at the little creatures behind him. Something about them looked nervous, shy at this point. It was obvious why. For the past few months the jester's animals had invaded this forest and hunted them. The Noe were a little apprehensive to venture into this region again because the creatures were last seen inhabiting this summer area.

Michael looked behind him and spoke to the little creatures, "It's okay. They're all gone." He turned to examine the territory one last time. It was peaceful. No threats. He continued, "This area is yours again. You are free to..." Michael was a little caught off guard when he turned back around and saw only one Noe standing behind him. A tired smile formed on his face as he looked at the little creature staring back at him. "Thank you," he said quietly. Michael then turned to the south and began his journey back to the village. As he took a few steps, he saw a few of the Noe who were behind him moving about in this region. It was a joy to see. He was thankful that the forest was theirs once again.

With his injuries, the walk through the forest took Michael most of the day to complete. With each step he kept telling himself the village was just around the corner. A part of him wanted to head back into the autumn section and see if he could find Corbeau, but he knew that more than anything, he needed more medical attention. The Noe had adequately cared for his injuries during the night, but he needed more advanced medical attention as soon as possible.

Michael arrived at the village just as the people were having their evening meal. Those who were standing outside quickly took notice of him and started calling out to others that one of the knights had returned. By the way he was moving, it was obvious to all that he was injured. As men and women came to meet him, a few went to inform Clara. It was just a moment later that the whole village was aware of his presence. There was much excitement among the villagers.

The knight was then led into a tent where he was seated on a table. He groaned as he stretched out his legs. The villagers began to clear from the tent as a dark-skinned man with glasses approached Michael. "Let me have a look at you." It was obvious that he was the doctor for this village. "Hold still now," he said quietly as he looked at the injury on Michael's head. He examined the paste-like substance the Noe had put on the side of his head. "It looks like our little friends took care of you."

Michael chuckled slightly. "Yes... they truly did. Not sure I would've made it without them."

At that moment, Clara burst into the tent. "Michael! You're back." She stepped further into the tent as questions began to flood her mind. "Are you okay? What happened?"

"It was the jester." Michael paused, wincing in pain as the doctor was still examining his head. "The disease he created was made from the blood of dragons. It made the animals he infected stronger, and it made them crave evil. Unfortunately, Corbeau found his supply and became tempted by it. He took it and became one of them."

Clara eyes grew wide. She tried to speak but the words didn't come. Michael continued, "His anger consumed him and we fought. It didn't end well for either of us."

The doctor interrupted, "I'll be right back." He exited the tent in search of more supplies.

Michael swung his feet off to the side of the table, facing Clara. "King Sebastian's assassin approached me when my back was turned. He knocked me into the winter region where, I assume, I laid unconscious for the night."

"Do you think he and Corbeau are still there in the autumn quadrant?"

Michael shook his head with a distant look in his eyes. "I don't know for sure, but the more I thought about it today, the more I would guess they are both gone by now. In the morning I'd say we send an exploration team to see what became of them."

Clara nodded as she took in Michael's words. Her emotions were mixed—the news of Corbeau's betrayal and Michael's injuries were unsettling, but she was greatly thankful that Michael was alive and doing reasonably well. She pointed to the injury on his head. "I take it the Noe took care of you through the night."

"Yes, they laid me on a blanket, and ministered to my injuries." Michael paused and shrugged his shoulders. "And... there was even a group of them waiting for me when I awoke."

Clara gave a half-smile before speaking, "I could tell they took a special liking to you." Michael laughed slightly. The two sat for a while talking about everything that had progressed these last three days. They were comfortable with each other, and it felt like they had known each other for three years, not just three days.

Eventually, the doctor came back into the tent. "Sorry for my delay. I was looking for a thread to stitch your injuries."

Clara stood to her feet. "Well, I should be going. The villagers have a special celebration planned tonight to commemorate the death of the jester's creatures. Goodbye, Michael."

"Goodbye."

Clara walked toward the entryway of the tent. Before leaving, she stopped and turned toward the chief knight. "And Michael..." She hesitated a little before continuing, "I know you must be worried about Corbeau and your kingdom, Mendolon, but we would love for you to join us at the celebration. It would mean a lot to our people."

"Thank you," Michael said as he looked straight at Clara. "In all honesty, I am worried, but as I learned when I was a boy, I must try not to worry about tomorrow, for tomorrow will worry about itself."

This saying came from a renowned source and was familiar to Clara. She looked back at him and spoke confidently more of the words of wisdom, "Look at the birds of the air, they neither sow or reap, or store away in barns, yet the Heavenly Father feeds them; or look at the lilies of the field, how they grow. They neither toil or spin. Therefore, do not worry about tomorrow, for tomorrow will worry about itself."

Michael was caught off guard by her quotation. "You know the teachings of the Righteous King?"

"Of course," Clara was smiling at this point. "They're my guidance for each day. I don't know how I'd face life without them." She then turned and left the tent.

Michael now smiled to himself. Just hearing the words of the Righteous King made him feel more at peace. He closed his eyes, trying to relax. "Tomorrow will worry about itself," he mumbled under his breath as the doctor began again to work on his head.

❧❧

The knights, the Grimdolon warriors, and the soldiers congregated on the plains in front of Grimdolon's castle. King Jean-Luc had called for a gathering of all those who fought against the jester's creatures. The common beasts of the kingdom were also invited and most had responded and were in attendance. Thousands waited for Jean-Luc to appear from the castle balcony and deliver his news.

The beasts of the kingdom were a little nervous as soldiers of their enemy nation, Mendolon, were standing near them. It was safe to say that many citizens wouldn't have shown up if not for the fact that Grimdolon warriors were also in attendance. The Mendolon soldiers had remained overnight after the battle as they thought Sebastian might be extremely angry when he learned that they hadn't gone to war with the beasts.

Just a few minutes later, Jean-Luc appeared on the balcony with Belle by his side. They were dressed majestically in their king and queen attire. Belle was wearing an elegant purple dress and Jean-Luc had a matching coat. Etalon, Gideon, and Bernard stood behind the king and queen. Seeing their king and queen, the citizens erupted in cheering. Jean-Luc smiled as he waved to everyone. After a few minutes he lifted his hand, silencing the crowd. He then reached in his jacket and pulled out a small scroll. He then turned and saw his glasses on a table beside Bernard. He addressed the knight, "Bernard, my glasses, please."

Bernard reached and tried to grab the glasses. He was a little nervous and accidently fumbled them, dropping them to the ground. The glass inside the frames cracked. "Sorry," Bernard said regretfully before picking them up.

"Very well," Jean-Luc said as he rolled his eyes. He then unrolled the scroll and addressed the crowd as he read from it. "Beasts, men, women, warriors, knights, I come before you today to say 'thank you' for your work in vanquishing the enemies of Grimdolon." Belle laughed a little as Jean-Luc had to keep adjusting the glasses on his face to avoid the crack in the lens. Jean-Luc smiled, knowing his fiancée was finding this amusing. He continued, "Through this battle, we have shown the world that man and beast can work together and fight alongside one another." The crowd started clapping in approval.

He continued, "The situation with the soldiers of Mendolon is complex, and they are under threat from their king." A murmur of despair arose in the crowd. "But on behalf of our kingdom, they are welcome to stay here until a suitable plan is formed." He unrolled the scroll further. "Let me hereby say that we will first mourn and bury those who passed during the battle with the creatures..." Jean-Luc paused just a moment before continuing with greater fervor, "Then let us welcome our new guests and celebrate our victory in this battle. Tomorrow, we will decorate and open up the castle for a celebration of the harmony between beasts and men. Peace be to you all." The crowd then erupted in a joyous celebration. It was a wonderful sight as families hugged each other, and beast warriors shook hands and embraced the Mendolon soldiers at their sides. Many in the crowd didn't know what the future held, but for now there was peace and harmony between the beasts and mankind.

Belle turned to her future husband. "Great speech, my love. In a world of despair, you've brought them some of this world's greatest gifts."

Jean-Luc took off his glasses. "Oh yes? And what do you speak of, my dear?"

She spoke quietly, "The gifts of hope, joy, and peace."

Jean-Luc smiled in return as the crowd continued to celebrate.

EPILOGUE

A young, nine-year-old boy played outside in the northern section of Mendolon. Ten days had passed since the armies of Mendolon and the warriors of Grimdolon fought together against the jester's creatures. The boy's mother had heard of the invasion of the soldiers into Grimdolon, and this was the first day she felt comfortable with her son playing outside. Like others throughout the kingdom, she received word that the battle never took place. And though there was uncertainty among the citizens, the week of ease and peace seemed to slowly dissipate fears of a sudden war.

Currently, the boy was drawing in the mud with sticks and occasionally stopping to act like he was a knight with a sword in his hand. The boy had no brothers or sisters, but he often played with other children that lived close by. He stood straight up and began waving his stick around, acting like he was the chief knight fighting the dreaded Savage. "Yay, yay," he said as he pictured a fierce sword fight.

He suddenly stopped when he heard thunder in the distance. A feeling of disappointment arose within him; the boy didn't want to stop playing. He then looked up in the sky and saw that the sky was clear. He was puzzled as everything was clear in every direction.

It was then that he saw three large creatures flying toward him from the north. The boys' eyes grew wide as three dragons flew over his head. They each were three different shades of red, with one of the dragons being so dark that it looked black. The boy was overwhelmed and wanted to run, but he was paralyzed with fear and wet his pants.

The dragons paid no attention to the young boy as they flew overhead. The one in the lead let out a loud shrieking growl as they turned west toward the castle of Mendolon. As planned, they were going to present themselves before King Sebastian. Six months ago, after long negotiations, he made a deal with the dragons that they would be given scores of gold and free rein in Mendolon in exchange for protection and obedience to the king of Mendolon. The dragons welcomed the opportunity to live openly in the world of men.

The dragons flew many miles over the countryside and various villages. Many people took notice and ran in terror. The western markets particularly were filled with people who screamed upon seeing the creatures. All commerce stopped in an instant as citizens dropped their purchases and ran. Fathers and mothers picked up their children and took refuge in whatever possible way they could. Most had never seen a dragon before but had only heard the legends and read the stories. The dragons let out another shriek, but otherwise didn't take notice of the people.

Sebastian was waiting out on a balcony as he saw the creatures approach. In the courtyard of the castle below stood the royal servants and the Mendolon soldiers who remained completely loyal to him. There were seven hundred people total. The king had a good sense of which soldiers were loyal to him and he hadn't sent these soldiers into the battle against the beasts of Grimdolon because he didn't want any risk of losing them. These soldiers knew the dragons had a treaty with Sebastian and would not attack them, but naturally they still felt a sense of fear when they witnessed the dragons gliding over the castle.

Two of the dragons rested comfortably on top on the castle, and one hovered in the air over the crowd. Sebastian smiled deviously. He held his arms out toward the crowd as he spoke, "Yes... please welcome our new dragons of Mendolon." About a third of the soldiers began clapping nervously as fear still encompassed them.

Sebastian turned and looked over his shoulder. Behind him stood the two new guardians of Mendolon. The northern assassin stood rubbing his white beard as he took in the sight of the dragons. He was dressed elegantly like a person of royalty. In the past, he had always stayed north of Mendolon and served Sebastian whenever he traveled. Now everything would be different. He would live in Mendolon and serve Sebastian day to day in the kingdom as his advisor and personal protector.

Standing a few feet beside the assassin was Corbeau. He was dressed in new specialized knight armor. It was red and black in design and a black cape now flowed behind him. He was wearing the helmet he had picked up from the fight with Michael. It covered most of his face and particularly his new scar. His skin was pale and his hair was completely black as the dragon disease had fully taken over his body. In his heart was nothing but anger and malice. In place of his missing fingers were three metal claws. They worked on a hinge and could grip when he moved his thumb. It reminded him of his enemy, Michael de Bolbec. He vowed that one day he would use this new hand to take the chief knight's life.

Sebastian laughed as he looked back at the crowd. The dragons were at his service, he had two new personal warriors, and he had a supply of dragon disease at his disposal. Jean-Luc's army of beast warriors may have escaped the battle with his soldiers, but the kingdom of Mendolon now had lots of power and it was all under his control. He felt his kingdom was secure, and it would grow stronger over time. Any chance of a rebellion against his throne would also be diminished. His mind began drifting to conquering other kingdoms and growing in power. He smiled at the thought of these new opportunities.

Gideon walked away from Grimdolon's castle. He was going toward a meeting house where he would convene with the other knights. His steps were careful as Grimdolon's soil was rocky, and one had to be careful not to trip on an occasional rock stuck in the path. He had been meeting with Jean-Luc concerning the news he had heard coming from Mendolon. They all knew about the dragons and the new weapon of the Dragon Disease. Around two hundred of Mendolon's residents had fled the kingdom. Many came to Grimdolon. Sebastian had learned of this migration and quickly put a stop to it. He didn't want anyone else leaving the borders of Mendolon.

The aged knight passed a few families of beasts that were moving about the land. They smiled at him as he passed by. Even though more than a week had passed since Jean-Luc's celebration, there was still an atmosphere of hope and joy in Grimdolon. Gideon also felt better himself as he had recently received word that his wife and family, along with Michael's family, were dwelling peacefully in a southern kingdom. They left right after the knights fled Mendolon.

Arriving at the cottage, Gideon opened the wooden door and went inside. All the other knights were sitting, except for Bernard who seeing Gideon, was the first to speak up, "Gideon! How'd it go with Jean-Luc?"

"It went well," he said as he shut the door behind him. "He said that his scouts spot no military action thus far. It's as if Sebastian is trying to get a handle on his own kingdom before he advances any troops."

Gideon then stepped close to the others and took a seat. He rubbed the back of his head as he thought about what he was going to say next. He looked up at the knights and just spoke candidly, "I'm sorry to say too that the rumors about Corbeau are true… he has abandoned us, and he is now a puppet of Sebastian."

Many of the knights buried their head in their hands. It was as if the air was instantly taken out of the room. They had heard reports of Sebastian's two new enforcers and that Corbeau might be one of them, but in their heart of hearts they hoped that this rumor was false. Having one of their own betray them and dishonor the knight's code was truly unthinkable.

After a few moments of silence, another knight spoke up, "And what of Michael de Bolbec?"

Gideon sat back in his chair and nodded briefly before answering, "Yes… word came from Saison that he was injured in a fight with Corbeau and is recovering. I'm not sure how badly he is hurt… but I would guess that he will join us when he's recovered." They were thrilled to hear this news.

Bernard then spoke up, "But Gideon…"

"Yes, go on."

"What does this mean for us?"

"I'm not sure what you're implying, Bernard?"

"Well, since we're kicked out of our kingdom and are actually fugitives of King Sebastian… do we still operate as a brigade of knights? Or is it time to disperse and go to our families?"

304

Gideon looked up at his fellow knight and gathered his words carefully before speaking. He spoke with great resolve, "Let me be honest with you all." He stood to his feet as he continued. "This is not the end of the knights. We will regroup, watch Sebastian's moves, and then plan accordingly. We will look for opportunities to bring peace and security to our citizens. Our people... we will still fight for them and for our kingdom. We will always be the Knights of Mendolon."

About the Author

Tony Myers is a fiction author. He enjoys finding creative ways to illustrate and communicate truth. He and his wife, Charity, currently live in Waterloo, Iowa with their 4 children. Visit his website at www.tonymyers.net, or follow him on Twitter @tony1myers.

Also, check out these other titles from Tony Myers. Available at most online book distributors.

Singleton

"As someone with a lifelong interest in magic who has been fooling people as long as I remember, I love the chance to be fooled myself. As I read Singleton I was baffled. The first few pages of the book caught my attention just like the opening trick of a good magic show. From there I was kept in suspense as the mystery unfolded. Just when I thought it was impossible to tie together all the strange things which were occurring, Myers performs his best trick. In the last few pages of the book he brings the mystery to a satisfying yet shocking conclusion. Like a good magic show, Singleton leaves you wanting more. Fortunately, Myers has another book up his sleeve. If you are like me and enjoy a good mystery, then you may want to consider Stealing the Magic for yourself. If Singleton is any indication, it is bound to entertain and keep you in suspense."

- John Neely, Magician

Stealing the Magic

"Heart-pounding, easy-to-read, captivating and absolutely unpredictable! Stealing the Magic has transformed my view of Christian fiction. Stealing the Magic is a story of a young college student in search of what every person wants...acceptance. There are so many lessons that can be learned from this book. I will say this, you NEED to read the prologue and epilogue of this book! This book is brilliant!!!!"

- Aaron Moore

"Myers delivers a page-turning mystery that grips the reader with its relatable characters and compelling plot. A taut, satisfying story for young suspense lovers and seasoned readers alike."

- Pamela Crane, literary judge and author of the award-winning *A Secondhand Life*

18951286R00171

Made in the USA
Lexington, KY
26 November 2018